SEVEN MINUTES IN HEAVEN

ALSO BY SARA SHEPARD

SEVEN
MINUTES
IN
HEAVEN

A LYING GAME NOVEL

BY

SARA
SHEPARD

An Imprint of HarperCollins*Publishers*

HarperTeen is an imprint of HarperCollins Publishers.

Seven Minutes in Heaven
Copyright © 2013 by Alloy Entertainment and Sara Shepard

Produced by Alloy Entertainment
1700 Broadway, New York, NY 10019
www.alloyentertainment.com

ISBN 978-0-06-212822-5 (trade bdg.)
ISBN 978-0-06-227238-6 (int. ed.)

Design by Liz Dresner

13 14 15 16 17   LP/RRDH   10 9 8 7 6 5 4 3 2 1
❖
First Edition

Good girls go to heaven, bad girls go everywhere.

—HELEN GURLEY BROWN

PROLOGUE

The walk-in closet would be any girl's dream. A thick pink rug lay on the hardwood floor, perfect for bare toes first thing in the morning. Shelves and cubbies lined the walls, filled with designer purses and jewelry and dozens of shoes. Luxurious clothes in every color of the rainbow hung in careful rows: blouses and skirts in silk, cashmere, cotton.

For most girls, this closet would be heaven. For me, it was just another reminder that heaven was exactly where I wasn't.

Next to me in the narrow space, my twin sister, Emma Paxton, ran her fingers through the rich fabrics of my clothes, her heart clenched in a knot of grief. She has my exact chestnut hair and long legs, the same marine-blue eyes lined by dark lashes. She is my identical twin, after all. But even though I stood right next to her, hers was the only reflection in the three-way mirror at the end of the closet.

Ever since I died, I'd been invisible. But somehow I still lingered among the living, attached through forces I don't understand to the long-lost sister I never had a chance to meet. The sister who'd been forced by my killer to take over my life. Since my death, Emma had fooled all my friends and family into thinking she was me, Sutton Mercer. She'd been fighting tooth and nail to find out what happened the night I died, and she'd managed to eliminate my family and my best friends as suspects. But the leads were quickly dwindling, the clues drying up. And the killer was still watching, somewhere in the shadows, making sure she didn't step out of line.

Now Emma stood in socks and underwear, a dazed expression on her face as she stared up at my wardrobe. It seemed ridiculous that after everything that had happened—the losses she'd suffered, the terror she'd lived in—the simple act of getting dressed could feel so overwhelming. But maybe it was *because* of her losses, because of her terror, that the simplest choices had turned complicated in her agitated mind. Emma had never had this kind of closet in her old life. Placed in the foster system of Las Vegas after our mother, Becky, abandoned her, Emma moved from home to home with her secondhand T-shirts packed in a duffel bag. I had so many clothes, so many dresses: short and tight or long and flowing, in bright wild prints or plain blocked color, with sequins or ruching or lace trim. There were, of course, more than a half dozen in black to choose from.

Suddenly, Emma began to tremble. She sank to the plush rug, hugging her arms around her knees as tears rolled down her cheeks.

"What happened to you, Nisha?" she whispered. "What were you trying to tell me?"

It'd been nearly two weeks since Nisha Banerjee, my old rival, was discovered floating facedown in her pool. The announcement sent shock waves through the school. Nisha was involved in dozens of activities, and while she wasn't quite the queen bee I'd been, everyone knew her. The rumor mill started up almost immediately. Nisha was athletic and a strong swimmer—half the school had been to a pool party at her house at one time or another. How could she have drowned? Was it just a freak accident? Or could it have been something darker—a drug overdose? *Suicide?*

But Emma and I knew better. The day of her death, Nisha had been desperately trying to reach Emma, calling her over and over. Emma hadn't called back at first because she'd been so distracted by my secret boyfriend, Thayer Vega, insisting that there was something different about her and that he was going to find out what it was. By the time Emma did call her, Nisha was already dead, and Emma had a feeling that it wasn't a coincidence.

If Emma was right, if Nisha stumbled on some kind of information about my death, then she was the latest victim in my murderer's deadly game. Whoever killed me was still out there—and was willing to kill again to keep his or her secret buried.

Emma finally got to her feet, rubbing the tears away impatiently. Grieving for Nisha was a luxury she couldn't afford. She needed to figure out what happened the night I died, before someone else she cared about paid the price—and before the killer eliminated her, too.

1

WHAT A TANGLED WEB WE WEAVE

"It was almost two weeks ago that this local girl was found dead in her family's pool," the newscaster's voice intoned as an image of Nisha filled the screen on a Saturday in late November. Emma stood in front of Sutton's desk, streaming the local news coverage about Nisha while she got dressed for Nisha's funeral. She wasn't sure why she was watching; she knew the details already. Maybe hearing them repeated often enough would make her finally believe it was true: Nisha was really gone.

The newscaster, a slender Latina in a mauve blazer, stood in front of a contemporary ranch house that Emma knew well. Nisha's home was the first place she went as

Sutton, the night Madeline Vega and the Twitter Twins, Lilianna and Gabriella Fiorello, "kidnapped" her from the park bench where she'd been waiting to meet her twin for the very first time. Emma remembered how irritated Nisha had seemed when Emma walked into the party—Nisha and Sutton had been rivals for years. But over the past month, Emma had started to form a tentative friendship with the tennis team cocaptain.

"The girl was discovered by her father just after eight P.M. last Monday. In an official statement, the Tucson Police have determined that there is no evidence of foul play and are treating the death as an accident. But many questions remain."

The camera cut to Clara, a girl Emma knew from the varsity tennis team. Her eyes were wide and shocked, her face pale. NISHA'S CLASSMATE appeared at the bottom third of the screen below her. "A lot of people are saying it might have been . . . it might have been intentional. Because Nisha was so driven, you know? How much can one person do before they . . . they crack?" Tears filled Clara's eyes.

The camera cut away again, replacing Clara with a teenage boy. Emma did a double take. It was her boyfriend, Ethan Landry. NISHA'S NEIGHBOR, said the caption below his face. He wore a black button-down shirt and a black tie and was obviously leaving his house for the funeral. Emma's knees weakened at the sight of him. "I didn't know her that well," Ethan said. His dark blue eyes were serious. "She always seemed really together to me. But I guess you never know what secrets people are hiding."

The camera returned to the newscaster. "Services will be held this afternoon at All Faiths Memorial Park. The family has requested that donations be made to the University of Arizona Hospital in lieu of flowers. This is Tricia Melendez, signing off." Emma snapped the laptop closed and walked back into the closet. The silence left in the wake of the chattering newscaster felt deep and sepulchral.

She'd never been to a funeral before. Unlike most kids her age, who had lost grandparents or family friends, Emma had never had anyone to lose. She took a deep breath and started to flip through Sutton's black dresses, trying to decide which one would be appropriate.

I couldn't remember if I'd ever had reason to wear mourning black. My dead-girl memory was frustratingly spotty. I could remember vague, general attachments—to my house, to my parents—but very few concrete moments. Every now and then a memory would come back to me in a flash of sudden details, but I hadn't figured out how to predict them, let alone trigger them. I tried to remember my grandfather's funeral, when Laurel and I were six or seven. Had we held hands as we approached the casket?

Emma finally decided on a cashmere sweater-dress, taking it gently from its hanger and pulling it over her head. The fit was a little clingy, but the cut was simple. As she smoothed the delicate knit down over her hips, Clara's words echoed in her ears. *It might have been . . . intentional.*

Thursday had been Thanksgiving, and even though the holiday had been cheerless, Emma was at least grateful for a few days away from school and the wild speculation about Nisha. The gossip didn't sit right with Emma. She'd spent the weekend before with Nisha, and she hadn't seemed at all sad. Whatever insecurities had kept her and Sutton at odds seemed to have finally evaporated, with a little help from Emma's kindness. Nisha had even helped Emma break into the hospital mental health records to find out the truth about Becky's past. For two awful weeks, Emma had believed Becky to be Sutton's killer—she'd wanted to check her mother's file to find out if her behavior had ever been violent.

Now Emma picked up Sutton's iPhone, scrolling through the messages. The day Nisha died, she'd called Emma about a dozen times over the course of the morning, then finally sent her a single text: CALL ME ASAP. I HAVE SOMETHING TO TELL YOU. She hadn't left a voicemail, and there was no other explanation. Hours later, she'd drowned.

It could be a coincidence, Emma thought, tucking the phone into a black-and-white clutch with her wallet.

There's no proof that anyone killed Nisha, or that her death had anything to do with me.

But even as she thought the words, a grim conviction settled over the doubt and grief that occupied her heart. She couldn't afford to believe in coincidences anymore. After all, how many long shots had brought her here? Travis, her pothead foster brother, had just *happened* to stumble upon a fake snuff video of Sutton that he'd thought was Emma. She'd *conveniently* arrived in Tucson the day after her sister's death, after spending eighteen years without even knowing she had a sister. And now Nisha had died the very same day she urgently *had* to talk to Emma? No, not all of that could be chance. She felt like a pawn under an invisible hand, being moved without volition across a chessboard in a game she barely understood.

And she couldn't help but feel that Nisha had just been sacrificed in the same game.

I watched as my sister fumbled with a handful of bobby pins, trying to sweep her hair up into a French twist. Emma was hopeless at updos—at anything but a simple ponytail, really. I wished I could stand behind her and help. I wished that we could get ready together and that I could hold her hand during the funeral. I wished I could tell her I was right there when Emma felt so very alone.

A soft knock sounded at the door. Emma spit out a bobby pin and looked up. "Come in."

Mr. Mercer pushed the door open, wearing a tailored black suit and a blue-and-burgundy tie. The gray in his hair seemed more pronounced than usual; he'd had a lot of secrets to keep lately. Emma had recently learned from him that Becky was the Mercers' daughter—making Emma their biological granddaughter. Now that she knew it, she could see the resemblance. She had Mr. Mercer's straight nose and bow-shaped lips. But Mr. Mercer had kept Becky's reappearance from his wife and Sutton's sister, Laurel.

"Hey, kiddo," he said, giving her a tentative smile. "How are you doing up here?"

Emma opened her mouth to say *fine*, but after a moment she closed it and shrugged. She didn't know how to answer that question, but she certainly wasn't fine.

Mr. Mercer nodded, then let out a heavy breath. "You've been through so much." He was talking about more than Nisha. As if her friend's death weren't enough, Emma had recently seen Becky, her own mother, for the first time in thirteen years.

Emma had managed to prove that Becky was innocent of Sutton's murder, but the image of Becky strapped to a hospital bed, frothing at the mouth, still haunted her dreams. She'd spent so many years wondering what had happened to her mom, but she'd never realized how ill Becky was. How unstable.

She picked up the small black-and-white clutch she'd packed with tissues. "I'm ready to go."

Her grandfather nodded. "Why don't you come down to the living room first, Sutton? I think it's time to have a family meeting."

"Family meeting?"

Mr. Mercer nodded. "Laurel and Mom are already waiting."

Emma bit her lip. She'd never been to anything like a family meeting before and didn't know what to expect. She stood unsteadily on Sutton's black wedges and followed Mr. Mercer down the staircase and through the bright entryway. Crisp, early-afternoon light flooded through the high window.

The Mercers' living room was decorated in luxe Southwestern colors—lots of earthy reds and tans paired with Navajo chevron prints. Paintings of desert flowers hung on the walls, and a Steinway baby grand stood gleaming beneath one window. Mrs. Mercer and Laurel were already there, sitting close together on the wide leather couch.

As with Mr. Mercer, Emma could see her own resemblance to her grandmother now that she knew to look for it. They had the same marine-blue eyes, the same slender frame. Mrs. Mercer looked nervous, her lipstick torn where she'd been biting her lip. Next to her, Laurel sat with her legs crossed, jiggling one foot up and down anxiously. Her honey-blonde hair was twisted back in the exact updo Emma had been trying to pull off. She'd chosen a black pencil skirt and a button-down blouse for the occasion, and she wore a tiny gold bracelet with a charm shaped like a tennis racket. She was pale beneath the light freckles across her nose.

Emma sat down carefully on the suede wing chair across from Laurel and her grandmother. From the entryway, the clock gave a single resonant *bong*.

"The funeral starts in an hour," Laurel said. "Shouldn't we get going?"

"We will, in just a minute," said Mr. Mercer. "Your mother and I wanted to talk to you first." He cleared his throat. "Nisha's death is a reminder about what's really important in this life. You girls are more important to us than anything." His voice caught as he spoke, and he paused for a moment to regain his composure.

Laurel looked up at Mr. Mercer, her forehead creased in a frown. "Dad, we know. You don't have to tell us that."

He shook his head. "Your mother and I haven't always been honest with you girls, Laurel, and it's hurt our family. We want to tell you the truth. Secrets only drive us apart."

Emma suddenly realized what he was talking about. Neither Mrs. Mercer nor Laurel knew that she and Mr.

Mercer had been in contact with Becky. Laurel didn't even know Becky existed. As far as she knew, Sutton had been adopted from an anonymous stranger. As for Mrs. Mercer, she'd banished Emma's mother from the household years before. Emma shot a panicked look at Mr. Mercer. He clung to the back of the chair as if bracing himself.

Mrs. Mercer seemed to notice Emma's anxiety and gave her a weak smile. "Honey, it's okay. Your father and I have talked about this. I know everything. You're not in trouble."

Laurel looked sharply at her mother. "What are you talking about?" Her gaze shifted to Mr. Mercer. "Am I the only one who doesn't know what's going on?"

An awkward silence descended on the room. Mrs. Mercer stared down at her lap, while Mr. Mercer adjusted his tie uncomfortably.

Emma swallowed hard, meeting Laurel's eyes. "I finally met my birth mother."

Laurel's jaw fell open, her neck jutting forward in surprise. "What? That's huge news!"

"That's not all, though," Mr. Mercer broke in. His mouth twisted downward unhappily. "Laurel, honey, the truth is, Sutton is our biological granddaughter."

Laurel froze for a moment. Then she slowly shook her head, staring at her father. "I don't understand. That's impossible. How could she be your . . ."

"Her mom—Becky—is our daughter," continued Mr. Mercer. "We had her when we were very young. Becky left home before you were even born, Laurel."

"But . . . why wouldn't you tell me something like that?" Angry pink spots appeared in Laurel's cheeks. "This is insane."

"Honey, I'm so sorry we never told you before." Mr. Mercer's voice had a pleading note to it. "We thought we were making the right decision. We wanted to protect you girls from our own mistakes."

"She's my sister!" Laurel snapped, her voice shrill. For a moment, Emma thought she was talking about Sutton—but then she realized Laurel was referring to Becky. "You kept my sister from me!"

Emma's fingers clutched her dress, her knuckles pale from the force. After everything she'd been through, she was startled to find she was still afraid of a Class Five Laurel Tantrum. But she couldn't blame Laurel for her reaction. Emma had spent so much time thinking of Becky as her missing mother that she'd almost forgotten Becky and Laurel were sisters. Laurel was right; it wasn't fair that she'd never been given the chance to know her.

"Where is she? What's she like?" Laurel demanded. Emma opened her mouth to answer, but before she could, Mrs. Mercer spoke.

"Troubled."

That one soft word seemed to fill the room. They all looked toward Mrs. Mercer, who was quietly crying, her hand pressed to her lips. The sight of her mother in distress seemed to derail Laurel's anger. She bit her lip, and her eyes softened.

Mrs. Mercer continued, her hand lowering to her heart. Her voice was low and shaky, barely louder than a whisper. "Becky hurt your father and me so much, Laurel. She's a difficult person to care for. We decided that it would be better for all of us if we didn't have contact with her. She's done so much damage to this family over the years."

"It's not all Becky's fault," Mr. Mercer broke in, leaning forward. "She's mentally ill, Laurel, and your mother and I didn't really know how to handle that when she was growing up."

Laurel turned her gaze to Emma again, her face more wounded than angry. "How long have *you* known all this?"

Emma took a deep breath. She picked up a tasseled pillow from the chair next to her and hugged it to her chest like a stuffed animal, thinking of what *Sutton's* answer to this question would be. "I met her that night in Sabino Canyon. The night of Nisha's tennis sleepover."

Emma had done her best to piece together the night that I died, and bits of my memory had come back, too. I had seen Laurel that night, when I called her to pick up Thayer Vega, my secret boyfriend and Laurel's longtime crush, and take him to the hospital after someone—probably my murderer—had tried to run him over with my car. I could see the memory register on Laurel's face, too, her eyes widening as she made the connection.

"I'm sorry I kept it from you," Emma said, flinching as she thought of all the other huge secrets she was hiding from the Mercers. "It was really intense, and I just wasn't ready to talk about it yet."

Laurel nodded slowly. She toyed with the charm on her bracelet, conflicting emotions flitting across her face. Emma knew how she felt—the discoveries she'd made about Becky and the Mercers were still fresh for her, too.

The room was so quiet they could hear the family's Great Dane's breath from where Drake snoozed in a gargantuan dog bed near the fireplace. Mr. Mercer stared out the window, where a pair of cactus wrens were busily building a nest in the desert willow beyond. After a long moment, Laurel laughed quietly.

"What?" Emma asked, cocking her head.

"I just realized," Laurel said, a half-smile twisting her lips to the side, "this makes you my niece, doesn't it?"

Emma laughed softly, too. "I guess so."

"Technically, it does," Mr. Mercer added. He unbuttoned and rebuttoned his suit coat, looking visibly relieved to hear them laugh. "But since we formally adopted Sutton, she's also legally your sister."

Laurel turned to face Emma again, and even though her smile looked a little strained, her eyes were warm. "This is all really crazy . . . but it's kind of cool that we're related. Biologically, I mean. You know you've always been my sister. But I'm glad we're related by blood, too."

Quick flashes of memory crowded my mind of us as little girls. Laurel was right. We *had* been sisters. We'd fought like sisters, but we'd also taken care of each other the way sisters were supposed to.

Mr. Mercer cleared his throat, running his hand over his jaw. "There's one more thing," he said. Emma's eyes shot up at him. More? "Becky said some strange things to me before she left. It's hard to know what to believe. Becky isn't always   reliable. But for some reason my gut says she might be telling the truth this time. She says that she had another daughter. That Sutton had a twin."

Emma's heart wrenched to a halt in her chest. For one long moment her vision went blurry, the Mercers' living room turning into a smeared Dali-like landscape around her. They still didn't know the whole truth. When she'd looked at Becky's files two weeks before, Emma discovered that Becky had yet another daughter, a twelve-year-old girl who Becky said lived with her father in California.

"A twin?" Laurel squeaked.

"I don't know if it's true." Mr. Mercer looked down at Emma, his face unreadable. "Becky didn't seem to know where your sister—your twin—was now, Sutton. But her name is Emma."

"Emma?" Laurel turned an incredulous glance at Emma. "Isn't that what you called yourself at breakfast the first day of school?"

Emma picked at a snag in Sutton's dress, playing for time. She was spared answering when Mr. Mercer spoke again.

"Becky told you about her, didn't she?" he asked softly. "That night at Sabino?"

Her mind churning, Emma managed to nod, grateful that Mr. Mercer had provided an explanation. It was most likely true. When Emma had spoken with Becky last week, Becky had talked about Emma like she'd already told Sutton about her once. Either way, Emma knew she had to be very careful here.

"All she told me was her name," Emma said softly. "I should have told you. But I was so mad. I was trying to find out if you knew about her, too, see if you recognized the name. I thought maybe I could pick a fight and you'd have to tell me."

Another tense silence opened in the room. Out of the corner of her eye she watched Drake look up from his bed and glance around, wagging his tail tentatively. The second hand on Mr. Mercer's Cartier watch clicked audibly. It seemed ploddingly slow compared to Emma's own racing heart.

Mrs. Mercer finally broke the silence. "I'm so sorry we lied to you, Sutton. To both of you. You both have every right to be angry. I hope someday you can understand, and maybe even forgive us."

My own heart ached at the look on my mother's face, full of anguish. Of course I forgave her, even though I could never tell her that. I only hoped she'd be able to forgive herself when the entire truth came out, when she realized how dearly all those secrets had cost our family. That someone had used them against us—against me—by forcing Emma to take my place after my death.

"So what now?" Laurel asked, her eyes on Emma. Her jaw was set determinedly. "We have to find this Emma girl, right? I mean, she's our sister. Our niece. Our . . . uh, whatever."

Mrs. Mercer nodded firmly. "We're going to try to track her down. We would at least like to meet her, make sure she's safe and happy where she is. Maybe make her a part of our family, if she wants to be." She tilted her head at Emma questioningly. "Did she tell you anything else, Sutton? Where Emma might be, or what her last name was?"

Emma bit hard on the inside of her cheek to keep the tears from escaping. It was so unfair—they wanted to look for her, wanted to make her safe, and she was right in front of them, in as much danger as she'd ever been in. "No," she whispered. "Becky didn't tell me anything else."

Mr. Mercer sighed, then leaned over to kiss the top of Emma's head. "Don't worry," he said. "One way or another, we'll find her. And in the meantime—I promise that we'll be honest with each other from now on."

For one brief, frantic moment, Emma thought about coming clean. The idea terrified her—they'd be devastated. She would have to tell them that the girl they'd raised as their own daughter was dead—and that she'd helped to cover it up. But it would be a relief, too. She would have help in her investigation, maybe even protection. She would be able to let go of the heavy weight that had pressed down upon her since the first morning she'd woken up in Tucson.

But then she thought about the murderer, always watching her—leaving notes on her car, strangling her at Charlotte's house, dropping lights from the catwalk in the theater at school. She thought about Nisha, calling her over and over, and then, just like that . . . dying. She couldn't expose her family to that kind of danger. She couldn't risk it.

Mrs. Mercer cleared her throat. "I know you girls will want to tell your friends, but for the time being, I'd appreciate it if we could keep this information private. Your father and I are still debating the best way to go about searching for Emma, and . . . there's still a lot for us to talk about."

Laurel's jaw stiffened belligerently for a moment, and Emma was sure she was going to argue. But then she took

Mrs. Mercer's hand and squeezed it. "Sure, Mom," she said, her voice gentle. "We can keep a secret."

In the hallway, the clock struck the quarter hour.

"We need to go," Mr. Mercer said softly. "We'll be late."

"I have to run to the bathroom," Emma said, needing a second to compose herself. She grabbed her clutch and hurried down the hall. As soon as she was alone, Emma leaned over the sink. In the mirror, her skin looked milky pale, her blue eyes brighter than usual. *I'm doing the right thing*, she told herself. No matter what, she needed to keep her family safe.

I was glad Emma was looking out for my family. But as I stared into her face, so achingly like my own, I couldn't help but wonder: Who would keep *Emma* safe?

2

A GRAVE MATTER

"It is with much sadness today that we offer up our fare-
wells to Nisha. She was a vibrant, talented girl, and we
will miss her."

The funeral was a graveside service, set among the syc-
amores and salt cedars of the cemetery. The sun blazed
from its late-fall angle in the sky, sending a melancholy
sheen over the gray and white tombstones. Emma sat on
a folding chair between Madeline Vega and Charlotte
Chamberlain, Sutton's two best friends. Right behind
them sat the Twitter Twins, their cell phones in their purses
for once. Laurel sat next to them, hiccupping with silent
tears. The entire school had turned out, including most of

their teachers and Principal Ambrose. Emma caught sight of Ethan standing in the shade of a tree, wearing the black shirt and black tie he'd been in for the news interview.

The officiant, a broad-hipped woman in a white sari, went on. "It is especially cruel to lose someone so young. Nisha was brimming with potential. The temptation to dwell on all she could have done if she had survived is great. We want to lament how she might have changed the world, how she might have gone on to such great heights."

Behind the woman in the sari sat the coffin, its polished oak gleaming in the sunlight. It was closed; there had been no viewing. The service was shaping up to be a short one. Before the officiant had gotten up to deliver the final eulogy, there'd been a handful of scattered readings from Nisha's friends, and the Hollier High show choir had sung "Wind Beneath My Wings." Privately Emma could imagine Nisha snickering at the choice—she hadn't been a sentimental girl. But there hadn't been a dry eye in the audience. Charlotte had burst into gasping sobs, mascara running down her cheeks, and Madeline, pale and trembling, balled up her skirt in her fists.

I watched the crowd wistfully. Would I ever have a funeral? What would people say about me then? Would they cry? Watching the casket and the deep hole next to it, a chill went through me—somewhere, my own remains lay hidden, separated violently from my spirit and left to rot. I looked around again, half-hoping to find an ethereal Nisha. But I was the only ghost here as far as I could see.

The officiant had a resonant, musical voice, tinged with the same faint Anglo-Indian accent Dr. Banerjee had. "But I believe we do Nisha a disservice, focusing on what could have been. As we say our good-byes, I ask you not to dwell on what has been lost but to think of what we gained by having Nisha in our lives."

A small string ensemble played an instrumental arrangement of the Beatles' "Let It Be" as everyone rose from their chairs and started to mingle.

Charlotte dabbed at the corners of her eyes with a tissue she'd pulled from the depths of her bag. Her long red curls had been pinned up behind her head, but stray coils fell on either side of her round, freckled face. "I can't believe this is happening. I can't believe she's dead."

"I still can't believe people think she did this on purpose," Madeline said, her hazel eyes wide. She shook her head. "She was fine on Sunday, right?"

Sunday had been the night they'd orchestrated a fake séance to prank a girl named Celeste Echols. It had been the first Lying Game prank Nisha had ever participated in—though she'd been the victim of a few in her time. She'd definitely seemed to enjoy being a part of the production.

"I know. It just doesn't make any sense. She's such a good

swimmer," Laurel whispered tearfully. "I mean, she was."

"What do you think, Sutton?" Gabby asked. Emma looked up sharply. As always, the Twitter Twins' wardrobes were in perfect contrast. Gabby wore a simple sheath dress and pearl studs in her ears, her lipstick a carefully lined red. Lili, on the other hand, wore what looked like a black thrift-store tutu and a pair of knee-high combat boots, a small veil pinned into her hair.

"Yeah, it seemed like you guys were getting close lately. Did she seem sad?" Lili asked.

"Does it really matter?" Emma said, her voice breaking. "She's gone. The 'why' doesn't change that."

The girls fell silent. Across the lawn, Emma watched as the funeral officiant leaned over to talk to Dr. Banerjee, who hadn't moved from his seat, a faraway look on his face. Emma had seen the doctor several weeks before, when he had treated her mother. He'd been patient and kind, even when Becky had been violent. Now his worst nightmare was coming true—and so soon on the heels of his wife's death.

"Excuse me," she told her friends, and walked around the now-empty chairs toward where he sat.

People nodded at her as she passed. Coach Maggie stood with a group of tennis players, looking shocked and heartbroken. Clara was with them, tears running down her cheeks

The officiant hugged Dr. Banerjee one last time, then joined the crowd, leaving him alone. Emma hesitated. She wanted to tell him how sorry she was for his loss and that Nisha had become a good friend to her. But more than that, she wanted to find out what *he* thought about Nisha's death—and where his daughter had been before she died.

Before she could decide what to say, someone else sat down next to Dr. Banerjee. Her body tensed as she recognized Detective Quinlan in ceremonial dress blues, his hat in his hands. Quinlan was hardly a fan of Sutton Mercer— he had a file three inches thick on Sutton's Lying Game exploits, and he had arrested Emma for shoplifting two months earlier. She instinctively ducked behind a headstone a few feet away.

Quinlan's voice was a low, sympathetic rumble. Leaning back against the cool marble, Emma strained her ears to hear what he was saying. She caught "so sorry" and "tragic" and was about to back away from the two men when the word "autopsy" drifted to her.

Dr. Banerjee shook his head violently at whatever Quinlan had just said.

"Look, Sanjay." Quinlan's voice was patient but firm. "There weren't any signs of a struggle. No defensive wounds, no bruises, no handprints. It was just an accident."

"No." Dr. Banerjee's hands remained folded neatly in his lap, but his muscles were tight across his face. "Nisha has been swimming since she was two. She would have had to have tripped and hit her head for it to be an accident. But no bruises? No concussion?" He paused, his mouth writhing for a moment before he could speak again. "My daughter was murdered."

Quinlan hesitated, his lips downturned beneath his mustache. "There's more," he said softly. "I hate to tell you like this. But the examiner found extremely high amounts of diazepam in her bloodstream. That's . . ."

"Valium. Yes, I *am* a doctor," Nisha's father snapped. His knuckles went white as he squeezed his fingers together harder. "She doesn't have a prescription for Valium."

Quinlan sighed, rubbing his stubbled jaw. "I know. We checked her records."

"Then what are you . . ."

"I know it's hard to hear. But Nisha had a very bad year." Quinlan looked uncomfortable. He turned his hat over and over in his hands. "I don't want to sound like I'm accusing her of anything. But Sanjay, teens try new things and don't always know their limits."

Dr. Banerjee's voice was hard. "Her room was all torn up, Shane. Someone went through and ripped the place to bits. Someone was looking for something."

Quinlan shrugged. "There was no sign of forced entry, and we didn't find anybody's fingerprints in there. Only yours and hers. Nisha must have done that herself.

Sometimes people do strange things when they're in an altered state."

Dr. Banerjee sat very still for a long moment, looking down at his hands. His glasses were askew on his nose, and it gave him a slightly manic look. Quinlan looked awkwardly around. For a moment Emma almost felt sorry for him.

"Look," he finally said in an undertone Emma had to strain to hear. "If there are any people you have a funny feeling about—strange people hanging around the house, boys who seemed too aggressive with her—if she had any enemies, give me their names. I'll look into it. But right now, I have no evidence, no leads, no clues. Give me something to work with."

Dr. Banerjee shook his head. "She didn't have any enemies. None that I knew of." His hands came free from each other and flew to cover his face. "I don't know who would want to do something like this to my little girl," he groaned, his back shuddering.

Behind the monument, a surge of guilt welled up in Emma. Should she tell them about the calls and frantic text from Nisha? Her stomach tightened with anxiety. Quinlan's suspicions were always quick to rise when Sutton Mercer was involved. At best, he'd probably dismiss it as another attention-seeking prank. At worst, Emma would end up on a list of suspects, and her own story would crumble easily on inspection.

"I need a drink of water," Dr. Banerjee finally said. His voice sounded tense, as if he was fighting for calm. His face had composed itself, except for his eyes. They were bloodshot and wild.

Quinlan nodded. "Come on, Sanjay." With surprising gentleness he helped Dr. Banerjee to his feet, and the two men walked to the banquet table set up in the shade of a cedar.

Emma slumped against the tombstone, her heart hammering. So Nisha's room had been ransacked. But what had the killer been looking for? And did they find it, or was it still there in Nisha's bedroom?

Emma stared at Nisha's coffin for a long moment, the deep brown wood shining in the sun. "I'm so sorry," she whispered. Her gaze fell on the grave she'd been hiding behind. JESMINDER BANERJEE, it read. BELOVED WIFE AND MOTHER. Nisha's mom. She hadn't even thought of that—of course they'd bury Nisha by her mother.

Emma pushed herself up and walked across the green. The crowd was starting to thin. In the distant parking lot she could hear cars starting and doors slamming.

She passed a cluster of Hollier students who were standing close together near a weather-beaten mausoleum with an urn of wilting lilies in front of it. Garrett Austin stood between his younger sister, Louisa, and Celeste, his current girlfriend. Garrett had been Sutton's "official" boyfriend at the time of her death, although she'd been seeing Thayer secretly at the same time. When Emma had taken her place, he'd offered up his virginity to her as a birthday gift, and after she bolted in a panic, they'd broken up.

Garrett looked devastated. His eyes were red, his blond hair lusterless and unwashed. He'd dated Nisha for a few weeks, and even though they'd broken up, he was obviously not taking her death well. He glanced up and noticed Emma, staring at her blankly, as though he didn't quite recognize her.

Caught, Emma took a tentative step toward him.

"How are you holding up?" Emma asked awkwardly, touching his shoulder.

Garrett blinked, and then all at once his face darkened into a scowl. He jerked away from her hand, his arms taut with anger. She instinctively took a step back. He looked for a moment like he wanted to take a swing at her.

"What do you care? You barely even knew her," he hissed.

Behind him, Emma could see that Celeste looked shocked by his anger. Louisa glanced from Emma to Garrett, confused.

Emma felt frozen in place. Barely knew her? Sure, Emma had only known Nisha for a few months. But *Sutton* had grown up with Nisha.

"Garrett, I know you're upset . . ." Celeste started, laying her hand on his arm. He whipped around violently so that his nose was inches from hers. Emma's entire body tensed at the wild expression on his face. A nasty sneer twisted his lips.

"You don't know anything," he snarled. "Would you just shut up for five minutes? I'm starting to think Nisha was right about you."

Emma's jaw fell open. Celeste's expression darkened. "Is that so?" she snapped, the airy quality gone from her voice. "When did you have this cozy little chat about me?"

"It's none of your business," he shouted. By now most of the other students they'd been standing with had slunk away awkwardly. Louisa watched her brother with anxious, darting eyes.

Laurel materialized at Emma's side and grabbed her by the arm, steering her past them, toward the parking lot. "Come on," she whispered, even as Celeste's voice rose up angrily behind them. "Arguing at a funeral? How tacky."

"I can't believe he'd yell at his girlfriend like that," Emma said, feeling a little dazed. She let Laurel lead her past the rows upon rows of headstones.

Laurel stopped for a moment, raising her eyebrow. "Excuse me? You two used to go at it all the time."

Emma stared at Sutton's sister.

Laurel shrugged. "Come on, Sutton, he used to freak

out about everything. You not calling him back quick enough, you wearing too short a skirt, you not making one of his games. He's not exactly even-keeled."

"Yeah," Emma stammered, trying to cover her confusion. "I know. Come on, let's go."

They started walking again. Across the graveyard, Celeste and Garrett's voices were still audible, cutting tensely back and forth. Emma's head spun. Why had he said that she barely knew Nisha?

I didn't know either. But something told me Emma had better figure it out quickly. Garrett obviously had a short fuse, and Emma didn't want to be caught in the blast zone if he went off.

3

ALONE AT LAST

The next afternoon, Emma and Ethan walked up a bare, hilly trail at Tucson Mountain Park. Emma tightened a gray cashmere scarf around her neck, shivering at the cool wintry air. The rocks glowed reddish gold in the late-day sun, and Emma and Ethan clasped hands as they walked, their fingers interlacing.

Emma liked the barren landscape. She'd felt as if someone had been following her since the moment she arrived in Tucson, but there wasn't much cover on this wide expanse of trail. Sutton's killer would have a hard time sneaking up on her here.

As they walked she told Ethan about the Mercers'

family meeting. He listened carefully, his eyes ahead on the path. "They're going to look for me, Ethan, and it's not like I covered my tracks." She thought about every *CSI* episode she'd ever seen. It was ridiculously easy to trace peoples' whereabouts, if you had an Internet connection and a witness or two. "I don't know how long I have before they figure it out. And if they do, I'll be the number-one suspect. The killer has made sure of that."

They reached a promontory with a covered picnic area looking over the park. A fat raccoon glanced nonchalantly up from a McDonald's wrapper as they approached, then waddled off into the underbrush. Emma sat on the top of the picnic table, rummaging in her backpack for a bottle of water. She took a long sip, then handed it to Ethan.

"All of us are in danger." She looked up at him miserably. "You, me, my family. We have to solve this, and fast."

He slid an arm around her and pulled her against his side protectively. She rested against his shoulder, breathing in the clean-laundry smell of his flannel shirt.

"Okay, so we've ruled out Laurel, Thayer, Madeline, Charlotte, Mr. Mercer, Becky, and the Twitter Twins," he said, ticking Sutton's friends and family off one by one. "Are we totally sure it's not, like . . . a random crime? I mean, maybe it was a drifter or something?"

Emma shook her head. "The killer knows too much about Sutton for it to be random. Where she lives, what her schedule is, the importance of her locket . . . the killer took it right off her neck and left it for me, knowing that I wouldn't be a realistic stand-in unless I was wearing it." She shivered. "This murder was personal."

Ethan nodded. "I guess you're right."

"You know who we haven't looked into?" Emma said quietly. "Garrett." She filled Ethan in on Garrett's comment that she "barely knew" Nisha, and Laurel's revelation that Garrett had a temper with Sutton.

"Wow." Ethan rubbed his jaw thoughtfully. "I don't really know much about Garrett. We had AP History together last year, but we don't really move in the same circles. I know he was out a lot for some kind of family emergency in the spring, but I never found out what the story was."

Emma chewed on her thumbnail. On the one real date she'd had with him, Garrett had mentioned something about his sister. *Charlotte was there for me during everything that happened with Louisa*, he'd said. At the time she hadn't been able to come up with a subtle way to ask what he was talking about. "What about Louisa? Do you know her?" she asked.

He shook his head. "Not that well. She kind of keeps to herself."

"I've seen her with Celeste. I guess they've hit it off." Emma took another sip of water and sighed. "Garrett doesn't strike me as the mastermind type, though. Whoever did this has had to orchestrate a pretty complicated alibi—hiding Sutton's body and her car, getting me to come to Tucson, watching me to make sure I was playing along. But Garrett couldn't even pick a restaurant when we went out. He let me decide everything." She twisted a lock of hair around her index finger so tightly it cut off the circulation. "Then again, maybe he's just a really good actor. Isn't that the thing with psychopaths? They're manipulative, really good at putting up a front."

Ethan raised an eyebrow. "I didn't know my girlfriend was an expert on criminal psychology."

Her lips twisted into a wry smirk. "If I wasn't before, I will be by the time this is over." Another thought popped into her head then, one that made her sit up straight. "You know, I haven't been able to figure out how the killer got into Charlotte's house that night he strangled me. But if it was Garrett . . ." She looked at Ethan significantly.

His mouth fell open. "He dated her before he dated Sutton."

"He might have had the alarm codes," Emma agreed, then paused. "And then he dated Nisha."

They looked at each other uncertainly. *And then Nisha died, too.* The unspoken phrase hovered between them.

Ethan licked his lips. "If it was Garrett, that makes

sense. Maybe she saw something while they were dating, and only figured it out two weeks ago."

Emma sighed. "It's all speculation, though, isn't it? We don't have any evidence putting him at the scene."

"Yeah, but we definitely have enough reasons to suspect him," Ethan argued. "In murder cases the cops almost always look at husbands or boyfriends first."

Emma thought back to homecoming, when Garrett had cornered her in a broom closet to yell at her about their breakup. He'd been drunk, almost violent, twisting her wrist to hold her there against her will. And now she remembered something else—he'd mentioned Thayer. *Everyone saw that fight between you guys just before he left. He loved you.*

"What if he found out about Sutton and Thayer?" Her throat went dry at the thought. "He could have followed her to the canyon that night and caught them together."

"That would be a real motive," Ethan said.

She nodded, the hairs on the back of her neck spiking up. Suddenly the memories of her brief "relationship" with Garrett looked a lot creepier. He'd acted like he really thought she was Sutton, but maybe he'd been testing her, training her so that no one would figure out Sutton was dead. The image of Sutton's bed, covered in rose petals, floated back to her, and she shuddered. What if he'd been trying to turn her into the Sutton he'd wanted all along?

I racked my brain for a memory of my summer with Garrett. I didn't remember anything suspicious—but then, I didn't remember fighting the way Laurel said we fought, either. In the days after I first woke up from my death, I'd felt a sort of warm tingle toward Garrett every time Emma saw him or spoke to him. I'd thought for sure I'd been in love with him in life, even if I couldn't remember why. But now all I felt was an anxious flutter.

"I'll ask around," she said finally. "Maybe Charlotte or Mads knows something that could be helpful." *Or Thayer,* she thought, though she didn't say that out loud. Ethan had been jealous of Thayer from the start—and it hadn't helped matters when he'd caught Thayer kissing Emma a week ago. The very mention of his name was enough to provoke a good half hour of brooding silence from Ethan.

She looked out over the landscape, the mountain air cool in her lungs. A few miles away she caught sight of a hawk drifting lazily on a gust of wind. Ethan opened a bag of gorp and picked out an M&M, popping it into Emma's mouth. She crunched down on the candy shell and smiled at him. Suddenly she was simply happy to be with Ethan, away from prying eyes. They'd barely been alone since the night of Charlotte's party, when they'd made love for the first time. The memory sent a flush of bashful pleasure through her cheeks and made her light-headed.

"Did you grow up with all the playground folklore about M&M's?" she asked coyly. He cocked his head at her.

"Huh?"

"You know, the urban legends about what the different colors mean?" She took the bag of gorp from him, picking past the nuts and raisins to find more candy. "Orange ones are good luck," she said, holding one up. "I definitely need that." She popped it in her mouth. "Yellow are what you give someone if you just want to be friends." She dropped a yellow candy back in the bag distastefully. "Red are for confessing when you love someone. . . . Here, you can have this one. And green?" She gave him a wicked grin. "They're for if you want to get someone . . . excited."

Ethan's cheeks were pink, but a dazed grin spread across his face. "Excited, huh?"

She held one up in front of his lips, but he shook his head, pulling her suddenly into his lap. "I don't need that one," he whispered against her ear. "You already make me crazy enough."

Emma's skin tingled as he pulled her into a passionate kiss, one that gave way to more kisses. All her lingering worries—about the murderer, about Nisha, about her family—drifted away. While she was in Ethan's arms, she was happier than she'd ever been.

I was glad my sister was getting some action. Emma deserved whatever comfort she could get after all she'd been through, even if her lame attempt at dirty talk had me wishing I could stick my fingers in my ears. But she and Ethan were made for each other—and if there were no other silver linings to the trap my murderer had caught her in, I was at least grateful for that.

4

FAREWELL, MY FRENEMY

A few hours later, Emma pulled Sutton's vintage Volvo into Ethan's driveway to drop him off. Across the street, Sabino Canyon loomed ominously. Next door, the Banerjees' house was dark and silent.

Ethan's home, a sand-colored bungalow with paint chipping from the siding, was one of the smallest on the block. It looked like it had been nice at one point, but it'd fallen into disrepair. Emma suspected Ethan tried to maintain the place as well as he could, but it was hard for him to keep up with it with his dad gone—Mr. Landry had more or less walked out on them a few years ago, when Mrs. Landry had been diagnosed with cancer.

Ethan turned toward her. "Good night," he whispered, leaning across the gear shift and placing the softest kiss imaginable on her lips. She closed her eyes. For just a moment, nothing in the world existed beyond the place where her lips met his.

"Good night," she said, as he pulled away. He gave her a long look, then got out of the car and loped up the driveway to his house. The car's headlights threw deep shadows around him—long, skinny abstracts of his body. His clean-laundry smell still lingering in the car, she watched him as he climbed the steps to the porch and let himself in.

Emma smiled to herself, touching her mouth with her fingers as if she could somehow hold the memory of the kiss there. She watched as the light in Ethan's room snapped on a moment later and imagined him sitting down at his desk, opening his calculus book or turning on his laptop, his dark blue eyes thoughtful under his furrowed brow.

Cute Boy Hugely Distracting to Amateur Detective. The headline flashed before her eyes as if it were in print, an old habit of hers. She shook her head to clear it, then put the car in reverse and backed down the driveway.

As she turned onto the street, her eyes fell on Nisha's house. She paused with her foot on the brake. A low wall with wrought-iron filigree surrounded the yard, but she could see that most of the windows were dark. She could just make out the glimmer of the pool in the backyard. A sharp, painful ache cut through her heart. That was where it had happened.

Emma thought of what Dr. Banerjee had said about Nisha's room being ransacked. What if the killer hadn't managed to find what he was looking for? If Dr. Banerjee and the cops had already gone over the room, it was a long shot. But it was still worth a try. She pulled the car to the curb and put it in park.

The motion-activated porch light sprang to life when she was a few feet from the door. In contrast to Ethan's weed-strewn yard, the Banerjees had a Xeriscaped garden full of white river stones and flowering cacti. But there were signs of neglect here, too—half-rotten fruit lay where it had fallen under a fig tree. Twigs and leaves floated on the brackish water in an austere marble birdbath. As Emma approached the porch, a large tabby cat with matted hair meowed piteously at her, its lamp-like eyes shining in the dark.

Emma stopped at the door. The cat swam around her ankles, a low hopeful purr coming from its throat. She swallowed, her nerve faltering—was it insensitive to ask a grieving father questions about his daughter's death? What would she even ask, anyway? She glanced behind her at the dark, hulking shape of the canyon. The murderer could be watching her, even now. What if she made things worse for Dr. Banerjee? What if Sutton's killer decided that he, like Nisha, knew too much?

She rang the doorbell before she could change her mind. The sound of the chime ringing out so suddenly in the quiet evening made her jump. After a long moment, she thought she could hear footsteps, and then Dr. Banerjee flung open the door.

Even though it was just a little past seven, he wore a long tartan bathrobe hanging open over a pair of mesh athletic shorts and a coffee-stained T-shirt that read HOLLIER TENNIS DAD. His thick glasses were askew on his face, making one eye look grotesquely magnified while the other squinted blearily. His hair stood up in a wild cloud around his head.

Before Emma could say anything, the cat streamed past his legs into the dark hallway beyond. Dr. Banerjee watched it go with an abstracted frown. "Agassi?" Then he glanced up at Emma. For a moment he looked blank, as if he did not quite remember who she was. He blinked at her.

"Sutton," he said at last. "Hello. Did you bring Agassi home?"

"Um, I actually wanted to ask you something. About Nisha."

His eyes seemed to focus sharply, his look of mild con-fusion evaporating at once. "What is it? Do you know what happened to her?"

Emma bit her lip. "I'm sorry, Dr. Banerjee. I don't understand it either." She shifted her weight. "But I was wondering if I could . . . go in Nisha's room? I won't mess anything up. I just want to say good-bye."

Dr. Banerjee took off his glasses and polished them on the corner of his grimy shirt. When he put them back on, they looked more smeared than before. A sad smile quirked his lips upward ever so slightly. He reached out and patted her elbow. "Of course, Sutton."

Somewhere in the depths of the house, the cat let out a loud, pleading cry. Dr. Banerjee gave a start. "I suppose I should feed him," he said vaguely. His vision went a little distant again, as if the effort required to focus his attention had finally exhausted itself. He ran his fingers through his hair and left it wilder than ever. "Just let yourself out when you're done," he said, then disappeared down the hall.

The house was almost completely dark. A flower-shaped night-light in the hallway to Nisha's room gave off just enough illumination for Emma to navigate. Passing the gleaming bronze kitchen, she saw the remains of a week's worth of takeout piled on the counters. Pizza boxes and Chinese containers towered precariously. A fly circled a half-eaten samosa on a ceramic plate. A fallen pint of Ben & Jerry's sat in a puddle of melted Cherry Garcia.

Emma had been in Nisha's room once before, during her second week in Tucson. At the time Nisha had still been a suspect, and she'd snuck in during a tennis dinner to try to find clues. When she snapped on the light now she was surprised at how little it had changed since then. There was no sign of the mess Nisha's killer had made—it looked like Dr. Banerjee had put everything straight. The purple bedspread was smooth, eight fluffy pillows propped at the head like an ad for a five-star hotel. All of her books were alphabetized on the shelves. The only evidence that someone had recently disturbed the room was a drawer with a broken front panel in the dresser. Otherwise it looked like Nisha could have just stepped outside.

Emma stood uncertainly in the middle of the rug. She didn't even know what she was looking for, much less where Nisha might have hidden it. She would just have to hope she'd know it when she saw it. While she glanced around, Agassi slunk in around the door and leapt lightly to the bed.

Emma started with the dresser, looking through the neat stacks of sweaters and T-shirts, feeling at the back and under each drawer for a hidden compartment or a note taped out of sight. Nisha had kept her belongings color-coded and perfectly organized, and the sight of her pure white tennis socks arranged row by row sent a surge of grief through Emma. She got on her knees and examined the desk, felt under the bed, and even peeled back the rug on the floor. Nothing seemed out of place. She blew a lock of her hair out of her face and sighed heavily.

Nisha kept her photos behind a glass panel near her headboard. Emma knelt in front of it, her eyes darting over the collage. Most of the pictures were of Nisha playing tennis. There were also a few of her with a woman Emma assumed was her mother, elegant in pearl earrings and burgundy lipstick, and several of Agassi looking glossy and well groomed.

Then Emma noticed a new picture, one that hadn't been there the last time. It was an older photograph, slightly crumpled, and unframed. It showed three little girls in ice skates, arm in arm and laughing so hard that one of the girls on the end—a tiny blonde girl with hair in pigtails—seemed about to fall. They all wore poofy party dresses, and the girl in the middle had a tiara tucked into her dark hair. It was Laurel, Nisha, and Sutton. Sutton had a tooth missing. A purple glittery star had been painted on one of her cheeks. Emma turned over the picture. It was dated April twentieth, with the words MY EIGHTH BIRTHDAY.

Emma's lips twisted downward. Once upon a time, Nisha had been friends with Sutton—or at least friendly enough to invite her to a birthday party, friendly enough to skate arm in arm with her. It looked like Nisha had put it up recently, after she'd started hanging out with Emma.

For a moment I heard a distant sound of childish laughter echoing down the corridors of my memory. That day at the ice rink, Nisha and I had tried to teach ourselves some of the tricks we'd seen during the Olympics. Michelle Kwan made toe loops look so easy, but we spent most of our time falling flat on our butts and laughing at ourselves. I couldn't remember why we'd ended up hating each other so much. Maybe it had just been that we were similar in all the wrong ways. We wanted the same things, and we were both willing to fight for them.

Emma climbed back to her feet and sighed. If there had ever been any evidence here, it was already in the hands of the killer. After all, Sutton's murderer had been a step ahead of her since she first arrived in Tucson. Why would this time be any different?

She stood in the doorway, sweeping her gaze one more time around Nisha's bedroom. *Good-bye, Nisha*, she thought. *I'm so sorry you got pulled into this.* She turned off the light and started the long walk back down the hallway. At the kitchen door she drew to a sudden stop, biting the corner of her lip. Then, impulsively, she went to the counter and started to gather the empty food containers. She found a roll of paper towels under the sink and wiped the counters down, then loaded the dishwasher, moving as quietly as she could. Somewhere in the house she could hear the low murmur of a television set.

Then she stuffed the takeout boxes into a garbage bag and carried it with her, past the night-light, past the beautiful furniture and the brightly colored tapestries and the elegant vases and all the other things that Dr. Banerjee had shared, once upon a time, with his family—back into the darkness beyond.

Good-bye, Nisha. I added my farewell to my sister's. *I promise, whoever did this to us is going to pay.*

5

HER CHEATING HEART

After the final bell rang the next day at school, Emma slowly gathered her books from her locker. She wasn't sure she was ready to face the tennis team, not yet. It would be an emotional practice. Emma blinked away a tear, looking at her reflection in the tiny mirror inside Sutton's locker. *Pull it together*, she commanded herself, and slammed the door shut. Then she did a double take.

Thayer Vega was standing there, waiting to talk to her.

My dead-girl heart gave a lurch at the sight of him. A gray henley shirt pulled tight across his muscular chest. His dark hair hung down over one eye, and his backpack was slung casually over his shoulder. Thayer had been the only boy I'd ever loved, the one person who really knew me.

"Hey," Emma said, hugging her books to her chest and giving him a shaky smile.

In the past month, she and Thayer had started to establish a cautious friendship. He was a good listener, and when Becky showed up in Emma's life again, he was one of the few people she felt safe telling. She'd started to think the two of them could put his relationship with Sutton behind them and be friends—until he kissed her at Charlotte's party two weeks ago. She'd pulled away, but not before he had a chance to realize something was wrong. He'd confronted her two days later, saying he knew something was off about her; and while she'd managed to dismiss his accusations, she knew he was still suspicious.

A wave of relief swept over her as she remembered Mrs. Mercer's plea to keep the news about Becky's other daughter a secret—if Thayer found out that Sutton had a long-lost twin, Emma had a feeling it wouldn't take long for him to figure out who she really was.

"Hey," he said, hefting the backpack farther across his back. "Are you heading out to the courts?"

"I'm not in any hurry," she said, smiling ruefully. "It's going to be like a second funeral."

"I get that." He searched her face for a moment. "How are you holding up?"

"Me? I'm okay." Emma's voice sounded too high in her ears, strained and anxious. He just looked at her.

"Come on, I'll walk with you to the locker rooms," Thayer said.

"Did you guys have a good Thanksgiving?" Emma asked, trying to make small talk as they paced down the hall.

He gave a bitter bark of laughter. "The usual. Mom burned the turkey, and Dad threw a wineglass at her. Mads and I ended up sneaking out and getting Burger King."

She gave him a sympathetic look. Thayer's family was at best volatile, and at worst downright abusive. "Sorry, Thayer. That sounds awful."

He shrugged. "It was par for the course around Casa Vega. And neither of us was in much mood for family time anyway."

Emma nodded. "Yeah. Mom and Dad cooked a big turkey dinner because they'd already bought the groceries and they didn't want it to go to waste, but they should have just stuck everything in the freezer. No one had much appetite. Except Drake," she added, smiling at the memory of the Great Dane, who'd casually sauntered past a countertop and inhaled a platter of sweet potatoes.

The halls were mostly empty by now, with the exception of a few drama kids wearing black robes for the school production of *The Crucible*. A pimply boy carrying a tuba hurried out of the music wing and disappeared through the doors leading to the football field.

As they crossed the flagstones of a small courtyard, Emma heard a dark chuckle from a bench in the corner. It was Garrett, his gaze pinned sharply on her. He was alone, his gear bag slouched on the ground next to him. His eyes were hard and angry, his lips twisted with bitter amusement.

"You'd better not let Landry catch you sneaking around all buddy-buddy," he said, sneering. "Although I could stand to watch him kick your ass again, Vega. I should have done it myself ages ago."

"Mind your own business, man," Thayer shot back. He stood with his legs planted wide and crossed his arms over his chest. Emma tensed next to him.

"You're not in charge of who I hang out with, Garrett," she snapped, recalling Laurel's words. It sounded like he'd been more controlling than she would have guessed. Maybe, in the end, he hadn't been able to control Sutton. Maybe it had driven him crazy.

Garrett gave her a long, cool look, his smile broadening slowly "You are a piece of work, you know that? It's almost like you believe your own lies."

She drew in her breath sharply. Once she would have thought he was just referring to Sutton's infidelity. But maybe he meant *Emma's* lies about being Sutton.

Thayer's hands clenched into fists for a moment. Then he relaxed them, shaking his head slowly at Garrett. "Man, it's over. This is pathetic even for you. Come on, Sutton." He rested his hand gently on her back and steered her through the door to the athletics wing.

Emma glanced at Thayer from the corner of her eye as they walked. His face was stormy, a brooding frown creasing his forehead.

She bit her lip and took a deep breath. "You know Garrett knew about us, right?"

Thayer nodded. "I had a feeling. He's said some weird stuff to me since I got back."

"Weird stuff?"

"Just macho bullshit. Watch my back, that kind of thing." Thayer shrugged. "I brushed it off at first. We've never exactly been friends. But he cornered me at the school break-in party a few weeks ago, drunk off his ass. He was pretty aggressive."

Emma's throat went dry. She stopped walking and touched his arm. He stared down at her fingers on his sleeve for a second too long, then glanced up to meet her eyes. "Thayer, do you remember anything at all about the face you saw through the windshield that night at Sabino?" she whispered. "Do you think it could have been Garrett?"

"Garrett?" He blinked in surprise. "I don't know. I

really couldn't see anything, it was so dark." His brow furrowed. "Do you have some reason to think it was him?"

"No, not other than how angry he's been at both of us, I guess." She sighed. "There are too many things in my life that don't make any sense right now. I wish I had some answers."

They stopped in the sports lobby just outside of the locker rooms. Nisha's senior portrait, blown up and framed with black velvet, hung on a corkboard next to the ticket office. In the picture her cobalt dress was bright against her dark skin. She gave the camera a serious look, obviously trying to appear like the dignified future Ivy Leaguer she imagined herself to be, but the photographer had somehow caught the ghost of a smile on her lips. All around the picture, people had pinned notes and cards, poems and song lyrics and messages in pink sparkly pen that Nisha would have mocked as far too girly.

"It's just so awful," Emma whispered. Thayer nodded, the corners of his mouth turning downward as he looked at the picture, too. She sighed. "Well, I'd better get changed. Thanks for . . . for walking with me."

Thayer turned to look at her again, his gaze searching and intense, as though he was seeking something in her features but didn't know what. Emma ducked away, suddenly afraid of Thayer's hazel eyes.

"It's weird," he said quietly. "Something about you has

really changed. Sometimes it feels like you turned into a whole new person while I was away."

"Maybe I grew up," Emma replied, her heart lurching nervously. "Or maybe you did, and you're just seeing me differently."

Thayer shook his head. "I don't know much, Sutton, but I know nothing can change the way I feel about you."

Relief flooded my body—the boy I loved so desperately still loved me back. But it was tempered by a deep feeling of sadness. Thayer had so many more memories of our time together, whereas all I had were a few scattered scenes. Would I ever get those memories back?

Emma's breath felt strangely short. She glanced up at Thayer's wounded and confused expression, then looked quickly away. "I have to go."

"Yeah. Okay." He shoved his hands into his pockets. "See you, Sutton." He turned toward the glass double doors and walked away from her.

She and I watched his retreating form together. I wanted to call out and stop him, to somehow let him know that I'm still here—and still in love with him. But he didn't look back, not even once.

6

THE CANYON'S SECRET

The humming sound of potters' wheels provided a soothing background noise as Emma sat in the ceramics studio
on Wednesday morning, struggling to attach a handle to
a lopsided pitcher. She dipped her fingers into the bucket
of slip she'd dredged from the vat at the back of the room
and dabbed it carefully on her project. Madeline wrinkled
her nose in distaste.

"You got some of that stuff on your jeans," she said,
pointing to a splotch on Emma's thigh.

"Ugh. That'd better come out in the wash," Emma
grumbled, though she had bigger problems right now
than cleaning Sutton's J Brands.

"So where's Laurel?" Madeline asked, looking around.

"I guess she decided to skip." Emma shrugged. It wasn't like Laurel to cut class without the other Lying Game girls, but a lot of things had been weird lately.

"I wish I'd gone with her." Mads sighed as her mug collapsed yet again. "I can't stand much more of this."

Charlotte put her bowl down, reaching over to pat Madeline on the back.

"Here's something to look forward to," Charlotte said, smiling. "My mom decided we're going to Barbados for Christmas. And of course Daddy's on board. He's been on his best behavior ever since Mom found a naughty text on his phone. Anyway, I refused to go unless I could take friends. So pack your bags, bitches, because we're heading to the land of rum and Rihanna."

Madeline's jaw fell open. "Are you kidding me?"

"Do I ever joke about vacations?" Charlotte winked. "In a few short weeks we'll be lying on the beach, drinking out of coconuts, and watching boys on surfboards."

"Oh my God." Madeline gave an uncharacteristic squeal, her eyes bright. "I am *so* in!"

Charlotte looked at Emma expectantly. "Sutton? What about you?"

Emma could barely process Charlotte's invitation. The only "beach" she had ever been to was a fake one at a water park outside Vegas, with screaming children and a lazy river that was probably full of pee. Images of white-sand beaches and brilliant blue water immediately danced through her mind. But then she hesitated. "I'll have to ask Mom and Dad," she said.

That seemed confirmation enough for Charlotte. "Oh, you'll convince them. You always do." She laughed in excitement, launching into a description of the private house her parents had rented, the beach bars that served piña coladas every afternoon, and the celebrities who would be going incognito. "Rob Pattinson for sure, he's always there," Char was saying, but Emma wasn't really listening.

The truth was, she'd been looking forward to celebrating the holidays with the Mercers. She'd never had much of a real Christmas before. A few of her foster families had tried to celebrate the holidays but never really made Emma feel welcome or included. There were usually some impersonal presents from a charity drive—three years in a row, she had received cheap desk sets from well-meaning donors—and maybe a dry turkey dinner.

Emma was sure that Christmas with the Mercers would be different. She didn't care about presents, but she couldn't wait to see the living room bright with tinsel, fragrant with the smell of a tree. She imagined Laurel playing carols on the baby grand; Mr. Mercer singing along, totally off-key; Mrs. Mercer wearing an ugly Christmas sweater and a Santa hat as she baked sugar cookies. They would hang stockings and ornaments and drink eggnog by the fire—even though it probably wouldn't get below fifty degrees in Arizona. She knew it was hokey, but she didn't care. She'd never had a hokey Christmas to get tired of.

Plus, Ethan was here, not in Barbados. And she'd always wanted to corner a boy under the mistletoe.

At that moment the door to the pottery studio flew open, slamming against the bookcase behind it. Charlotte's bowl slipped from her hand and shattered on the ground. The school's front office manager, a kindly woman named Peggy, stood in the doorway. Her normally neat graying hair was coming loose from its bun. She glanced wildly around until she caught sight of Mrs. Gilliam, then strode quickly across the room to whisper something in her ear. Mrs. Gilliam's owl-like eyes fell on Emma.

"Sutton, you're needed in the office." Mrs. Gilliam was clearly trying to be calm, but she'd gone pale. Her bangles jangled discordantly as she gestured in Emma's direction. "I'll clean up your station; don't worry about that. You just go."

Emma's heart sank with dread. "What's going on?" she managed to ask through her choked throat.

Peggy spoke up this time, her nasal voice hushed. "Your parents are here to see you. Something has happened."

Laurel, Emma and I thought at once. Something had happened to Laurel. That explained why she hadn't been in class.

Emma was on her feet without fully realizing it, tearing through the door and out into the hallway. "Walk, don't run, Miss Mercer," Peggy called out behind her, but Emma took off at breakneck speed, past the SAY NO TO DRUGS! and WILDCAT PRIDE posters, her shoes sliding dangerously on the scuffed linoleum. She turned a corner and hip-checked a recycling bin, sending it rolling across the floor, but didn't stop.

Just as she was about to turn into the front office, she ran full-on into someone—someone who smelled familiar, like freshly mown grass, mint gum, and hospital. It was Mr. Mercer.

"Thank God," he mumbled, his eyes racing over her features like he was checking each and every one of them. He pulled her in and hugged her tight. "You're okay."

He was still wearing a lab coat and hospital ID; he'd obviously come straight from work. For a moment Emma just stood there, rigid in his arms, her heart still racing. How had the murderer attacked this time? Did Laurel's death look like a suicide, like Nisha's?

Then a shaky voice spoke up from behind Mr. Mercer. "Sutton, what's going on?"

Emma broke away to peer over his shoulder. Behind

him, Mrs. Mercer stood, her eyes swollen with tears. And next to her was Laurel.

"Oh my God," Emma exclaimed, flying at Laurel and hugging her tight.

For once, I was grateful for Emma's tendency to show more emotion than I ever would. She needed to hug Laurel enough for the both of us.

"Um, good to see you, too?" Laurel tried to joke, though she was clearly shaken. She took a step back and twisted a lock of hair nervously around her finger.

A single hot tear cut down Emma's cheek. "I just thought . . . I was worried that you . . . you weren't in class . . ." She looked up at Mr. Mercer, frowning. "What's going on, Dad?"

"Let's step outside," he said softly, taking Emma by the elbow and leading her toward the door. Laurel and Mrs. Mercer followed.

They exited by the student parking lot. A small strip of lawn stretched out between the building and the sidewalk, a beat-up picnic table carved with graffiti of ages past chained to a handicapped parking sign. A few feet away, Sutton's beloved Volvo glittered in the sun. Mr. Mercer guided everyone gently toward the table, gesturing for them to sit down.

The chasm of dread in Emma's chest opened wider as her grandfather sat slowly next to her. He inhaled deeply, and then, finally, he met her eyes. What she saw there stopped her ragged breath in her throat. She knew what he would say a heartbeat before she heard it.

"The police found a body in Sabino Canyon," he said. "They think it's your sister."

Emma's hands clenched against her thighs. A panicked feeling clawed inside her chest, more and more frantic, until she couldn't push it down any longer. She opened her mouth and let out an anguished sob.

The sunny afternoon fragmented into a thousand pieces, like a mirror breaking before my eyes. My parents and my sisters fell away from my vision. And just like that, I was back in the canyon, on the last night of my life.

7

A HAND IN THE DARK

Becky's footsteps fade away into the velvet darkness, until there's no sound in the canyon but the wind echoing mournfully through the trees. This late, even the crickets are silent. The moon looks ghostly, shining through tattered clouds and casting strange shadows all over the clearing, warped and grotesque. Far below me, the lights of Tucson sprawl at my feet. I feel more alone than I've ever felt in my life.

The breeze is sharp on my damp cheeks, and I rest my hands over my face for a long moment, hiding from the world like I did when I was a kid. Between the darkness and all the crying I've done tonight, my eyes are starting to feel strained. The pressure of my palms soothes me, shutting out my surroundings—but it can't shut out the memories that keep flashing through my brain. The fight with Thayer, after I'd spent so long looking forward to seeing him. The accident, the terrible crunching sound of Thayer's leg snapping as my own car plowed into him, driven by someone I couldn't see. My father, coming to tell me that I was his granddaughter, that my biological mother is his daughter Becky. And then Becky herself—my sad, tormented birth mom—telling me that somewhere out there, I have a twin sister.

I think of my old dream, where my reflection would step out of the mirror and we'd play together. I would always wake up feeling peaceful and somehow sad. I never wanted to leave her, this other girl who looked like me and yet wasn't. A part of me has always known, I realize now. A part of me has always missed her.

Anger spikes through me. I lean down and pick up a handful of rocks, throwing them as hard as I can out over the side of the canyon. The muscles in my shoulder flex and burn with the effort. I'm mad at Becky. I'm mad at my grandparents. Because they couldn't work out their own problems, I've been kept from my twin. I've been denied the one person who might have understood me, who might have made me feel less alone. It hurts, even more than the years of wondering why my birth mother abandoned me, why my parents loved Laurel more. It hurts because without this missing piece, I will never feel complete.

"Selfish!" I shriek, releasing another stone into the night air. "You're . . . all . . . just . . . selfish!" My voice echoes around the canyon, bouncing back at me fainter and fainter until it's gone.

Then my hands are empty. I stand there for a moment, my breath heaving, my fingers clenched. I could pick up more rocks. I could throw them all night.

But suddenly I think of Becky's ravaged face, thin and tear-streaked, its faint resemblance to my own unmistakable. I remember the stricken look on my grandfather's face as I screamed at him earlier tonight. And the rage begins to seep out of me, like water from a sponge.

I am a long way from forgiving them. But maybe, just maybe, they've already punished themselves enough for their mistakes. They've already suffered more than I would wish on any of them.

Something snaps in the bushes. I stop and listen, my heart pounding, but whatever it is goes silent. Some nocturnal creature on its way home, probably. Turning away from the cityscape, I sit on the bench again, exhausted. I should start heading back down to the parking lot, and across the street to Nisha's so I can make someone drive me home. But I don't want to see any of my friends right now. They're always waiting for me to show the slightest sign of weakness. The only person I'd let see me when I'm vulnerable like this is Thayer.

I pull out my phone and scroll to Thayer's number—I have no service out here, but I just want to look at his picture. It's my favorite photo of him, gazing out over Wasson Peak. Thayer normally smirks for the camera, and even though I love that signature cocky smile of his, I managed to take this picture before he realized it. This thoughtful, serious side of Thayer—this is who he is when he's with me.

I sigh, looking at the picture and blinking back tears. I love Thayer. When we're not fighting, we're perfect together. We make each other stronger. The only thing that's keeping us apart is the secrets we've been hiding, the lies we've been telling. Thayer was the one who wanted to keep our relationship a secret. And I agreed. I didn't want to hurt Garrett or Laurel or Madeline.

But I'm tired of lies. All our sneaking around is just as bad as the secrets my parents kept from me. We've hurt people, including each other. I'm not afraid of how real our love is, and I don't care who knows it.

I take a deep breath of the cool, crisp night air. I'm going to break up with Garrett and go public with Thayer. Garrett will be hurt, I know. His face will turn purple with rage, and he'll say some mean and ugly things. But isn't it kinder, in the end, to rip off the bandage now? To stay with him any longer would be leading him on.

I open up an e-mail on my phone from our secret account and start to type, overcome by the sudden need to say all this, to get it down while the emotions are fresh and raw. Dear Thayer, I begin.

And then I keep writing. I tell him everything I've held back so long. That I'm ready to move on to the next stage of our relationship. That I love him. It all comes pouring out of me.

And then I hear another noise, another soft rustling in the bushes. I pause, my nerves singing. It doesn't sound like an animal to me.

Someone is in the canyon with me.

"Hello?" I call. Maybe Becky came back to tell me more about my sister. Or maybe my dad came to pick me up.

But no one answers.

My blood picks up speed again, my pulse thudding in my ears. I save my draft and stand up from the bench, but I can't see beyond the trees and boulders that circle the little clearing.

It could be Madeline—Thayer could have called her from the hospital. Maybe he asked her to come pick me up and she decided to mess with my head a little first, punish me for being out here with her brother. I deserve it.

"Is anyone there? Say something," I yell. I sound braver than I feel. "Come on, it's late, I'm not in the mood for this shit."

I take a few steps toward the source of the sound, willing myself not to look scared. Someone might be videotaping me from the trees. In the Lying Game, you never know when one of your friends is getting footage of you looking like a moron, or setting you up for a fall. You're always waiting for your comeuppance. It used to be fun. I used to crave that adrenaline rush, that feeling of being just a little out of control. But that was back when we had an emergency brake. Before I destroyed it.

Just a few weeks earlier, I'd pretended to stall my car on the train tracks. It was a good prank. But during that stunt I'd done the unforgivable: I'd said, Cross my heart and hope to die, *the* phrase we were only supposed to use if we were really in trouble. At the time it seemed like a great idea. Our pranks were starting to get predictable and stale. We'd gotten so used to each other's tricks we could see one coming from a mile away and derail it before it had a chance to really get good. Breaking the safe-words' hold on us was the only way to keep the game interesting.

But since then, the game has gotten a little too interesting. My friends fake-kidnapped me a week later and filmed my sister strangling me into unconsciousness with my own locket. It left a big bruise on my throat; I went through three bottles of concealer in a week trying to cover it up. Garrett caught sight of it one night when we were waiting to get a table at Cafe Poca Cosa and freaked out—he asked what had happened, but I just shrugged off his question. What happens in the Lying Game stays in the Lying Game.

Before that night we'd never actually gotten physical with each other. The stakes have gone up, and it's not as fun as I expected—I've been twitchy since then, constantly waiting for the other shoe to fall. And now there's no going back. Once you've broken a rule like that, you can't fix it.

"Mads? Char?" I take another step toward the trees, squinting into the darkness. My mouth has gone dry. I think of the stranger in my car, bearing down on Thayer. Whoever hit him could still be out here, hiding in the shadows. I try to swallow but it's like I've got a throat full of sand. A few yards away an owl gives a soft, chuckling hoot, making me jump.

"You guys?" My voice sounds too high. I clear my throat and try again. "Whatever, bitches. Your lame stalker act isn't fooling anyone." I turn back to the bench, my hands shaking as I throw the bag over my shoulder and start for the trail.

I'm tired of not being able to trust anyone—not even my best friends. Maybe it's time to end the Lying Game. I try to imagine their reactions to that idea. Charlotte will go all alpha on me and tell me it's not mine to end. Madeline will wheedle and coax. Laurel will get sullen and claim I'm only ending it to hurt her after she worked so hard to get in. But I hate that tonight of all nights, after all I've been through, I'm literally freaking out because I think my own friends are up to something. That's not how friendship is supposed to work.

The path to the parking lot is steep and treacherous, covered in roots and rocks. I start down it slowly, leaning back to counterbalance myself as I go. When the moon disappears behind a dense cluster of clouds, I have to feel my way in the dark. That's when I feel someone's hand on my shoulder.

"Sutton," growls a voice behind me, rough and angry. The smell of whiskey mingles sickeningly with that of spearmint.

But I know that voice. And as soon as I realize who it is, I know just how much trouble I'm in.

It's Garrett.

8

THE GAME'S AFOOT

Emma's lungs seized as if she'd had the wind knocked out of her, the breath frozen painfully in her chest. "My . . . my sister?"

Across the table, Mrs. Mercer stifled a sob, and Laurel put a comforting arm around her shoulders. Emma turned to look at Mr. Mercer, noticing for the first time the mud on the elbows of his lab coat, the twig snagged in his shoelaces.

"I'm sorry, Sutton," he murmured. "Yes. It was Emma. I identified the body."

The body. Someone had finally found my body. After so long, it almost didn't feel real.

Emma's breath kept catching in her throat so that she felt just a step away from hyperventilating. The world slid in and out of focus around her. Of course, she'd known all along that Sutton was dead . . . but somehow, hearing this made it feel more *real*.

"That is," Mr. Mercer went on, his eyes haunted, "there wasn't much to identify. Her body wasn't . . . wasn't in good shape. But they found her driver's license in her bag." His voice cracked. "The picture. God, Sutton, I just—it looked *just* like you."

Emma's gut wrenched violently. Her driver's license? As in *Emma's* driver's license? Her wallet, along with her duffel bag, had been stolen on her first night in Tucson. If the police had found it with the body, that meant two things: one, that the murderer had been the one to steal her things—which she'd suspected but hadn't been able to verify.

And two, the killer had gone back to the scene of the crime to plant evidence.

"*Garrett* had gone back," I corrected my sister silently. I could still feel that hand on my shoulder, that voice in my ear, as if no time at all had passed since the night in the canyon. Garrett. It seemed so obvious now. He'd been so jealous. So violent. Why had I stayed with him, knowing all that? How could I have been so stupid?

"The police thought she *was* you, at first. They thought

it was some kind of fake ID," Mrs. Mercer said softly. Her cardigan was buttoned wrong, and her hands kept fluttering nervously to her mouth as if she wanted to stop the words from coming out of it. "But of course, you aren't missing, and that body had been in the canyon for . . . for a few months, at least. They called us down, and we explained about Becky and that we'd just found out about Emma ourselves."

Emma put her hands over her face. Her heart hammered so loudly in her ears that for a moment, she couldn't hear anything else. She tried not to think about Sutton's body—a girl who looked just like her, but . . . well, decomposed. But now that she knew it was real, the image was hard to shake. "Who found her?" she whispered through her hands.

"A kid," Mr. Mercer said. "A freshman at the university. He was hiking off the main trails and found her at the bottom of a ravine. She was covered with leaves, so no one could see her from the trail. But he saw her . . . her foot sticking out."

I strained my mind, trying to connect myself to what they'd found there in the canyon. Even though Emma didn't want to imagine the body, I couldn't help it. Was I a skeleton now, empty eye sockets staring at the sky? I felt a strange sort of detachment. Even though I had lived in it for eighteen years, that body wasn't me; not anymore.

Emma drew her hands away from her face. She took a deep breath, and finally her lungs filled all the way. The world suddenly seemed to have a surreal brightness, as if the sky and trees and mountains were oversaturated with color. Laurel sat staring at her, her mouth drawn into a small button in her face. Mrs. Mercer's eyes were moist with compassion. Next to her, Mr. Mercer put a hand on her back and rubbed gently.

No one seemed to have any suspicions, yet, that the body wasn't Emma's. At least there was that.

"How did she die?" Emma's voice was barely a whisper.

Mr. Mercer hesitated, exchanging glances with his wife. Something unreadable darted across his face and was gone.

"They won't know for sure until after an autopsy," he said. "It appears that she fell off the cliff. A lot of her bones were broken."

Of course. The killer had made Sutton's death look like an accident, or possibly a suicide—just like Nisha's. For all intents and purposes, Sutton Mercer—or now, Emma Paxton—had simply stumbled to her death.

Would they ever find proof that I was murdered? I tried to go back to the memory, to Garrett's hand on my shoulder, hoping I could trigger the rest of it. I wanted to know how he'd done it. But it was just like trying to go back to sleep to continue a dream that was interrupted. I couldn't do it.

"They wouldn't answer any of my questions when I identified the body," Mr. Mercer continued. "They said the investigation was 'ongoing,' whatever that means. So we'll just have to wait for the medical examiner's report to know for sure." He ran his hands over his eyes violently, like he was trying to rub away the memory of what he'd seen. "When I first saw her, I was sure it was you. Even though my brain was telling me it couldn't be, that she was too long dead and I'd just seen you this morning, I was absolutely certain it was you. She was wearing a pink hoodie I could have sworn I'd seen you in before. I've never been so scared." He pulled her into a rough hug. "But you're okay. Thank God you're okay."

Mrs. Mercer's shoulders shuddered as she started to cry again. Laurel grabbed her purse and rummaged inside, coming up with a small packet of Kleenex that she handed to her mother. Emma felt her own lip tremble at the sight of her grandmother so disconsolate. She clasped her hand over her mouth to keep from letting out a sob.

"I just don't know what to feel," cried Mrs. Mercer. "I'm so relieved it's not our baby. I'm so grateful for that. But Emma . . . Emma was ours too. I know we never knew her. But now we never will."

The sight of Mrs. Mercer and Laurel crying together was the final straw. She couldn't do it anymore. It wasn't fair. The Mercers had a right to know that it *was* their baby down in the canyon. They had the right to be able to grieve Sutton.

"I have to tell you something," she said, her voice sounding flat and distant in her ears.

"No!" I screamed, trying to somehow get Emma's attention, make her hear my voice just once. I appreciated her motives, but she wasn't going to accomplish anything by coming clean now. How did she plan on solving my murder from behind bars?

"I—" Emma stared out over the parking lot as she spoke, unable to meet their eyes. The sun bounced off the windshields of the cars. From where she sat she could see Sutton's vintage Volvo, which her sister had restored with Mr. Mercer's help.

"What is it, honey?" Mrs. Mercer asked gently. But Emma didn't answer. She'd just seen something.

A note was tucked under the Volvo's windshield wiper.

A cold calm descended on Emma. She stood up, moving robotically. Her mind was eerily still as she walked to the car and carefully pulled back the wiper to grab the piece of paper. She held it in her hand for a moment, feeling the Mercers' eyes on her. She knew without looking where it had come from, but if she didn't open it, if she didn't see the familiar, blocky handwriting, she could still pretend to herself that the note could be anything. From anyone. A parking ticket, a flyer for a party, a love note. Anything but what it really was.

But she had to open it. Because the person who had left it was probably still watching.

She unfolded the note. It was on the same lined notebook paper as the other notes she'd gotten. The handwriting was rigid, the letters carved so deeply into the paper they almost tore through it in a few spots.

Sutton didn't do what I told her, and she paid for it. Don't make the same mistake. Keep up the game, or Nisha won't be the only person you care about who dies for your sake.

Her gaze shot up. She looked frantically up and down the rows of cars, trying to see who might have left it. How long had it been there? How had the murderer known so quickly that the body had been found? The parking lot glittered serenely around her. Several rows away, two girls in aviator shades got out of a silver Miata, one sipping a Frappuccino. Then Emma glanced toward the school, and her blood ran cold.

A boy sat staring out a window, a notebook open on the desk in front of him. His lips were twisted into an ugly, knowing smirk, a look of delighted malice lighting up his eyes. He watched her hungrily, almost eagerly, like he couldn't wait to see what she'd do next.

It was Garrett.

Emma refused to look away. Adrenaline surged through her body, and she held Garrett's gaze, determined not to reveal how terrified she was.

"Sutton?"

Back on the lawn, Mr. Mercer had taken a few uncertain steps toward her. Mrs. Mercer and Laurel watched her with wide eyes from the picnic table. Emma propped herself up against the side of the car.

"What is that? Are you okay?" Laurel asked, frowning. "You look like you've seen a ghost."

If only, I thought grimly.

"Flyer. For a car wash," Emma muttered, shaking her head. "Sorry. I . . . I guess I'm kind of in shock." She glanced again at Garrett. He had turned back to his notebook and was scribbling something frantically. Then, without glancing at her, he lifted the notebook so she could read what he'd scrawled there.

BITCH.

Lined paper, block letters. Scrawled with a savage intensity. Her knees started to tremble. Still staring straight ahead, Garrett put the notebook back down. He didn't look at her again—but he didn't have to. She knew he'd already seen everything he needed to see.

"Let's get you all home," Mr. Mercer said, shuffling them into his SUV. As they pulled away from the school, Emma risked a glance back toward the window, but the glare from the late-afternoon sun hid Garrett from view.

It didn't matter. I could picture him just as clearly as if he'd been in front of me. Garrett—sweet and affectionate Garrett, my over-eager boyfriend—had another side. An angry side. A temperamental side. And that night in the canyon, a violent side.

9

BAD COP, BAD COP

"I'll get it," Emma called into the kitchen, grabbing the money that Mr. Mercer had left on the entryway table. The doorbell rang again. No one had been in the mood to cook dinner, so they had decided to order gourmet pizza from a place called Flying Pie.

All afternoon she'd been folding and unfolding that note, staring down at the angry scrawl, thinking of the look on Garrett's face from that window as he watched her. *Nisha won't be the only person you care about who dies for your sake.* She read the words over and over. The thought paralyzed her. Everyone, *everyone* was at risk now—and the killer was a step ahead of her at every turn. She couldn't make a move without endangering someone she loved.

Since she got home her phone had been chiming with texts, but she turned it off without even checking it. Mads and Char, Thayer, *Ethan*—the thought of talking to any of them made her stomach squirm. Especially Ethan. What if the text was intercepted somehow? What if the murderer found out that Ethan knew her secret? Her very first threatening note had said *Tell no one*.

"Coming," she yelled, as the deliveryman knocked. She opened the door. "Thanks for wait—" But the words died in her throat. It wasn't the pizza guy.

It was Detective Quinlan.

He wore a badly fitting brown suit, immaculately clean and pressed, and his shoes shone like he'd just pulled them out of the box. His expression was unreadable behind the soup-strainer mustache that hung over his upper lip. His eyes were the cold gray of granite.

"Good evening, Miss Mercer," he said. "I'm very sorry for your loss."

Emma gave a jerky nod, fighting to stay calm. She should have expected this—the cops would have questions, and the Mercers were Emma Paxton's next of kin

My sister had to be on her guard. I'd spent the better part of my life trying to outsmart that man, and he wasn't as dumb as he looked.

Behind her, footsteps sounded as Mr. Mercer entered

the room. "Detective," he said, coming forward to shake the man's hand. "I expected you tomorrow."

"You folks are on my way home. I thought I'd swing by and see how you're doing."

Mr. Mercer gave a wan smile. "A little shell-shocked, mostly. Come on in."

Quinlan's mustache twitched almost imperceptibly. "Thanks so much."

Mr. Mercer led the detective into the kitchen, Emma trailing behind them with her heart pounding in her ears. Mrs. Mercer and Laurel were at the kitchen island laying out plates and napkins for the pizza. They both stopped in their tracks when they saw Quinlan. He gave an apologetic smile. "Sorry to interrupt right at dinnertime. I know it's been a long day."

"Not at all," Mrs. Mercer said. She put down the pile of plates. "Can I get you something to drink, Detective? I can put on a pot of coffee."

"Don't trouble yourself, Mrs. Mercer." He glanced around the room, picking up a pineapple-shaped serving dish from the counter and examining it in his hands.

Emma walked over to stand by Laurel, who gave her a wide-eyed, furtive look. Mrs. Mercer gestured for Quinlan to sit in one of the dining chairs, then took a seat across from him, her husband standing behind her with a hand on her shoulder.

The detective took a tiny notebook out of his breast pocket and flipped it open. "I've been talking to Las Vegas, and here's what I've got so far. Emma Paxton went missing on September first after an argument with her foster family. No one's heard from her since. Her foster mother reported her missing, but because there were no signs of abduction or foul play, she was assumed to be a runaway. Foster kids take off all the time. Emma was just a few weeks away from turning eighteen, so LVPD figured she'd just gotten a head start on setting out on her own." He clicked his pen a few times and glanced up at Emma. "What we're trying to figure out is how she ended up here. Is there anything you can tell me about that, Sutton?"

Emma took a deep, controlled breath, trying to quell the rising panic in her chest. If they were investigating Emma Paxton, it wouldn't be long before they checked Sutton's Facebook account and found out the twins had been in contact. She had to tell them as much truth as she could without giving herself away—or else she'd get caught in a much bigger lie.

She licked her lips. "Y-yes," she stammered. "She messaged me on Facebook the night before she disappeared. We made plans to meet in the canyon the next day."

Mr. and Mrs. Mercer's heads both shot around to stare at her. "What?" Mr. Mercer asked, his eyebrows arched up as high as they could go. The color had drained from Mrs. Mercer's face. Next to her, Laurel gaped soundlessly.

Emma stared down at her feet—she didn't trust herself to meet anyone's eyes. "I'm sorry I didn't tell you earlier," she said, inventing rapidly. "I wasn't sure if it was real or not. She never showed up where we agreed to meet, and I assumed it was all some sort of prank." She thought back to that night—how eager and hopeful she'd been, how excited to finally meet her family. Grief twisted in her chest.

Laurel snaked her arm reassuringly through Emma's. "Was that what you were trying to tell us earlier this afternoon, back at school?"

"Yes," Emma agreed quickly, grateful for Laurel's explanation. "I waited for her for hours."

Quinlan's pen scratched quickly across the page, the only sound in the thick silence. Emma looked up at the Mercers, their faces full of sadness and confusion. The gray streak in Mrs. Mercer's hair seemed to stand out more starkly than usual, her face lined. She looked strangely old.

"And you didn't tell anyone about this? Didn't worry about your sister?" Quinlan said skeptically.

Emma met Quinlan's eyes. Inside, her heart was racing, her nerves on fire. But she gazed steadily at the detective for a long moment. "This all happened right after I met my birth mom, Detective Quinlan. Do you know anything about my birth mom?"

Quinlan glanced at Mr. Mercer. During Becky's most recent stay in town, she'd been arrested for pulling a knife on a stranger during a psychotic break. Emma was willing to bet it wasn't her first run-in with the law.

"Yes," he said finally. "I know about your mother."

Emma could feel her lip trembling, but she held her head steady. Mr. Mercer took a step toward her as if to comfort her, but she didn't turn her gaze from Quinlan.

"Becky has problems," she said. "She skips town any time she gets a little upset. How was I supposed to know Emma wasn't just like her?" The bitterness in her voice—anger directed at Becky—was genuine. A single tear streaked down her cheek. "And like I said, I wasn't totally convinced it wasn't a prank. I didn't want everyone to see me acting . . . desperate."

Mrs. Mercer gave a strangled groan and buried her face in her hands. Mr. Mercer looked torn between comforting his wife and going to his daughter. But before he could move, Laurel spoke.

"In case you haven't noticed," she said curtly, "we're grieving."

A rush of gratitude for my sister filled me.

Quinlan pursed his lips slightly, jotting something down in his notebook, then flipped back a few pages to look something up. "All right," he said. "Miss Paxton's time of death is estimated to be between August thirtieth and September first. Were you in Sabino Canyon between those dates?"

Laurel gave a little jump, and Emma knew what she was thinking. The thirty-first was the night Thayer and Sutton had been out in the canyon on a date; when Thayer was hit by someone driving Sutton's car, and Laurel had to come take him to the hospital. But it was Mr. Mercer who answered.

"Sutton and I were both at Sabino Canyon on August thirty-first." He glanced at Mrs. Mercer. "We met Becky there. It was a pretty emotional night. Sutton didn't know about Becky until then."

Quinlan turned his steely gaze back on Emma. "Was this before or after you'd found Emma on Facebook?"

"Just before," she said. "Becky told me about Emma, and a few hours later I got the message from Emma herself."

Quinlan's hairy eyebrows arched high on his forehead. "That's quite the coincidence."

Emma shrugged, though a thin sheen of sweat had broken out at her temples. "I assumed Becky had gotten in touch with Emma right before she came to see me. After all, *Emma* is the twin that Becky raised. *I'm* the one she gave away. The one she didn't want." She let her voice waver, then hoped she wasn't overdoing it. "If she wanted us to finally meet after all these years, it stands to reason that she would go to Emma first."

A long and awkward silence followed this speech. Mrs. Mercer was still hiding her face in her hands, weeping silently. Laurel seemed to be examining the brown mosaic tile on the floor. Emma swallowed hard.

"Okay," Quinlan said, drawing out the second syllable skeptically. "So can you explain why you walked into the station two days later calling yourself Emma Paxton?"

The question dropped like a bomb. Mrs. Mercer's hand flew away from her face as she whipped around to stare at Emma. Next to her, Laurel went rigid. Mr. Mercer blinked at Quinlan.

"She did *what?*" he asked, his face sheet-white.

"Yup. First day of school, Sutton came into the station insisting that she wasn't Sutton but Emma, and that something terrible had happened to her twin. I blew it off as another prank. Now, though . . ." He shook his head. "Now I'm not so sure."

Emma's collar suddenly felt like it was choking her. She swallowed hard, forcing herself to hold Quinlan's gaze.

"Well, yeah," she said softly. "It *was* a prank. I'd just found out I had a twin. It wasn't like I knew anything had happened to her. Like I said, she didn't show up when we were supposed to meet." She held his gaze, trying to channel a little of Sutton's attitude, trying to imagine how Sutton would handle being interrogated when her long-lost sister had just died. "I was *mad*. Mad at my parents, mad at Becky, mad at Emma for standing me up. I was hoping you'd call me on it. That you'd tell my parents, and then I'd find out if Emma was even real."

She looked away from Quinlan to her grandparents. Mrs. Mercer stared miserably at her, her eyes glassy with tears. Mr. Mercer looked stern for a moment, like he might chastise her, but then he looked away as though ashamed.

"I'm sorry," Mr. Mercer said, blowing air heavily out through his mouth. "You're right, Sutton. We should have told you the truth much sooner."

Not bad, I thought, oddly proud of Emma's performance. She did a good angry Sutton Mercer. I must have been rubbing off on her after all.

A stab of shame shot through Emma's chest. Now Mr. Mercer thought he was in the wrong, when none of this was his fault. *I hope someday you can forgive me*, she thought. But all she said was, "It's not important anymore."

Quinlan sat very still in the chair, watching her evenly. He let the silence stretch out a heartbeat too long before speaking again. "I have one more question, and then I'll get out of your hair for the evening. Sutton, we've been looking at Nisha Banerjee's phone records to try to figure out what may have happened in the hours leading up to her death. It looks like she called you and texted you . . ."—he glanced at his notes—". . . eight times all together."

Emma nodded. She'd been expecting this ever since the funeral. "I was busy and didn't answer. I tried to call her back later, after tennis, but by the time I called her . . ." She trailed off helplessly.

The detective raised an eyebrow. "So you have no idea what she was messaging you about?"

"No. I wish I did." Emma's voice broke. "Maybe I could have helped her." Laurel gave Emma a stricken look and squeezed her arm. "I asked Dr. Banerjee about it, but he didn't know either."

"What does that have to do with Sutton?" Mr. Mercer asked, frowning at Quinlan. The detective shook his head.

"Probably nothing," he said. "But it seemed unusual. Nisha didn't make a habit of calling anyone that frantically. I'm just trying to make sure we have all the facts." The detective stood up, closing his notebook and sliding it back into his breast pocket. "Sutton, I really need to see those Facebook messages. We're trying to come up with a timeline of what happened to Emma, and they'll help. Can you come by the station on Friday?"

Emma wanted to ask Quinlan some questions, too— about the state of the body, whether there was any evidence of murder or footprints nearby or anything—but he was already looking at her strangely, and she didn't want to set off any more alarms in his head. Instead, she just nodded. "Sure I'll come after school."

Quinlan paused where he stood, looking around at each of them. His gaze lingered longest on Emma. "I should warn you, this is going public tomorrow."

"Public?" Emma asked, frowning.

"There's a press conference scheduled for eight A.M. I'm guessing the media are going to have a field day with it. You should be prepared for that."

Mrs. Mercer rose from her seat. "Can't we keep this quiet?" she asked pleadingly. "We haven't even had time to take this in."

Quinlan looked sympathetic, but he shook his head. "There's already a half dozen news helicopters circling over the spot where we found her. I'm afraid the story's going to hit pretty hard." He pulled his wallet from his back pocket and removed a business card. "I'll leave this here. Give me a call if you remember anything else that you think might be of use."

"Of course," Mr. Mercer murmured. "I'll see you out, Detective Quinlan."

The detective followed Emma's grandfather back to the front door. As they passed her, Quinlan flashed her a sharp look, his eyes glittering brightly. Then he was gone.

Emma braced herself against the kitchen island, the strength flooding out of her all at once. She'd managed to dodge the truth one more time. But she had a feeling Quinlan wasn't done with her yet. How much longer would she be able to conceal her identity, now that the cops had found Sutton's body?

Emma's secrets—and mine—were unraveling faster than she could build new lies to cover them up. And I knew from experience what happens at the end of a Lying Game.

You get caught.

10

STAND BY YOUR MAN (AND VICE VERSA)

The last bit of evening light illuminated the cracked wood of Ethan's front steps when Emma pulled up outside his house a few hours later. Ethan sat on the creaky porch swing, a can of root beer in one hand and his laptop propped on an enormous wooden spool used as a table. When he saw her, he jumped to his feet and walked quickly toward her, his face disappearing into the shadows as he left the porch's warm glow.

"What's going on?" he asked, before she could say anything. "Charlotte and Madeline said you'd been pulled out of class, and I couldn't find you. Why didn't you answer my texts?"

She stumbled forward into Ethan's arms. "They found her," she whispered, burying her face in his T-shirt. "Sutton's body. In Sabino Canyon."

She felt his body tense, then curl protectively around her. "That explains it." She looked up at him quickly. He jerked his head toward the canyon in answer. "I sat out here watching the cops turn into the parking lot all afternoon. The place was crawling with reporters, too."

A groan escaped her lungs. "There's going to be a press conference, Ethan," she said. "It's all going to come out. And look."

She handed him the crumpled ball of paper that had been left on her windshield that afternoon. He took his arms from around her to smooth the note flat against his thigh, then held it up to the light. A sob bubbled up from inside her while he silently stared at the note.

"The killer is threatening my family and my friends now!" she exclaimed. "Ethan, this person is watching me *all the time* to make sure I don't mess up. I'm putting the Mercers in danger. I'm putting *you* in danger!" Tears ran down her cheeks. "I've been so selfish. I should never have told you the truth! I never should have let you help me with the case. And now it's not just the murderer we have to worry about." She wrenched out of his grasp, taking a few steps back. "The cops. The media. They're going to figure it out. I don't want to drag you down with me. I couldn't bear it if something happened to you." She looked wildly around, suddenly afraid the killer was here, watching her right now. The street was quiet now, but anyone could be out there in the darkness.

Ethan closed the distance between them and pulled her against his chest. She struggled for one panicked moment and then melted into his embrace.

"I'm not letting you go through this alone," he said fiercely. "I don't care what anyone thinks. No matter what, Emma, I'm here for you. With you. You can't leave me now."

"If they find out who I am, they'll think I killed her. And you'll look like my accomplice." She pressed her face against his shoulder.

"I don't care," he said, his voice muffled, his face buried in her hair.

Her tears dampened the cotton of his shirt. "Ethan, I don't want what happened to Nisha to happen to you, too."

He took Emma by her shoulders and held her a little apart from him, forcing her to meet his gaze. Half of his face was in shadow, but his eyes shone with determination. "I'm not going to let that happen."

She desperately wanted to believe him. The idea of going through the investigation without him felt like sending her heart through a shredder.

"Ethan," she whispered. "I think Garrett might be the killer."

His eyes widened. "Did you find proof?" he asked.

She told him about seeing Garrett in the classroom, about the way he watched her unfold the note. "He just sat there grinning at me. Like he was having the time of his life watching me squirm."

Ethan's jaw tensed. With another glance up toward the canyon, he took her hand and led her onto the dimly lit porch. Two small brown moths flung themselves at the bare bulb that hung over the house numbers. Ethan's telescope sat near the railing, angled toward the sky. Next door, Nisha's house was dark and silent. Emma ran her fingers through her hair nervously. The whole street felt haunted to her now.

Ethan's laptop sat open, a cursor blinking placidly on an open document. Dostoyevsky's *Crime and Punishment* sat splayed out, spine up, on the seat next to it. "Oh, sorry. Were you doing homework?" she asked, another pang of guilt cutting through her. She wondered how much of Ethan's schoolwork she'd interrupted since she'd arrived in Tucson.

He sat down on the porch swing, picking up the computer and setting it on his lap. "It's not due until the end of the month. I was just trying to get a head start." As he spoke, he exited the document and pulled up Facebook.

Emma loved the way his hands flew over the keyboard, doing everything with the shortcuts he'd programmed, never using the mousepad. Even though his computer was old and dented, Ethan had painstakingly built the machine inside.

"What are you doing?" she asked, sitting next to him on the swing. She'd stopped crying, but now the salt of her tears was drying on her face and making her skin feel stiff. Rubbing at her cheeks, she cuddled against Ethan's shoulder as he pulled up Garrett's profile.

"I want to know what Garrett was up to the night of Sutton's murder," he said. He handed her the can of root beer, and she took a small sip. The bubbles churned in her fluttering stomach.

"Good thing his profile is public," Emma said, craning her neck to see. "We're definitely not friends anymore." The screen filled with hundreds of pictures of Garrett— scoring at soccer, shirtless and oiled up on a beach somewhere, lifting a glass to the camera at a fancy res- taurant. In a few he stood by his sister, an arm wrapped protectively around her.

The most recent update read: *RIP Nisha B. You'll be missed, baby girl.* Before that, though, most of his status updates were pretty banal, things like *Anybody see The Voice tonight? CeeLo brought his parrot!!!* or *Only five more months before I never have to do a trig proof again.* Sometimes he linked to soccer news or *Saturday Night Live* clips. It looked like he posted several times a day.

"Go to the night of the thirty-first," Emma said, her hand on Ethan's shoulder. He scrolled backward through the months, slowing when he hit September. Emma winced when she saw the phrase *Garrett went from being "in a relationship" to "single,"* updated on her birthday.

"Nothing interesting," said Ethan. She leaned in and peered at the monitor. Then her eyes fell on Garrett's last post before Sutton's murder, late in the afternoon of the thirtieth.

Do you ever get tired of all the lies people tell?

Emma and Ethan exchanged glances. "That could be about Sutton and Thayer," Emma said quietly. Ethan nodded. Then they saw a status update from September first, and shivered. It was updated at 2:38 A.M.

Eventually, people always get what's coming to them.

I stared at the screen, my mind churning, willing the words to spark my memory to life, to take me back to that night so I could finally see how he had done it. But I couldn't remember past that point when he grabbed my shoulder and said my name. *Sutton.* He'd said it like it was the dirtiest, most insulting word he'd ever heard.

"Garrett would probably have known about the snuff video," Emma said softly, rereading the September first update. "It wouldn't have been hard for him to steal it from Laurel's computer sometime when he was at the house."

Somewhere far away an ambulance siren wailed. The dogs up and down the street howled in response. Emma gazed out at the canyon, looming like a dark shadow, like a secret.

"I don't get it," Ethan said. "Stealing it and hoping you'd see it . . . that seems so complicated. Why wouldn't he just Facebook you from Sutton's account?"

"I didn't use Facebook much when I was Emma. It's not like I had a lot of friends. My profile was hidden." She sighed. "And Garrett needed me to come out to Tucson and take over Sutton's life, *fast*. If he did any research on me, he'd have known about Travis. What better way than to label that video *Sutton in AZ* and slip it to my slimy foster brother? Obviously I'd look for a girl who looked just like me. Then once I did, he replied to me as Sutton."

Ethan stared at her. "Emma, that makes it sound premeditated. Like he planned all along to use you to cover up the murder. Which means he already knew you were out there, somehow."

The thought sent an icy thrill down her spine. How would Garrett have known about Emma, when not even the Mercers knew she existed? But it would all fit in with knowing about Travis.

Emma glanced over at Nisha's house, which was

completely dark. She wondered if Dr. Banerjee had gone to stay with friends or family. Maybe he was at the hospital, burying his grief in his work like he'd done when his wife died. She could just make out the short organza curtains in Nisha's bedroom, motionless now.

"How are we going to prove that he did it, though?" she asked, laying her head back against the siding of the house. Ethan stared at the computer screen thoughtfully.

"If we had access to Garrett's texts or e-mail, we'd be able to see if he sent the link," he said. "Even if he deleted the messages. That stuff stays on record forever. You just have to know how to pull it up."

"I'll keep an eye on him," she said. "Maybe I can figure out a way to get my hands on his phone."

"Be careful." Ethan looked worried. "He's dangerous, Emma. Especially now. He's probably getting desperate."

"Well, so am I," Emma said, sounding tougher than she felt.

And so was I. I'd never felt so helpless, so hopeless. I finally knew who had killed me—and I couldn't tell a soul.

11

REALITY TV BITES

"The girl's body was found just a half-mile off Upper Sabino Canyon Road, at the bottom of this scenic overlook." The newscaster, the same woman who had covered Nisha's death just a few days earlier, was now wearing a poofy yellow North Face vest. Emma guessed that must be her "outdoorsy" look. She stood in front of a picnic area with green-painted benches and an awning, wisps of hair flying free from her ponytail in the breeze.

Mrs. Mercer passed a basket of steaming rolls to Emma, her eyes never leaving the fifteen-inch television they'd propped at the end of the island. The Mercers almost never ate dinner in front of the TV, but there seemed an unspoken consensus to do so tonight.

Emma and Laurel had both been surprised when the Mercers said they would be missing school that day—until they looked out at the front lawn and saw the crowd of news vans gathered outside. The Mercers had refused to open the door, but any time they saw someone in front of a window the reporters started shouting questions. "Sutton! Sutton, did you know Emma? What do you think happened to her, Sutton?" So Laurel and Emma had spent most of the day in the kitchen, baking cookies and flipping through magazines. "You are looking for answers in the wrong places," Emma's horoscope had said, and she rolled her eyes. *Tell me something I don't know.*

For most of her life, Emma had wanted to be an investigative reporter when she grew up. But now that she was experiencing a media siege firsthand, she wasn't so sure. The reporters felt like nothing so much as vultures, circling her family, waiting for one of them to show signs of weakness.

The TV screen cut to a young man with glasses and a long blond ponytail, standing in front of a dormitory building on campus. "She was covered up with leaves and branches," he said, his voice breaking. "All I could see was her . . . her foot, sticking out at a weird angle." He looked terrified, blinking in the bright light like a nocturnal creature out during the day. *This will haunt him for the rest of his life*, Emma thought sadly.

The reporter returned. "The body has been identified as Emma Paxton from Las Vegas, Nevada." The previous year's school photo flashed on the screen. Emma had worn a vintage wrap dress she'd scored from a garage sale in Green Valley. Her bangs were shorter then; she'd grown them out to match Sutton's longer hairstyle. Her smile was maybe a little more guarded than Sutton's, a little less confident. Still, the image made the Mercers stir in their seats. Mr. Mercer dropped his fork onto his plate of untouched lasagna, and Mrs. Mercer stared at the screen with a rapt, shocked expression.

"It's so weird," Laurel said. "She looks just like you."

All Emma could do was nod.

Watching news coverage of her own death was dizzyingly surreal. She felt weirdly exposed every time her picture appeared on-screen, as if the Mercers would suddenly be able to see that the girl in the photo was sitting right in front of them. The newscasters had said her name so many times it was almost easy to believe that poor Emma Paxton, foster kid, *was* dead—that she really was Sutton Mercer now.

It was weird for me, too. I watched as my parents grieved for a girl they'd never met when their own daughter was gone. Would I be buried in Vegas, far away from my family and friends? Would my headstone say my sister's name? What if Emma never found my killer—would she live as me forever, until she was finally buried as Sutton Mercer at the ripe old age of ninety?

"Paxton went missing almost three months ago from Las Vegas, after an argument with her foster family. Clarice Lambert, her guardian at the time, spoke with our Nevada correspondent."

Emma choked on a mouthful of water, sending it down the wrong pipe. She coughed, clutching her throat.

"Honey?" Mrs. Mercer put a hand on her back.

"I'm okay," she said quickly. "Just drank too fast." She took a deep breath, wiping the corners of her eyes. There on the screen, in front of the little bungalow house she'd stayed in for a few short weeks, stood Clarice and her son, Travis. Clarice was wearing a strappy sundress meant for someone much younger than she was, her platinum hair piled high on top of her head. She had a mildly shocked, scandalized expression on her face. Travis slouched next to her, a baseball cap pulled askew across his ear and a sanctimonious expression on his wide, fishy lips.

"She was obviously a troubled girl," Clarice said. "She stole from me, she lied to me, and when I tried laying down the law, she took off in the dead of night. Never a note or a message saying where she was going. Of course

I worried, but there wasn't anything I could do. She was almost eighteen."

Emma's body twitched involuntarily. Clarice had all but kicked her out of the house after Travis had framed her for stealing from her purse. Why was the news even talking to her? She didn't know anything about Emma.

Travis had the microphone now. "Emma was a wild girl," he said with a smirk. "She was into all kinds of crazy stuff. I found a video of her online, getting held down and strangled and . . ." His next word was replaced with a loud beep. "She always had money, too. Maybe she was involved with some kind of fetish dungeon or something."

I goggled at the TV—would they show the snuff video? I didn't want my parents to see me like that. They both stared at the screen, my mom with a disturbed grimace, my dad looking confused. I wondered if he'd ever even heard the phrase "fetish dungeon" before, much less in connection with anyone he might be related to.

Across the table, Laurel set her glass down with a loud *thunk*. Emma glanced up at her, her mind shooting back to what she'd learned of the snuff video. Laurel had masterminded that prank—and she'd been the one with the movie saved on her hard drive. What if she recognized what Travis was describing? But Laurel just toyed with her food, a distracted look on her face.

The newscaster's voice came back. "When investigators tried to find the video, they found no trace. Whether it's been since taken down, or was a case of mistaken identity, is still under investigation. Meanwhile, LVPD, who is assisting the Tucson police with the investigation, discovered a locker checked out to the missing girl at the Greyhound station, containing clothes, what seem to be journals, and around two thousand dollars in cash."

Emma's insides lurched. They had her journals? Her cheeks felt like they were on fire. She imagined the police flipping through the cheap composition books, guffawing over the phase in junior high when she'd dotted all her i's with hearts, or reading her fake headlines out loud to a room of beat cops. *Girl Goes Stag to Homecoming, Stands by Refreshment Table All Night*—she imagined Quinlan and his buddies reading it aloud and erupting in laughter. The very thought made her want to hide her face in her hands.

The cameras jumped back to the newscaster, who held her microphone to her lips and looked seriously into the camera. "Meanwhile, the Tucson Police Department has refused to give an official cause of death, saying the case is still under investigation. But our sources tell us Paxton was hoping to meet up with her biological family in Tucson. Whether she made it to them is unknown. The family has so far declined our requests for an interview." At that, Mrs. Mercer hit the remote, and the sound muted.

"Requests?" she snapped, curling her lip. "You spent most of the day on our front lawn, you gargoyle." Then she sighed, and started gathering dishes. "Poor Emma. It sounds like she could have used our help."

"What do you mean?" Emma asked, glancing up at her grandmother.

"Just, if she was as troubled as those people said . . ." Mrs. Mercer trailed off, then shook her head. Her face darkened. "I wish we'd known about her sooner. This is all Becky's fault. It's always Becky's fault. She lies, she steals, she keeps secrets, and she doesn't care who she hurts along the way."

"Kristin," Mr. Mercer said softly. But his wife scowled, grabbing the Pyrex dish of lasagna from the center of the table. She moved so violently a small splatter of sauce flew free and landed on her sweater, but she didn't seem to notice.

"You know it's true. She kept us in constant agony, wondering where she was and if she was okay. And for some insane reason, she didn't tell us about this other little girl who we could have . . ." Tears sprang to her eyes. "This little girl we could have saved."

Mr. Mercer stood up and gently pried the dish from her

hands. He set it back on the table and pulled his wife into his arms. She broke down then, sobbing against his chest as he patted her back. Laurel and Emma looked at each other with wide, frightened eyes. Emma had never seen Mrs. Mercer this emotional, and from the look on Laurel's face, she hadn't either.

Emma couldn't help but agree with Mrs. Mercer. She wanted to forgive Becky—Becky was her mother, after all—but sometimes she was so angry she could scream. What had been the point of keeping Emma if she was only going to abandon her five years later? What had been the point of separating the twins?

It was so unfair. If Sutton hadn't died, if Emma hadn't come out to Tucson to find her, the wheels might have been set in motion on their own, by Becky's confession to Mr. Mercer. What would it have been like if the Mercers had come for her as a family? She imagined being called out of class in Henderson, just like she had been the day they found Sutton's body. But in this alternate reality, she was summoned to meet her family. Her real, blood family. She pictured it: Mr. Mercer, gentle and reassuring; Mrs. Mercer, a nervous but excited smile twitching the corners of her lips; Laurel, wary at the possibility of a new rival but hopeful, eager to be liked. And Sutton. Her sister. Her twin.

"What was she like?" Laurel asked softly, breaking Emma's thoughts. Emma gave a start, her mind racing to come back to the present. To the reality where Sutton was gone, and she was alone.

"What was who like?" she asked.

"Emma," she said. "You talked to her, right?"

Emma ran her finger along the condensation on the outside of her glass. "Just a little bit. I didn't know much about her." Then, because she couldn't resist, she added, "I know her foster mom had just kicked her out of the house. She sounded kind of awful."

"Who, that woman with the tacky lounge-waitress hairdo?" Laurel said. "She *looked* awful."

"Now, girls," Mr. Mercer said, frowning at them from where he still stood with Mrs. Mercer in his arms. "You don't know that. It can be hard to know what to do for someone who's troubled. I'm sure that woman did her best for Emma."

Emma knew he was speaking more about his own relationship with Becky than anything, but she was glad that Laurel at least had sided with her.

Mrs. Mercer wiped her eyes with a pineapple-print cloth napkin, then let go of her husband. "Did anyone want dessert? There's some ice cream in the fridge."

"No thanks, Mom." Laurel threw her own napkin down in front of her. Emma shook her head, too. Her stomach felt like a lead weight.

Mr. Mercer pulled a chair out for his wife. She sat down, her eyes still damp, and he set about clearing the rest of the dishes. The plates and silverware clattered together, echoing around the silent kitchen. On the muted TV Santa Claus delivered pizzas in his sleigh, the phone number for a regional pizza chain painted on the side.

"Do we have to go to school tomorrow?" Laurel asked, sucking her lower lip anxiously. Mr. and Mrs. Mercer exchanged uneasy glances from across the room. Then Mr. Mercer came back to the table, wiping his hands on a dish towel.

"I wish I could hide you girls from this forever," he said, "but I don't know if you should miss any more school. We talked to the principal this afternoon, and she promised me there would be no press allowed on campus. I know it won't be easy. I'm sure your friends have a lot of questions for you."

Emma rolled her eyes. That was an understatement. All day long she'd been fielding texts from Madeline and Charlotte. WHAT IS GOING ON???? Charlotte had asked, while Madeline had seemed excited that a "mega-foxy" reporter had cornered her outside campus to ask if she knew Sutton. THIS IS SO CRAZY, she'd texted, along with a photo taken from her phone of a line of news vans just off campus.

The Twitter Twins' updates had been the most useful

real-time description of the school day. Early in the morning Gabby had tweeted:

Media circus at Hollier. How'd the paparazzi find me again?

Lili had followed up shortly after:

Life expectancy of teen girls seems to be plummeting in Tucson. Be careful, everyone.

They'd chronicled each rumor as it circulated and had live-blogged the school assembly at which the principal had announced the discovery of another body. Gabby's last post had read:

Hollier High needs a hero. Sutton Mercer, come back and lead your people!

She knew the halls were going to be buzzing with rumors the next day, and she would be at the center of it. Even imagining it made her heart beat faster—but not nearly so fast as it did a moment later when the news came back from commercials.

A male reporter with a shellacked helmet of hair stood in front of a coffee shop, talking to a girl wearing an apron over a vintage Bad Religion T-shirt. She wore a pair of black plastic-frame glasses, and her dark hair was spiked in a short, edgy pixie cut. Tears glittered in her eyes. Emma hurried to turn the volume back up.

"—just don't understand how this could happen," the girl was saying, wiping at her eyes. "Emma was my best friend."

Before she could stop herself, Emma jumped to her feet, banging her knee on the table leg. Vibrations of pain shot up through her hip, but she ignored them.

The girl on the screen was Alex Stokes—Emma's best friend from Henderson. The one person she'd been in contact with since coming to Tucson. She was standing outside of Sin City Java, where she was a part-time barista.

The Mercers gawked at Emma, alarm plain on their faces. She'd knocked her chair over, and she stood gripping the side of the table, her knuckles white. Her grandfather looked from her to the TV set, and then back to Emma, his eyes round and baffled. "Do you know that girl?"

Emma sat down slowly, shaking her head no, but they still stared. Laurel's glass hovered halfway to her lips, frozen in midair. Mrs. Mercer gave her a worried look. Emma cleared her throat and forced herself to speak. "It's just that that girl seemed to care about Emma a lot. No one else seems to miss her. It's just so sad."

Emma stared at her friend's face. Alex was the only person from her old life who actually cared about her; she also happened to be the only person who could blow Emma's cover.

Since coming to Tucson, Emma had been lying to Alex, just like she'd been lying to everyone. She'd told her friend back home that she and Sutton were getting along perfectly, that the Mercers had welcomed her to stay with them for a while. She'd been texting Alex on and off for the past three months—long after "Emma Paxton" was supposed to have died.

And now Alex could blow all of her lies wide open. All she had to do was mention the texts she'd gotten from her best friend, apparently from beyond the grave, and Emma would be through.

"We were joined at the hip," Alex said. And then she looked directly into the camera, tears hanging from her long, dark eyelashes. "We used to meet at the rec center and talk for hours."

And just like that, relief flooded Emma's body. Alex wasn't going to expose her. Alex was covering for her. The "rec center" had been their own private code for any kind of rule-breaking. It started when Emma was staying with the Stokeses; one night Alex had slipped out past her curfew for a date with a boy from UNLV. When Alex's single mom came home early and asked where her daughter was,

Emma had stammered out that Alex was swimming at the rec center. They both laughed about it later. *Good thing my mom's internal clock is all screwed up from working nights,* Alex had teased, *or she'd have wanted to know why that pool is open at midnight on a weeknight.* From then on, "rec center" was synonymous for "I've got your back."

Emma suddenly missed her old best friend more than ever. Hearing the news of her own death had made her feel horribly alone—as though she were a living ghost, invisible to the people around her. But here was Alex, clear as day, telling her she was on her side.

"I think I need to lie down for a little while," Emma said cautiously. "May I be excused?"

"Of course." Mrs. Mercer was still watching her with concern evident on her face. "Do you need anything, sweetheart?"

"No, I'm all right." Emma gave a wan smile. "Just tired." She stood up and carefully pushed her chair in against the table. She could feel their eyes follow her out the kitchen door.

It was all she could do to keep from taking the stairs three at a time. She forced herself to walk slowly, passing the gallery wall of family photos that ran up the stairwell. She knew the pictures by heart now, every smile, every outfit, the patterns on the wrapping paper in birthday and Christmas photos. It was a highlight reel of Sutton's life, not hers—and yet after so much pretending, sometimes it was hard to remember that.

When she got to Sutton's room, Emma rummaged at the bottom of the biggest desk drawer, where she'd hidden the old BlackBerry she'd brought with her from Vegas. Sure enough, Alex had messaged her. WHAT THE HELL IS GOING ON? ARE YOU OK?

Emma winced, wishing Alex were in front of her right that minute so she could throw her arms around her with relief. She hit the button to reply.

I CAN'T EXPLAIN RIGHT NOW. DON'T CONTACT ME AGAIN—IT'S DANGEROUS. THANK YOU FOR EVERY-THING. LOVE YOU ALWAYS.

Her heart was sick at the knowledge that she was about to cut off one of the few people in the world who really knew her, but she forced herself to hit SEND, then powered down the BlackBerry. In Sutton's underwear drawer she found a box of tampons—her go-to hiding place from her foster kid days. No one ever thought to look in someone else's tampon box. She shoved the phone inside and stuck it in the back of the drawer.

There. Hopefully Alex would keep a low profile until this was all over and Emma could explain. The last thing she needed was for her best friend to end up on the mur-derer's hit list—or get Emma herself thrown in jail.

But I couldn't help wishing Emma had broken the BlackBerry and thrown away the pieces. After all, they'd found the Greyhound locker. Nothing was safe, not anymore. Emma needed to hurry up and prove that Garrett killed me—before he pinned it on her.

12

DOWN THE DRAIN(PIPE)

"It's like she was lying to her journal," Emma said, sprawled on her stomach across Sutton's luxurious bed. With no other clues, she had turned back to Sutton's cryptic diary for answers. But it was just as confusing as all the other times she'd read it—even with Ethan's help trying to interpret it. It was around ten that night, and they'd been on the phone for almost an hour, sifting through the various entries with no luck.

"*July 20—C is being a real c-word if you know what I mean. She needs to get over it.*" Emma turned the page. "*July 21— Yum yum yum, got G Burberry Sport for our 1 mo. anniversary and he smells so good.* Nothing about Garrett's temper or the fights they had or the fact that she was still sneaking around with Thayer. She had all these secrets, and she didn't even admit them to herself." She snapped the book shut in frustration.

"It makes sense, though." On the other end of the line she could hear a soft crunching sound. She pictured Ethan with his legs up on the railing of the porch, a bowl of salted popcorn in his lap, wearing the blue flannel shirt that always smelled like vanilla. She couldn't help the little shiver of pleasure that trilled along her spine at the image. "Her friends were always looking for ways to get her. She wouldn't want to give them anything that they could use to prank her."

Emma sighed, rolling over on her back and flipping through the book for the hundredth time. What would it have been like if their situations had been reversed— if Sutton had been forced to figure out who Emma was through *her* journals? Her twin would probably be as annoyed as Emma was now—after all, none of her cutesy fake headlines or lists had any real information in them. Emma had always been careful not to put in too many details or names. In a foster home you never knew who was going to get into your stuff.

"It just feels like the harder we look, the less we find," she said. "I've dog-eared all the pages that say anything about G, but none of them are of any use."

"We have to keep looking. This guy is smart—but somewhere, somehow, he slipped up. I'm sure of it. We just have to figure out how."

A soft knock sounded at the door. "One second!" she yelled, covering the receiver. Then she dropped her voice. "Hey, I need to go. See you tomorrow, okay?"

"Love you," he whispered.

Her toes wiggled at the sound of his sexy baritone saying those two little words. For a moment after she ended the call, she clutched the phone against her heart and smiled. Then she got up off the bed, smoothed her hair, and went to the door.

Mr. Mercer stood in the hall, dressed in a short wool jacket and holding Drake's leash in one hand. "Looks like the media have gone home for the night. Want to come on a walk?"

"Yes!" Emma had never felt so stir-crazy in her life. She was almost relieved to have to go back to school the next day. Anything would be better than doing nothing.

Drake had caught sight of the leash and was skidding in circles around the entryway when they came down the stairs. His tail flew back and forth wildly, and when it hit the accent table at the foot of the stairs, the photos of Laurel and Sutton propped on top collapsed like a set of dominoes. He reared up and pawed at Mr. Mercer, whining with excitement.

"Down!" Mr. Mercer said, trying to sound stern, but the sight made Emma smile. She pulled on a purple Juicy Couture puffer jacket she'd found in Sutton's closet while Mr. Mercer snapped the leash to the dog's collar.

The night was crisp and so clear the stars looked like perforations in the sky. Christmas decorations had started to spring up throughout the neighborhood. Poinsettias in terra-cotta planters flanked a few desert-scaped walkways, and one family had strung colored fairy lights around a towering saguaro cactus in their yard. The Paulsons had gone completely overboard—they'd assembled a giant inflatable snow globe, its constantly running fan roaring as it circulated fake snow through a winter scene that featured both Santa and Frosty the Snowman. When Emma and her grandfather stepped close to the yard they activated some hidden trigger that started playing "Deck the Halls" from a tinny speaker behind the mailbox. Drake eyed the production warily, pressing protectively against Emma's leg as they walked past.

Mr. Mercer seemed surprised by the decorations, as if he'd lost track of months. "I haven't even had a chance to ask you girls what you want for Christmas," he said.

"Oh, right," Emma said, feeling suddenly warm despite the chill. No one had ever asked her what she wanted for Christmas before. She knew Sutton had no problem asking for designer clothes and goods from her parents, but all she wanted was to solve her sister's murder. And stay a part of this family.

Mr. Mercer sighed, his breath puffing out into the cold night air. "I know it's hard to even think of presents at a time like this."

"I'm sure I can come up with something." She put on a deadpan expression that made him chuckle.

They walked in silence for a little while. Mr. Mercer moved with his shoulders strangely hunched, as if protecting himself from something Emma couldn't see. He seemed tired and introspective, and she wondered if it was the loss of a granddaughter he didn't know affecting him so profoundly, or something else entirely.

"Have you heard from Becky?" she asked tentatively.

"No," he said, his voice low. He looked ahead into the darkness. "I want to try to get word to her, but who knows where she is by now? And maybe it's better that she doesn't know. What would it help? She lost track of Emma so long ago. It might be best if she never learns what happened to her."

The idea put a lump in Emma's throat. Becky hadn't been in her life for thirteen years, but the idea that Emma could die and Becky would never even know it made her feel small and alone. She could have suffered terribly every single day since Becky had left her—she could have died hundreds of times over, and Becky wouldn't have had a clue. She'd never realized it before, but now that she did, the thought sat hard and cold over her heart.

I knew how Emma felt. Every single time I watched my adopted father put an arm around her shoulders, I was sure that would be the time he realized that she was an impostor. That he'd finally see that I was gone. It wasn't jealousy, exactly—I didn't begrudge Emma that love— but the world had moved forward, and no one had noticed that the girl living my life wasn't even me.

Emma played with the zipper pull on her jacket, her voice suddenly small. "Dad, did you suspect? Before Becky told you, I mean? Did you ever think there might have been two of us?"

Mr. Mercer turned to look at her, his lips twisted in thought. "No. But then again, you yourself were such a surprise it was hard to know what to think. Becky was only eighteen when she came home with you. We hadn't seen her for more than six months. We hadn't even known she was pregnant, and then all of a sudden she rang the doorbell with you in her arms. It was just before Thanksgiving, and you were only a few months old." A fond smile curved across his face. "You were such a sweet baby. And tiny, impossibly tiny. Becky told us you'd been several weeks premature—of course, now we know that your size was because you were a twin." His voice caught for a moment, then he recovered. "We loved you from the moment we saw you. We would have loved both of you, if only we'd known."

Emma nodded. "Mom's taking this really hard, isn't she? The news about Emma?"

They were passing under a streetlight, and in its lurid yellow light she could see the deep shadows in Mr. Mercer's face. "Of course she is. We both feel terrible. Sutton, Emma was just like you at the beginning. Thinking about how difficult things were for her is hard, because it's so easy to imagine *you* in her place. It could just as easily have been you that Becky kept secret from us. And now . . . well, it's too late to do anything for Emma. And that breaks your mother's heart, and mine."

As they turned a corner, headlights lit up behind them. Emma glanced around to see a midsized Audi, creeping slowly in their wake. She drew in her breath, instantly on edge. "Let's go this way," she said, lacing her arm through Mr. Mercer's and tugging him down a side street. Drake's tags jingled as he trotted along ahead of them. She wanted to see if the Audi would follow them. Sure enough, the headlights turned, too.

"Is that someone you know?" Mr. Mercer asked, glancing over his shoulder. She pulled him ahead, walking faster. She passed a mailbox with tinsel garlands wound up the pole and hung another right. Who did she know with an Audi? It was hard to see in the dark, but it looked white. Or maybe silver . . .

"Silver," I whispered, suddenly knowing who the car belonged to. I'd been in that car almost every day last summer.

Garrett, Emma thought, only a moment behind me. Her heart pounded as the car crept closer. Garrett had picked her up in that car the night he'd taken her out for their picnic. She clutched Mr. Mercer's arm. "We need to go home," she muttered urgently.

"What's wrong, Sutton?" he said, trying to look behind them at the car. "Who is that?"

"Just trust me. Keep walking." She pulled him along behind her, cutting across a corner lawn now to keep as far from the car as she could. For a moment she thought about bolting, but then she realized it would do no good— Garrett would be able to catch them. He'd already run someone over in a car once; if he wanted to do it again, there'd be nothing to stop him.

With a sudden roar of the motor, the car lurched around the corner after them, angling its nose to block their path. Drake barked furiously. Next to her, Mr. Mercer tightened his arm through hers. She shuddered as the door flew open and braced for Garrett in all his rage, ready to push Mr. Mercer down and stand in front of him, if she had to.

But it wasn't Garrett. It was a skinny, pointy-chinned man wearing a denim jacket and a shabby brown knit scarf. He wore wire-frame glasses, and he was fiddling with a digital audio recorder as he approached them.

"Ted and Sutton Mercer?" A shameless grin spread across his face. "Care to give me a statement for *The Real Deal Magazine*?"

Mr. Mercer looked outraged. He straightened himself to his full height and hugged Emma to his side with one arm. "You almost ran us over!"

The reporter's grin didn't falter. "Just trying to get your attention. Come on, pops, don't you want your side of the story to be told?"

Emma's temper flared. "Not by some hack from a second-rate gossip rag."

The man laughed out loud. "I've already heard it all, sweetheart. Save your insults for the fat girls at school."

Drake hadn't stopped barking. Now he gave a low, threatening growl.

"We have no comment to make at this time," Mr. Mercer said firmly. Emma noticed that he'd given some slack to the leash, and Drake had gotten closer to the reporter. The reporter seemed to have noticed it, too. He held his hands up in the air and backed slowly away.

"It's your prerogative. But the story's going to be big, and there's gonna be a lot of dirt that comes out. I guarantee it." He leaned slowly down to place a business card on the curb. "If you start to feel like you aren't being properly represented in the media, give me a call. My number's on the card."

The reporter backed into the side of his car, eyeing Drake the whole way. He groped around for the door handle, and then he was off, leaving Emma, Mr. Mercer, and Drake in a cloud of exhaust.

Emma strode over to where the card lay and plucked it up. Then she ripped it into tiny pieces and threw them in the air. Mr. Mercer watched her with an unreadable expression on his face.

"Did you know that was a reporter?" he asked.

"I . . . I suspected," she stammered.

He sighed, putting his hand on her shoulder. "I wish I could protect you from them, Sutton. They're going to be all over the place." He rubbed Drake behind the ears. The dog's tail whipped wildly back and forth. Then he laughed. "'Second-rate gossip rag'?"

Emma broke into a sheepish grin. "That's right. Those reporters are the ones who are going to need protection." She held up her fists and pretended to box.

I trailed behind my father and sister as they walked back toward home. I wished Dad could protect Emma, too—I wished he could keep all the danger now threatening her at bay. But I knew as well as Emma did that it had to be the other way around. She was the only one who could protect him. It hadn't been Garrett in the car this time. But sooner or later, he'd make good on his threats. He'd come for our family, and when he did, she had to be ready.

13

SISTER ACT

Since she'd taken Sutton's place three months earlier, Emma had gotten used to the wide berth given her by most of the students at Hollier High. Sutton was notorious, after all, and no one wanted to get caught in the crossfire of a Lying Game prank. But the following day, when the crowds parted before her and Laurel as they made their way down the hall, it felt different. On either side she could hear barely stifled whispers.

"Did you hear the dead girl was her sister?"

"Her *twin* sister."

"Yeah, right. I don't care what you say, this is some

kind of prank. Remember last year, when she told everyone she'd been carjacked?"

Emma kept her breath steady and even as she walked, trying not to let panic overtake her. She had never gotten used to everyone looking at her, and now they weren't even bothering to hide it. If she ever needed to channel Sutton's bitchiest attitude, it was now.

She rounded a corner to see Charlotte and Madeline standing by her locker. When they caught sight of her they hurried forward to meet her, both of them looking pale and worried. Charlotte carried two paper coffee cups and tried to hand her one and hug her at the same time.

"There you are," she murmured, her voice low. "Are you okay?" Emma took the cup gratefully. The night before, she'd set up a three-way video-chat with Charlotte and Madeline to tell them everything that had happened. She hadn't wanted to have to explain more than once. By then they'd seen the news—Madeline couldn't stop saying that it was "so weird," and Charlotte had seemed almost hurt that "Sutton" hadn't told them about her twin. But to their credit, both girls had seemed more worried about her than anything else.

"Don't you have somewhere to be?" Madeline barked at a short boy in a flannel shirt who seemed to be lingering a few feet away, listening. He jumped and scuttled off, looking terrified. She sighed, running her hand over her sleek, jet-black hair.

Emma smiled her thanks. "I can't believe these people."

"*I* can't believe how calm you are," Charlotte said, eyeing Emma. "I'd be a mess."

"Well, my sister's a great actress," Laurel said, looking steadily at Emma as she spoke.

Emma squirmed under her friends' stares. She adjusted her purse on her shoulder. "Well, I'm not as calm as I look. In fact, I need some air. I'm going to step out, okay?" And before they could say anything in reply, she hurried out the glass door into the courtyard. She took a deep, grateful breath. Soon she would have to go back in there, enter another classroom, and deal with more questions and stares and snide whispers, but for this one moment she could just *be*.

The courtyard was deeply shadowed, the morning sun still too low to touch the corners of the little square. She was alone—everyone else was on their way to class. A handful of acacia trees in terra-cotta planters dotted the area. She took a step toward the shade-dappled benches.

Then a hand shot out and grabbed her wrist. She shrieked, instinctively stepping back, but the hand clenched tighter around her. And then she saw who it was.

Thayer.

Dark shadows hung under his eyes, which shone with a

manic gleam. He stood looking down at her, still holding her arm in a tight grip, and Emma was suddenly and painfully aware how much taller and stronger he was.

"You need to tell me the truth," he hissed. "Now."

Emma looked around frantically, but no one saw them. The bell for class rang inside.

"Let go of me, Thayer," she said sternly.

Thayer's eyes narrowed, but he dropped her arm suddenly, as though she'd been on fire. "I know you're not Sutton," he said. He took a deep, ragged breath, running his hands through his hair like a man possessed. "You're the twin, aren't you? You switched places with her. I don't know why or how. But I knew you weren't her. I've known it since the first time I saw you."

Thayer. Part of me wanted Emma to reach out and touch him, so that I could feel him, if only for a second.

But she just flipped her hair and stared at him coolly, doing her best to mask her racing heart. "Thayer, you're being crazy. I never even *met* Emma."

At that, Thayer let out a cry—something between a snarl and a scream—and grabbed the front of Emma's shirt, yanking her forward. The muscles in his neck were rigid. "Tell me the truth," he growled, his breath hot on her face. Emma whimpered, trying to pull out of his grip, but he wouldn't let go. "Don't lie to me! What did you do to her?"

"Thayer, stop it!" I yelled uselessly. "She's trying to help me." But I was powerless—powerless to talk to him, powerless to soothe him. I could only stand and watch.

Tears welled up in Emma's eyes. For a moment, Thayer's face was a grotesque mask, twisted in rage, but when he saw that she was crying, something in his expression shifted. He let go of her shirt so abruptly she stumbled. Then he was pacing back and forth in a short, tight course, like a panther searching for its prey.

Emma hugged herself, trembling uncontrollably, and wiped the tears from her cheeks. Thayer's hands were clenched into fists, and every movement he made seemed tense with barely controlled power. But when he stopped and turned back to her, the anger had melted away, leaving nothing but anguish.

"Please," he whispered. He took a step forward, but stopped when he saw her flinch. "I just need to know. Is she—" He choked on the word. "Is she dead?"

Thayer's hazel eyes searched her face with desperate longing, moving over her features, trying to find the girl he loved inside them. Emma's heart twisted in her chest. She wished she could tell him how trapped she felt. How deep her own grief ran. How sorry she was to have hurt him. But a cruel, nagging voice recited the threat in her mind. *Sutton didn't do what I told her, and she paid for it . . . Keep up the game, or Nisha won't be the only person you care about who dies for your sake.*

Garrett had already tried to hit Thayer with her car. If he *killed* Thayer, she would never forgive herself.

Summoning every ounce of Sutton Mercer coolness she had left, Emma leveled a steely glare at the boy in front of her.

"How dare you?" she asked, her voice as sharp and cold as glass. Thayer opened his mouth to say something, but she talked over him. "My sister *died* in that canyon. Everyone at school is looking at me like I'm a freak. And now you accuse me of taking her place in some kind of sick *Parent Trap* plot?" She pulled herself up to her full height, poking a finger at his chest savagely. "Are you high? Or just jealous? You'd love it if I were Emma, because that would mean I hadn't really dumped you for Ethan at all. Well, guess what? That's exactly what happened. You were gone. I fell in love with Ethan. End of story. What you and I had is over . . . and maybe we shouldn't bother trying to be friends if you're going to be so cruel."

Thayer's hand fell limply away from her, and he stood there dazed, like she'd slapped him. She fought the urge to reach out to him, to take it all back, her throat burning with every word. Hurting him was the only way to keep him safe. She picked up her purse and turned to go back into the school.

"Hey, Emma?"

And before she could stop herself, she paused.

"I thought so," he said in a low voice.

Emma turned, desperate to say something, anything, to fix her mistake—but Thayer was already gone.

I'd been waiting all these months for someone to realize Emma wasn't me. But now that it had finally happened, all I felt was cold, sick dread.

Because what Thayer knew could kill him.

14

EAT YOUR HEART OUT, NANCY DREW

Emma found Ethan on his way to German class. "Thayer knows," she whispered urgently. Ethan stopped short, his jaw working soundlessly for a moment.

"What? How?" he finally asked, his voice low. She pulled him toward an alcove behind a potted plant. A large picture window looked out over the soccer field.

She bit her lip. Thayer had suspected ever since he'd kissed her at Charlotte's party. Ethan knew about the kiss—he'd caught them—but she didn't want to bring it up again.

"He called me Emma, and I reacted," she admitted, shame washing over her anew. "I'm such an idiot."

"No, you're not," Ethan said fiercely. Emma gazed into his dark blue eyes, where anxiety vied with something else—a fierce vigilance, maybe. And even though she knew that Ethan couldn't really protect her if the murderer was determined to kill again, his solid strength was comforting. She felt her muscles slowly unclench, calmed by his presence.

Emma sighed and leaned her head against Ethan's shoulder. "I mean . . . he doesn't have a way to prove it. But what if he catches me in a lie? What if he figures something out?"

Ethan's eyes narrowed. "The only way he could know for sure is if he did it. I still say he's suspicious."

She shook her head impatiently. "Thayer was on his way to the hospital when Sutton died. There's no way he could have gotten back to the canyon with a broken leg. He was probably high on painkillers by that point anyway."

Ethan gave a noncommittal snort, which she took to mean "Okay-fine-he-has-an-alibi-but-I-don't-have-to-like-it." She opened her mouth to tell him how desperate Thayer had seemed to know the truth, how he really just wanted to know if it was the girl he loved at the bottom of that canyon, but before she could speak, Ethan's gaze shifted. He was staring at something out the window.

"Look!" he hissed. She turned to look where he was pointing.

Garrett and Celeste had appeared on the soccer field. Emma couldn't hear a word through the glass, but it was obvious they were shouting at each other. Celeste kept shaking her head no, her long blonde braids dancing around her head. Garrett's face was an ugly red, screwed up in rage. He shook his hands violently in front of her, looking like he wanted to strangle her.

I knew that expression. I knew that face. It surprised me, how familiar it suddenly was. New memories floated hazily to the surface. I remembered his mood swings, his bad temper. I remembered him punching a locker and leaving a dent in the metal, walking away from me in a rage. I remembered how his fingers left spots of blood on the clean linoleum behind him.

"Wow," Emma breathed. They both watched as Celeste threw one hand up dismissively, then turned to walk back toward the school. Garrett stood staring after her for a long moment, his chest heaving with anger. Then he turned away and stormed off across the field, toward the small cedar grove that separated campus from the busy street beyond.

"That was . . . intense," Ethan said uncertainly.

"Now's our chance," Emma said, straightening up. Ethan frowned.

"Our chance for what?" he asked, but she glanced up and down the empty hall, not answering. She grabbed

Ethan's hand and hurried down the hall to where the senior lockers were.

Garrett's locker was in a cul-de-sac around the corner from a Coke machine. It was obvious which was his—the good-luck sign the soccer boosters had made for the finals still hung there proudly in red and gold glitter letters. Emma walked quickly to it and examined the lock.

"What are you doing?" Ethan whispered.

"What we should have done a long time ago," she said, setting her jaw. "You keep a lookout, okay?"

He nodded, leaning back against the lockers and staring over her head.

She slowly twisted the combination to zero, and then, crossing her fingers on both hands, she delivered a sharp little kick to the base of the locker. The door sprang open, shuddering with a wobbly metallic sound in the empty corridor. She glanced up and down the hall to see if anyone had heard.

"Where the hell did you learn that?" Ethan asked, looking impressed.

She grinned. "My friend Alex taught me, back in Henderson."

The locker smelled strongly of peanut butter and some kind of musky aftershave. A hooded sweatshirt hung on the hook. Books were neatly stacked on the top shelf, surrounded by assorted bits of clutter—a plastic comb, a handful of loose change, an athletic mouth guard in a plastic case. Hanging on the inside of the door was a magnetized mirror, a faded *Sports Illustrated* picture featuring Mia Hamm celebrating a win by ripping off her shirt, a photo of Garrett and Louisa standing in front of the Grand Canyon, and a snapshot of Celeste curled up in an overstuffed armchair in a book-lined study.

"What are you looking for?" Ethan whispered, peering into the locker.

Emma shook her head. "I don't know. Maybe this is pointless. I guess he's not going to have a sign saying I DID IT on the inside of his locker." She chewed her lip, her eyes running across Garrett's things. "I read that some killers keep mementos of their crimes so they can relive them later." She shivered, imagining the kinds of things she would find in his locker if Garrett had taken a keepsake. It would have been horrifying to find a lock of Sutton's hair or a piece of her clothing—or worse.

She crouched down to unzip a Nike duffel bag slouched on the floor of the locker, but all it held was a pair of soccer cleats, white socks, mesh shorts, an enormous green plastic water bottle—and a flask of something that smelled like bourbon. She zipped it back up, still kneeling, and sighed.

"I guess it's a bust," she said, disappointed. Ethan didn't

answer. She looked up at where he stood next to her, frowning. "Ethan?"

He was gazing at something on the top shelf. He reached slowly upward, and carefully, as if it were something dirty, he picked up a tiny silver key hanging on a metal tag.

"Ethan?" She rose slowly to her feet. "What is it?"

She held out her hand, and he let the key fall into her palm. It was small—too small to be a house key. On one side of the metal fob, she could just make out the word ROSA. A second word was too scratched to decipher. Below that was the number 356.

She frowned. "Does this mean something to you?" She didn't know anyone named Rosa at Hollier.

"Flip it over," Ethan said, his eyes round in his face. She cocked her head quizzically. He nodded at the key fob in her hand. She turned it over and stared down at it.

On the reverse side of the tag, someone had scratched the initials S.M. into the metal. Her hand started to shake so hard the text blurred in her vision. Ethan moved toward her, putting a hand on each of her shoulders to hold her steady.

"What does it mean?" Her voice was a hoarse, pleading whisper.

Before Ethan could answer, the sound of footsteps echoed from around the corner. Emma shoved the key into her jeans pocket and shut the locker as quietly as she could. Then she looked frantically around for somewhere to hide.

"Here," Ethan breathed, backing her against the wall and gazing down into her eyes. She struggled for a moment, disoriented—but then she fell still as she realized what he was doing. He pressed his lips to hers, and even though her blood was still rushing in her ears, for one sweet moment the kiss took over and her panic subsided.

"Oh! I'm sorry!"

They both looked up to see Celeste, who had stopped in her tracks when she saw them. She was dressed with her usual Arwen-of-Middle-Earth flair, in a green tunic printed all over with Celtic knots and a pair of leggings. Bangles jingled on her wrists, and dozens of mismatched silver earrings hung from her multiple ear piercings. Her eyes were bloodshot, her voice thick with tears. She wiped furiously at her face and tried to force a smile. "I didn't mean to, uh, interrupt."

Emma gently pushed Ethan away from her. Celeste stood uncertainly in the hallway, looking everywhere but at them. Emma could see a folded piece of paper in her fingertips. She must have been about to put a note in Garrett's locker.

"Are you okay?" Emma asked.

Celeste shifted her weight, her bracelets jangling

musically against one another. She usually had an airy, ethereal sensibility, but today she seemed weighed down with sadness.

"I'm fine. I mean, you know how Garrett is."

Celeste was clearly trying to sound dismissive, but the words hit Emma like an electric shock. She didn't know how Garrett was, not really—but standing in front of her was someone who did. She glanced at Ethan, who stood a little apart, looking anywhere but at Celeste. "Hey, Ethan, can I meet up with you later?"

He looked startled for a moment. She widened her eyes meaningfully at him, trying to communicate that she wanted to talk to Celeste alone. He jumped up from where he'd been leaning on the wall, fumbling at his books. "Oh, uh, yeah. I should get to class anyway. See you, Celeste."

Ethan's footsteps disappeared down the hall. The Coke machine hummed loudly. Emma fidgeted with her purse strap. "I know we're not exactly friends, Celeste, but I—I just don't want you to get hurt."

Celeste sighed, glancing up through her wet lashes to meet Emma's eyes. "He's an Aries. They're always intense, you know?"

"Um, right," Emma said. She bit her lip, thinking about what she'd just seen through the window. Garrett hadn't looked intense—he'd looked like he wanted to hurt someone. "We used to fight a lot when we were together. He has a . . . scary temper."

Celeste leaned back against the wall of lockers, watching Emma warily, like she was reluctant to confide too much. Emma couldn't exactly blame her—the Lying Game girls had pranked her a few weeks ago. But after a moment Celeste spoke, her voice quiet, tentative.

"It just all comes back to Louisa. The weird thing is that Louisa is actually doing okay. I mean, her mom put her in therapy, so she's had help. But the whole thing, like . . . *broke* him. His spirit is so wounded. I keep asking him to meditate with me. It helped a lot, after my parents got divorced. But he won't even try."

Emma nodded carefully. "So you think he's angry because of . . . because of what happened with Louisa?"

Celeste gave her an odd look. "Yeah. Of course."

"Oh, well, I never heard the whole story. I knew he was upset about it, obviously, but I don't really know *what* he was upset about," Emma fished.

The color drained from Celeste's face. She glanced back over her shoulder as if checking for eavesdroppers. "I shouldn't have said anything, then. It's not my business to spread around."

Emma mentally swore. Gossip always flowed freely at Hollier, and the one time she needed it, it dried up entirely.

"I'm not trying to pry," she backpedaled. "I just think you should be careful. I mean . . . Garrett's pretty volatile, Celeste."

Celeste narrowed her eyes suspiciously. Sutton Mercer wasn't exactly known for her concern for others.

"Well, um, take care," Emma said, recognizing her cue to leave. She tucked Sutton's purse under her arm and walked away.

"Hey, Sutton?"

Emma paused and turned around. Celeste stood in the middle of the hall, hugging her shoulders.

"I heard about your sister," she said. "I'm sorry." Then she turned and disappeared, leaving Emma with more questions than answers.

But something Celeste said had awoken a strange, tingling memory at the back of my mind. It stayed maddeningly out of reach, just beyond my memory, but I could feel it there. Something had happened to Garrett's little sister—something very, very bad.

Maybe bad enough to turn her brother into a killer.

15

BEHIND ENEMY LINES

Garrett's house was a small hacienda on a quiet street near the country club, surrounded by slate tile, low stone benches, and succulents in earthen pots. Enormous golden fish drifted lazily in a koi pond beneath a small cluster of paloverde trees. A dark blue Subaru Outback was parked in the drive, but Garrett's silver Audi was nowhere to be seen. Emma sat in Sutton's car across the street for nearly ten minutes, taking deep, steadying breaths and watching the house. Finally, she braced herself and got out of the car.

School had just let out. Garrett would be in the Hollier weight room with the rest of the soccer team for the next two hours—the season was over, but they worked out together year-round. Thoughts of Garrett had haunted Emma all day. His face red and angry as he screamed at Celeste; the smirk on his lips as he'd held up the sign that read *BITCH*; the small, shiny key with her sister's initials scratched on the tag. She'd wandered through all of Sutton's classes in a fog, waking up only during fourth-period German to stare intently at the back of Garrett's head as if she could read his thoughts if she just tried hard enough. Finally, she couldn't take it anymore. She was going to hunt for answers—even if it meant putting her own life at risk.

She was going to try to get into Garrett's bedroom.

No one knew she was here. She hadn't told Ethan she was coming. He would have figured out a way to stop her. But she couldn't find the proof she needed if she never tried.

Garrett's street had felt strangely vacant as Sutton's GPS led her to his house. No traffic rushed by, and no one in the neighborhood seemed to be outside doing yard work or enjoying the golden November sun. The only thing she could hear was the soft, constant chatter of birds overhead. A few blocks away, someone at the country club yelled, "Fore!" It was punctuated by the soft *pock* of a ball being smacked in the distance.

As she set foot in the Austins' yard, a bizarre, high-pitched cry tore through the air. Emma jumped, panic surging in the pit of her stomach. Another cry broke out, and then another, again and again, echoing off the flagstones. It sounded like a girl's voice, wailing in pain.

Each keening cry seemed to cut through Emma's chest. She spun in circles, looking for the source of the sound. For a split second she was sure that Garrett had another victim here, somewhere on his property. But then two enormous peacocks came hustling out from the backyard, their tails dragging behind them. One of them tossed its head back, its throat shuddering as it gave the cry she'd mistaken for human. Emma shrieked as they beelined for her. She jumped up onto a stone bench next to the pond just as the birds swooped toward her. They flanked her, angling their heads to glare at her with their beady eyes.

The front door opened, and a thickset woman with sandy blonde hair stuck her head out, calling, "Rocko! Salvador!" Then she saw Emma cowering on the bench. Her eyes widened, and she bustled through the doorway. The peacocks pivoted their heads on their long necks to look at her, and one stalked toward her, looking hopefully at her hand. "Shoo!" she said. "I don't have any corn, you wretched things."

This had to be Garrett's mom. She had the same hair, the same molasses-brown eyes—though where her son was all muscle, she had the rounded corners of a teddy bear under her loose linen pants and brown sweater. Amber rings glittered on every finger, amber drop earrings hung from her lobes, and a pair of cat-eye glasses hung at her chest from a chain made of amber beads.

Emma held her breath as the woman made warding-off motions with her hands while the birds stood and stared balefully. She didn't know what Garrett might have told his mother after their breakup, or what kind of relationship Sutton had with her boyfriend's mom to begin with. But when the peacocks had finally strutted away around back, the woman broke into a warm smile.

"Sutton!" she exclaimed. She extended a hand to help Emma down from the bench. "It's been so long! Sorry about the boys," she said, sighing toward the peacocks. "They've been so aggressive lately. I don't know what's gotten into them."

Emma gave the woman a tentative smile. "I'm sorry I, uh, got them all riled up. Thanks for saving me, Mrs. Austin." As soon as the words left her mouth a cloud moved over the woman's expression.

"That's Garrett's stepmother's name, dear," she said coolly. "Remember? My maiden name is Ramsey."

Emma cursed herself inwardly. Of course—Garrett's parents were divorced. But as quickly as it had appeared, the woman's darkened expression passed. "Besides, why are you calling me Mrs. anything? You always used to call me Vanessa."

Vanessa. Something stirred at the back of my mind. As usual, it was almost impossible to nail down a specific memory, but I could grasp at fragments. I remembered having dinner with Garrett's family, picnic-style on the floor of their living room. I remembered the impression that there was a lingering sadness around her, though I wasn't sure why. Was it a remnant of a bitter divorce, or something darker? I struggled again to conjure up a memory of Garrett's sister—*what had happened to her?*—but nothing came to me.

Emma took a deep breath. "Sorry, Vanessa. It's been a long time."

The woman patted Emma's shoulder, smiling wistfully. "It has, hasn't it? But I'm so glad to see you now. Does this mean you and Garrett are friends again?"

Emma hesitated. Garrett's mom was nothing like she'd expected. She seemed so sweet; the idea of lying to her made Emma a little nauseated. But she had to get into Garrett's room somehow.

"We're trying," she said evasively. Vanessa nodded, and for a moment, she looked tired.

"I know how difficult he can be sometimes," she said, her voice low. "But you meant so much to him. I'm glad you're trying to stay in each other's lives. I always thought you were good for him, Sutton."

Emma bit her lip. "You did?"

"Of course." Vanessa had a dimple in her left cheek, the same as Garrett's. When she smiled, the years peeled off her. "You were the only girlfriend he ever had who didn't let him get away with murder."

Emma forced a hollow laugh at Vanessa's choice of words. "Oh, I don't know about that." She cleared her throat. "I stopped by because I think Garrett has my Wildcats sweatshirt. Is he here?"

Vanessa shook her head, her amber earrings swaying with the movement. "No, I'm afraid he's still at school. Pumping iron, I think he calls it?" She had a gasping, breathless laugh. "He won't be home for a few hours."

Emma pretended to be disappointed, pursing her lips in a pout. "Oh, man. I was really hoping to wear it this weekend. They're playing New Mexico, and I always wear that shirt when I watch the game with my dad."

"Why don't you run up to his room and see if you can find it?"

Emma felt a pang of guilt at how easily the woman suggested it. "You don't mind?"

"Not at all. If you're brave enough to enter that mess, you have my blessings." Vanessa opened the front door with another laugh. Emma followed her into an entryway with cherry-wood parquet flooring and antique bronze light fixtures. The window over the door was a stained-glass image of the sun coming up over the mountains, and the light filtering through it cast an orange glow over the room. She stared around for a moment. This wasn't what she'd expected Garrett's house to look like at all. The decorations were luxurious and eccentric. Garrett had always seemed so bland to her.

Then again, she clearly didn't know anything about Garrett at all.

Emma turned and gave Vanessa her best impress-the-adults smile. "Thank you so much. I'll just be a minute."

"Take your time, sweetie." Garrett's mother enclosed her in a quick hug that smelled like jasmine perfume and potting soil. Emma's heart ached a little. Vanessa reminded her of her best friend Alex's mom, who'd always treated her like family.

She gave Garrett's mom another little wave and took the steps two at a time, her heart picking up speed. The stairs opened onto a landing that looked over the living room. The high, slanting ceiling was made of red tin, stamped with an elaborate vine pattern. Creepy ambient music seeped out from under one of the closed bedroom doors. A large collage hung on the door at eye level—it looked like the artist had ripped up pictures of fashion models and then pieced them back together into surreal, alien forms, some with animal bodies, others with machine parts replacing arms or eyes. Emma thought it was safe to assume that was Louisa's room. The room after that was a blue-and-yellow tiled bathroom—and the one after that, she guessed, would be Garrett's. She tentatively cracked the door and peered inside.

Bingo.

Vanessa hadn't been exaggerating. Garrett's room looked like a bomb had gone off in it. His dark green bedspread slumped half on the bed, half on the floor. Dirty clothes were strewn around on every square inch of the floor, and a pervasive smell of sweaty socks filled the air. PowerBar wrappers and empty Gatorade bottles collected on every surface. Pictures of soccer players and Italian race cars were tacked all over the walls, and a jock strap dangled from the little gold figurine topping an MVP trophy on his desk.

Emma's eyes darted uncertainly around the room. If Garrett were hiding something about the murder, where would it be—and *what* would it be? She opened his desk drawers, sorting through unorganized piles of paper clips, highlighters, and thumbtacks. There was evidence of his current romance with Celeste, in the form of a chunk of violet quartz next to his computer—Emma assumed it was for focusing his chi or something like that. A photo of Celeste sitting on a swing and gazing off into mid-distance sat behind it.

A few picture frames lay facedown on the desk, where they'd been knocked over by a hastily flung windbreaker.

She picked them up and turned them over—and as she did, her heart started to slam against her chest.

In one, Nisha beamed at the camera in tennis whites. And in the other, Sutton gave her best movie-star pout from a lounge chair, dressed in a jade-green bikini and a flowered sarong.

The frames shook in her hands. Why would he have these here, on his desk, after both girls had broken up with him?

I stared at the pictures. What did he think about when he looked at them? Did he relive what he'd done to us? Did he tell himself that I'd deserved it for hurting him? A shiver moved through me as I looked at my own coy smirk, frozen forever in time.

Emma set the pictures back where she'd found them. She suddenly felt a lot less safe than she had a moment before. She backed toward the door, stumbling over a stray hiking boot on the way.

As she turned to go, she kicked an orange prescription bottle with the tip of her toe. A few pills rattled inside. She frowned, stooping to pick it up.

It was Valium.

Time froze. She stared at the crisp black print on the label until the letters didn't make sense, until they looked like a jumble of alien signs. Detective Quinlan's voice floated back to her. *The examiner found extremely high amounts of diazepam in her bloodstream.* Nisha hadn't had a prescription. But Garrett did.

"What are you doing in here?"

The voice cut through Emma's thoughts like a knife. She jumped, throwing the bottle to the floor, and looked up to see Garrett's sister in the doorway.

Louisa wore cut-off jean shorts, bright green tights, hiking boots, and a large black T-shirt that draped off one shoulder. Her dyed-black hair was cut in a shaggy bob, and she wore dozens of black jelly bangles on her arms. She stood in the doorway, looking both curious and mildly annoyed. Emma hadn't even heard her open the door.

"Oh . . . uh, hi, Louisa," she stammered, fastening a bright smile on her face. "Long time no see." Louisa raised an eyebrow. Emma swallowed. "Your mom let me in. I thought I'd left a sweatshirt here, but I don't see it. I mean, I don't know how I could find it in this mess." She gave a nervous laugh, but Louisa didn't smile.

The younger girl gave her a long, steady look. Emma squirmed. She felt like she was being memorized for a police lineup. But finally Louisa spoke.

"You should stay away from Garrett."

Emma blinked. There was no malice in Louisa's voice—just a blunt matter-of-factness. But her brow was crumpled in a worried frown.

"I'm not trying to make any trouble," Emma said carefully.

Louisa shrugged. "It doesn't matter. Look, Sutton, I'm not just trying to be bitchy. He's seriously worse when you're around. I don't know what happened between you guys, but these past few months he's been a total wreck. There's no way you guys are going to be buddies after all that, okay? Just stay out of his life. You owe him that."

A chill crawled up Emma's spine. "He's been unstable since the breakup?"

Louisa gave an impatient snort. "Since before that. The night before Nisha's party he came home hysterical at like three in the morning. He wouldn't tell me where he'd been, but he was hyperventilating and pacing. It took me the rest of the night to get him to calm down." She sighed. "I thought you guys had broken up, but then you were together at Nisha's, so I didn't know what to think." She gave Emma a tiny, almost apologetic smile. "I'm not saying it's your fault, Sutton. We both know my brother has problems. But you make them all so much worse. If you really want what's best for him, you'll stay far, far away." And with that, she left.

Emma stood paralyzed in the middle of Garrett's room, Louisa's words tossing around in her mind. *We both know my brother has problems . . . but you make them all so much worse.*

A sick, twisted fear washed over her. The night before Nisha's party was the night Sutton died. Was his mood frantic because he'd just murdered her in cold blood?

Frustration raged through me. I felt like I was choking on all the things I couldn't tell Emma. If only I could beam my memories straight into her head. If only I could show her what I knew—that Garrett had been in the canyon with me. That he'd killed me.

I'd kill him myself, but thanks to him, I was less than a shadow: silent, intangible—and helpless.

16

LAW AND ORDER: LONG-LOST TWIN UNIT

Later that afternoon, Emma pulled Sutton's Volvo into a parking space outside the police station for her interview with Quinlan. Mr. Mercer had offered to meet her there, but she'd told him not to. She'd lied to the Mercers enough already; she didn't want him to witness this, too.

By now the drab gray building was familiar to her. This was where she'd first tried to report Sutton missing, only to be accused of crying wolf. This, too, was where she'd been brought after she was arrested for shoplifting, when she'd first read Quinlan's file on her twin.

Every time she'd been there before, a sleepy, muted feeling had permeated the air, almost as if the station were underwater. But now officers strode quickly and purpose-fully through the labyrinth of desks behind the reception area. Phones jangled from every corner, pitched just slightly off from one another so their tones clashed pain-fully. A flat-screen TV had been installed on the wall of the waiting area, tuned in to the national news. The sound was off, but the headlines sprang up swiftly along the bot-tom of the screen. She gave a jolt as she realized that the silver-haired CNN reporter was standing outside Sabino Canyon's visitor center. His lips moved soundlessly. GIRL'S BODY FOUND WEDNESDAY, said the blocky text under his handsome face. TPD HAS YET TO RELEASE AN OFFICIAL CAUSE OF DEATH.

So it's gone national, she thought grimly. No wonder the station was looking sharper than usual.

Behind her the door opened and then closed, a blade of sunlight cutting quickly across the room and then disap-pearing again. She glanced away from the TV and gasped.

Travis Lambert, her old foster brother, stood there looking as smarmy as ever, though he'd obviously tried to dress up. He wore a button-down shirt that bunched around his waist where it was badly tucked in, and he'd shaved off the pathetic little strip of hair on his upper lip.

Next to him was a balding, middle-aged man in a tai-lored gray suit. He carried a briefcase, swinging it back and forth like it was some kind of weapon. They walked to the reception desk, where a female officer with thin, penciled-on eyebrows sat typing on an ancient-looking computer.

"My client's here to see Detective Ostrada," drawled the man with the briefcase. The officer gave them a skeptical, unimpressed look, then picked up a phone receiver and hit a button.

"Ostrada? The witness you requested is up here."

Emma took a few steps backward and sat on the low bench in the waiting area, trying to look like just another citizen waiting to talk to a cop. *Stay calm*, she ordered herself. *He hasn't seen you. And even if he does see you, you're Sutton Mercer. You have no idea who the hell he is.* She softened her gaze so that she could look as though she were staring into space while keeping Travis in her periphery. The last thing she wanted was to make eye contact.

The officer hung up the phone and stood up. "You can follow me," she said, sounding like she didn't really care if they did or didn't. She opened the gate that separated the reception desk from the rest of the station, and the lawyer stepped through.

Travis lingered for a moment, his hand on the gate. *Go on*, Emma urged him. *Straight through the gate and out of my sight.* But instead he pivoted slowly, his pupils flaring with recognition when his eyes landed on the bench. Emma fought to keep her face neutral, to act like he was just someone a girl like her wouldn't have the time of day for. She was Sutton Mercer now—not poor, powerless Emma Paxton, with a whole journal titled *Comebacks I Should Have Said*. She pretended to be captivated by a poster on the wall over his head with McGruff the Crime Dog peering suspiciously over the lapel of his trench coat.

"Travis?" the lawyer said, sounding mildly impatient. "Come on, we have a meeting."

"Coming," he said in a singsong voice. Then, staring right at Emma, he pursed his lips to kiss in her direction before pushing through the gate and disappearing into the back.

Her stomach twisted in knots, a sick, shaky feeling sweeping through her. Of course she was still poor, powerless Emma. So long as the murderer kept playing with her like she was his puppet, so long as she had to hide the truth from everyone she loved, she would still be as helpless to control her own fate as she had ever been as a ward of the state back in Vegas.

Emma uncrossed and recrossed her legs on the bench, shifting her weight, wondering why in the world Travis was even here. Maybe they just wanted someone else to identify the body. Maybe he was there to tell more lies about Emma, about how wild and perverted she'd been.

Her thoughts were interrupted by Detective Quinlan, who was now standing at the gate holding it open for her.

"Thanks for coming down, Miss Mercer. Please follow me."

As Quinlan led her past the clusters of desks, she was intensely aware of all the eyes following them both. Everyone in the office seemed to know who she was and what she was there for. A paunchy, buzz-cut officer gawked openly as she passed. A woman whose black hair was twisted in a high pompadour on her head took a surreptitious photo of her with a cell phone.

Who knew the police force would be just like a bunch of high school kids, I thought bitterly.

Quinlan led Emma down a linoleum hallway to an interrogation room at the back of the station. Like everything else in the building, the room was drab and industrial gray. A faded silk fig tree stood in a plastic pot in one corner, thick dust on its fake leaves. She glanced nervously at Quinlan. "How come we're in an interrogation room?" she asked, trying to sound like she was joking. "Do I, uh, need a lawyer?"

Quinlan's mustache twitched slightly. "No, no, Miss Mercer. Not to worry. This is just a casual conversation." He moved to the far side of the table, then tossed two manila folders onto the table, side by side. The tab on the thicker one read SUTTON MERCER. The other read EMMA PAXTON.

Emma stared at the thin folder with her name on it. What could possibly be inside? The only time she'd ever gotten in trouble with the law in her old life was the night she and Alex had broken curfew to see a punk show on UNLV campus, and the officer then hadn't even written them up—he'd just driven them home and handed them over to Alex's furious mother, which had been bad enough. Was the file only for information about the body they'd found in the canyon? Her fingers ached to flip it open, but that was obviously impossible with Quinlan right in front of her.

I wanted to see inside just as badly as Emma did—especially if there was information about my body in her file. Every time I tried to imagine my corpse, an overwhelming sense of curiosity took hold of me. I'd never liked creepy things when I was alive—I didn't watch slasher movies or medical dramas or anything like that. But the urge to see my body was like an itch just out of reach. It wouldn't go away until I'd scratched it.

Quinlan, meanwhile, was busy fidgeting with a digital recorder he'd set on the table. "Can you please state your name and date of birth, Miss Mercer?"

Emma repeated Sutton's name and their birthday, and after he'd replayed the recording to make sure it was working, he clasped his fingers together and rested them on the table. "All right. Can you please tell me again what you know about Emma Paxton?"

Emma swallowed hard. The recorder both made her

feel better and not—she didn't like the thought of the lies she'd have to tell being recorded in her own voice, but on the other hand it would document anything Quinlan said, too. He wouldn't be able to bully or intimidate her if he wanted to use the recording as any kind of evidence.

"Well, like I told you," she said slowly, "I met my birth mom for the first time in Sabino Canyon on August thirty-first. She told me I had a twin named Emma. That same night I got a message on Facebook from a girl named Emma Paxton. Her picture looked exactly like me. We messaged back and forth a few times, and we made arrangements to meet the next evening back at Sabino. I went the next night to meet her, and she never showed up, so I went to Nisha Banerjee's party instead. I didn't really think about her after that—I assumed the Facebook messages were either a lame prank from my friends, or that Emma was just a flake like my birth mom."

"Can you show me those Facebook messages?" Quinlan asked. She nodded, pulling them up on her iPhone and handing it across the table. The night before, she'd sat up staring at her Facebook exchange with Sutton, trying to see if there was anything incriminating that she hadn't realized. As far as she could see, the messages were safe.

Quinlan's eyes flickered up to meet hers. "'Don't tell anyone who you are until we talk—it's dangerous!'" he read out loud. "What was that all about?"

Emma's throat felt dry. "I wanted to surprise my parents with her," she said, beads of sweat gathering at her temple. "I was afraid someone else would find her before I did and think she was me. I didn't want her to give it away."

Quinlan's eyebrow twitched, but otherwise his face was motionless. Somewhere overhead the air conditioning kicked on, and a blast of cold turned her sweat clammy.

"Pretty weird coincidence," Quinlan said. "The night you found out about her was the night she messaged you?"

Emma nodded, shrugging. "Yeah. I know it's weird; I thought so, too. But like I already told you, *Becky's* weird. Maybe she was in contact with Emma, too."

Quinlan pushed the phone back across the table. Emma slid it into her pocket, her skin crawling under his gaze. He was watching her intently, his gray eyes sharp and glinting. She tried not to squirm away from making eye contact.

"Do you know anything about her foster family?" he asked then. She shook her head.

"I saw them on TV yesterday, but she didn't tell me anything about them." She frowned slightly. "I thought I saw her foster brother—what's his name, Travis?—out front in the waiting area. Does he know anything about what happened to my sister?"

The corner of Quinlan's eyebrow twitched again, but

besides that his face didn't move. "We're hoping he can help us with a timeline," he said. He picked up Emma's file, opening it near his chest. She strained her eyes to try to see over the top of the page, but he kept it at a close angle to his body.

"Okay, now, what can you tell me about Nisha Banerjee?" Quinlan's voice was almost conversational, his face neutral and earnest, but a blade of cold shot up Emma's spine. She stared at him blankly.

"What about her?" she asked. She fought to keep her fingernails out of her mouth, instead sliding her hands under her butt on the chair. Quinlan gave her a disingenuously curious look.

"Well, her phone records show that she called you over and over the day she died. She apparently had something really important to tell you. What was so urgent?"

Emma shrugged, trying to look more wistful than terrified. "I've already told you, I wish I knew. She died before she could tell me. But what's that got to do with Emma?"

"I don't know, Sutton. You tell me." Quinlan closed the file and set it down, then crossed his arms over his chest. He stared at her for a long moment, as if expecting her to volunteer more information.

Alarm bells went off in my head. I knew this game too well. Quinlan and I had played cat and mouse for the past few years. His bullshit radar was hair-trigger keen. Emma needed to step very carefully.

Quinlan leaned back in his chair and interlaced his fingers behind his neck. "You know, when I first got word of this, I was sure it was a prank. *Sutton can't have a twin,* I thought—one of you is more than enough. Still, something isn't adding up."

Emma straightened in her chair. Her hands trembled, but she tossed her hair over her shoulder. "Hey, thanks for recording this. I'm glad whoever's going to listen will hear you harassing a grieving teenager without her parents in the room."

That seemed to startle him. He glanced at the recorder, then back at her. "Look, I'm just saying, given your history the whole thing seems kind of far-fetched."

"Yeah, well, I didn't get to write my own life," Emma snapped. *That was true enough,* she thought. "Sorry you don't like the plot."

Quinlan held up his hands defensively. "All right, I'm sorry. You're right." He sighed. "Can you just do me one favor, though?"

"What?" she asked, narrowing her eyes.

"Can I swab your cheek?" She frowned, but he persisted. "I don't want to go into details, but your sister's body wasn't in great shape when we found it. We just want to make sure that she is your biological twin. A quick

DNA test will resolve the whole thing."

Emma bit her lip. There was something about it that she didn't like—Quinlan's rapid-fire questioning had left her feeling vulnerable and confused. But there was no way a DNA test could incriminate her—she and Sutton would be identical, and refusing would seem suspicious. She nodded.

Quinlan extracted a Q-tip from a clear plastic tube in his briefcase. She opened wide, and he ran it along the inside of her cheek, peering into her mouth like a dentist. Then he briskly slid the swab back in the tube and slammed his briefcase shut.

"Wait right here," he said. "I'll be back in just a few minutes."

With that he turned to the door and was gone.

An uneasy feeling descended on me in the silence left in his wake. I didn't trust Quinlan. He was almost as crafty as I'd been. And now he was out of sight. But that also meant that Emma was alone—and he'd left the files on the table. It was finally time to see how I'd died.

17

BODY OF EVIDENCE

Emma counted to ten, holding her breath so she could hear Quinlan's movements as he went down the hall. A distant door opened and shut, and then there was silence. When she was sure he was gone, she grabbed the file that listed her own name.

She flipped it open—and immediately dropped it. The file landed on the table in front of her, gaping open. Paper-clipped to the inside of the folder was a photo of a skeleton.

Emma's throat went dry. She'd known there would probably be post-mortem pictures in the file, but she hadn't stopped to imagine what they'd look like. She couldn't swallow; her tongue felt like sandpaper inside her mouth. But she took a deep breath and squared her shoulders. What if there were clues the cops hadn't known to look for? She had to see those pictures.

The body's empty eye sockets stared straight up at the sky. Brightly colored leaves partially covered it, red and gold and brown. Scraps of skin still clung to the bones, and its long hair spread out behind it, dried out and bleached red by sun and exposure. The skull's awful grin was a strange contrast to the faded pink hoodie still zipped around the corpse's torso.

I gazed at the picture, unable to tear my eyes away from what little remained of the body I'd left behind. Staring at the skull, I could just trace out the memory of my own features—there were my high cheekbones, my narrow chin. But I didn't feel much connection with the bones in the picture. They didn't have anything to do with me anymore. Weirdly, Emma's body felt more like mine than my own did.

There were other photos, paper-clipped behind the first, capturing the body from different angles. It looked like Sutton had been wearing yellow cotton shorts the night she went to the canyon. Close-ups revealed splintered bones, and one showed a jagged hole near the crown of the skull.

The more she looked at the pictures, the stranger

Emma felt. She'd known for months her sister was dead. Between the killer strangling her in Charlotte's kitchen and dropping a theater light next to her in the school auditorium, and most recently, what happened to Nisha, there was really no room for doubt. But still, *still*, there had been some small, hopeful part of her that thought Sutton might walk back into town someday, laughing at the success of her best Lying Game prank yet. Staring down at the pictures of the body, though, there was no room left for hope or fantasy.

This was what had happened to her sister. This was all that was left of her.

Of course, everyone thought this was Emma's body. There was nothing to tell them apart—not even the DNA in their bones. Looking at Sutton's dead body was like looking at pictures of *herself* dead.

A dry spasm shot through her, and bile filled her mouth. She went to a low metal garbage can and spit into it, wishing desperately that she'd asked Quinlan for a glass of water before he'd left.

She went back to the table and sat down again, shaking slightly, fighting to suppress her nausea. On the other side of the folder were stacks of forms and reports, collated and stapled. She picked up a facial reconstruction sketch that showed a young woman's features, from the front and then again in profile. It was almost spookier than the actual remains—there was something uncanny about seeing her own face, drawn by someone who had never actually seen her but who had built the image up from her sister's bones. All the details were right. The artist had gotten the features perfectly, but something was off in the eyes and the lips. Of course, those would be the hardest things to imagine with only the skeleton for a guide.

Next she picked up a diagram of the crime scene, sketched from multiple angles, that showed both the body's distance from the road and the spot the investigators thought she'd fallen from, high overhead. Her breath caught as she recognized the area on the map: Sutton had fallen from a precipice very close to the spot where the girls had held their fake séance just a few weeks earlier.

She thought back to the faint voice she'd heard in her head that night, so familiar in her ear. It had told her to run. It had sounded like it was coming from far, far away. But maybe it had been closer than she'd thought.

It had come from me.

Finally there was the coroner's report. The medical examiner had enumerated Sutton's injuries, and the list was long. On one page he'd sketched the locations of the wounds and fractures on a schematic outline of her body.

Victim has more than a dozen separate bruises and thirteen lacerations over her limbs and torso. Victim's tibia and three ribs are fractured, and left shoulder is dislocated. Victim also suffered depressed skull fracture directly over right eye, causing subdural hematoma and massive hemorrhage.

Emma bit hard on the inside of her mouth, her blood salty and metallic on her tongue. Her sister had died in a lot of pain, and a side note mentioned that it looked like wild animals of some kind had "disturbed" the body. Emma didn't want to think about that. She turned the page.

These injuries are all consistent with an accidental fall.

The words froze her in her seat. *Accidental* fall?

I froze, too. They thought it was an accident? How was that possible? I reached frantically through my memory to conjure up the last image I had of that night in the canyon. Once again I felt Garrett's hand on my shoulder, his voice in my ear. I willed myself to turn around, to face him and find out what he had done to me—but the memory went dark. All I could pull up was that sickly sense of vertigo I'd had when Quinlan had first announced that I'd fallen. Garrett must have pushed me over the side—but there had to be a clue, some indication that he'd done it on purpose. What happened to me—what had happened to Emma and Nisha since—had been no accident.

Emma's head spun wildly. It was just like Nisha's death, covered up and made to look accidental.

Then, at the bottom of the report, two lines in bold type caught her eye.

CAUSE OF DEATH: CEREBRAL CONTUSION CAUSED BY BLUNT FORCE TRAUMA

MANNER OF DEATH: UNDETERMINED

She blinked. *Undetermined.* So maybe they weren't so sure it had been an "accidental" fall, after all.

She kept shuffling through the folder. A stack of grainy surveillance camera stills were stapled together with printed-out e-mails from the Sabino Canyon visitor center, addressed to Quinlan. *We're eager to help in any way we can*, the sender had written. *The camera takes one picture on the hour every hour. We installed it three years ago after a spate of vandalism in the parking lot—it's not set up to monitor activity on the trails.* Emma quickly ran her index finger through the dates attached to the pictures until she found the ones taken on the night of the thirty-first. Her eyes searched for any familiar car, any familiar person. Any clue she hadn't caught before.

From the photos it seemed that there'd hardly been anyone in the canyon that night, and she didn't recognize any of the cars. Sutton's Volvo was nowhere to be seen.

Maybe the murderer had already stolen it by the time the picture was taken, or maybe she and Thayer had parked somewhere secluded.

Picture by picture, hour by hour, the parking lot emptied. At one point two new cars appeared—cars she knew. Mr. Mercer's SUV and Becky's rusted-out brown Buick. That must have been when Sutton had run into her father, and then, not long after that, into Becky. An hour later the cars were gone. Maybe the murderer had walked from somewhere, or had been dropped off by a taxi, just as Emma had been the following day.

She turned the page, and I felt an electric shock pulse through my being. There at midnight, under the sallow yellow light of a street lamp, sat a familiar silver Audi. I could just barely make out the sticker on the bumper. It read WHAT'S LIFE WITHOUT GOALS? The letter O in GOALS was replaced by a soccer ball.

I knew that car. I knew the dark, kidney-shaped stain on the passenger seat where I'd spilled a cup of coffee. I knew the cheesy shearling throw in the backseat, where I'd curled my legs up under me and quirked a finger, beckoning its driver to come close for a kiss. I knew the dent he'd left in the rear driver's side door one night when I'd told him he'd had too much to drink, when I refused to give him his keys. I could see his soccer-muscled leg flying toward that door even now, crumpling the fiberglass with his heel.

It was Garrett's car. And now that wasn't all I could see. I felt the memory coming before it took me. It welled up like an undertow, and dragged me down, down, down— back to the last few moments of my life.

18

WHAT GOES UP . . .

When I feel the hand on my shoulder I spin around, fear tight in my throat. For a moment I can't believe my eyes. Garrett stands inches behind me, his features clenched in a bitter scowl. He's close enough that I can smell the whiskey on his breath. His hair is a wild tangle, and one of his knees is skinned below his khaki cargo shorts. The scrape oozes blood down his calf.

"What are you doing here?" I gasp, staggering a few steps back. Behind me the trail slopes sharply away. I catch my balance on a boulder.

His laugh cuts through me like a knife. By now I'm used to Garrett's mood swings, his erratic behavior, but that doesn't mean I like them. Good Garrett might be a sweet, earnest puppy dog—*lovable and easygoing and maybe even a little vulnerable—but Bad Garrett is a whole different story. And just my luck, guess which one of them is here now?*

He squints at me through the gloom, his eyes bloodshot and unfocused. "No need to ask what you're *doing here," he sneers. "You look like a slut in those shorts."*

I should ignore him. I should turn and walk down the mountain without saying another word. But like I always do with Garrett, I rise to the bait. "You liked these shorts just fine the other day," I snap. Just a few days earlier we'd gone to see some boring superhero blockbuster together, and he'd been so distracted by my legs draped over his lap that we didn't do much watching.

"That was before you were wearing them at midnight in the middle of nowhere," he says. His words slur sloppily together. "Are you trying to get attacked?"

I know why he's saying this, where his venom is coming from, but that doesn't mean it doesn't hurt. I turn away from him to hide the tears in my eyes. "Go home, Garrett. You're drunk, and you're being a real asshole."

But he reaches out and grabs my arm. "Stop trying to act like you're so innocent," he hisses. "Stop trying to make me feel like the bad guy. I know what's going on."

"You don't know anything," I say angrily. After everything I've already been through tonight, I don't have any patience for one of Garrett's temper tantrums. "And I really don't appreciate you acting like I'm a total ho just because I want to . . ." I can't

finish the sentence. All summer, I've been hoping that Garrett and I could cement our relationship, that we could finally take it to the next level. I think part of me has been hoping, deep down, that if we finally make love I'll be able to commit to him and him alone, that I'll be able to let go of Thayer and quit all the sneaking around and lying. I've given Garrett about a thousand opportunities to seduce me, and he's rebuffed me at every turn. It's almost enough to make a girl doubt her own charms—except I know it's just Garrett's own weird hang-ups holding him back. He's been funny about sex, ever since what happened to his sister.

Now, though, I'm glad we didn't go all the way. I don't want to be with him anymore. What Thayer and I have is so much more real than anything between me and Garrett. I just can't believe it's taken me this long to see it.

"I know what you've been doing out here, who you were with," Garrett says. He lets go of me, and I stumble backward. My wrist is tender where he gripped it.

"Why? Have you been following me?" I think about the feeling I've had all night that someone's been watching me, and my skin crawls. "That's gross, Garrett."

He gives a derisive snort. "You know, I went to Nisha's house tonight. Looking for my girlfriend?" He says the last word almost sarcastically. "Since that's where you told me you were going to be tonight, after all. But they said you hadn't been there all night."

I shrug. "I decided not to go to Nisha's lame party. So what?"

"So I was pulling out of her driveway and just happened to see you running up the trail. I thought I'd come up and surprise you. But you weren't out here alone, were you?"

The clouds around the moon shift, casting weird wispy shadows over the trail. To my left, Tucson sparkles like it's made of fairy lights. To my right is the drop-off to the ravine. This is the part of the trail my father used to warn me about— when I was a little girl he'd make me hold his hand as we passed the drop. He'd always told me that the cliff was too steep for climbers to rappel down, and that there were bodies no one had ever been able to retrieve at the bottom. A shiver runs up my spine.

"Admit it," Garrett says, his voice ragged. "You were with Thayer, weren't you?"

My mouth goes dry. I don't even have the heart to deny it anymore. But I don't want to admit the truth right now either— not in the middle of nowhere, when he's this drunk, this angry. Before I can move, he rips a sapling up by its roots and snaps it in half, screaming with rage.

"Goddamn it, Sutton!" His voice echoes, ricocheting around the ravine below. He throws the broken halves of the little tree over the side, and I watch as they are swallowed by the darkness. "How could you do this to me? I love you." He pulls at his own hair, grabbing it with his fists.

Terror flashes through me, and suddenly I think of the

shadowy figure behind the wheel of my Volvo as it crashed down on Thayer. Of the driver who hijacked my car to run down the boy I love. A bleak realization starts to blossom inside of me. I take a step away from him. "How long have you been following me?"

"Long enough," he sneers. My heart twists in my chest. This is Garrett, I try to tell myself. Sweet, dopey Garrett. He'd never run anyone over with a car—not even Thayer. Right?

But then the moon comes out from the clouds, and I can see the muscles in his neck and shoulders taut with barely restrained rage. His jaw is clenched into a twisted rictus grin, his eyes flashing wildly. The thought comes to me with a sudden dull thud of my heart—maybe this isn't Bud Garrett after all. Maybe this is a Garrett I haven't seen until now. Insane Garrett. Violent Garrett.

"What did you do?" I breathe.

He laughs, and it's a bitter, broken sound. "I don't have to explain myself to you." He takes a step toward me, grinning nastily.

A rush of anger flashes through me, burning my fear away. For a moment it's almost like I can hear the sickening crunch of Thayer's leg snapping again, like I can hear his voice call my name, weak with pain. I clench my fists, pushing my face close to Garrett's. "You're so fucked up," I whisper. His eyes widen.

"Me?" He takes another step toward me. I stand my ground, even though he's inches from my face now. "Who's the liar here? Who's the slut?" On the last word he shoves me, a short, hard push. I stumble but catch my balance before falling. "Who's the one who just . . . can't . . . tell . . . the truth?" With every word he pushes me farther back. My blood is pounding in my ears, and this time it's as much from anger as it is from fear.

"We're through, Garrett!" I stare up at him, and it's like I'm seeing him for the first time. The sweet boy who brought me lilies of the valley for our first date, who sent me dozens of playlists filled with songs that made him think about me, who held my hand so innocently when we walked side by side—that boy is gone. Did he ever even exist? The person in front of me is a monster, damaged beyond all repair.

He freezes, and for a moment it looks like nothing is alive but his eyes. They burn with a frenzied light. I don't know how I ever thought they looked soulful. "We're not through until I say we're through," he grits out.

Pebbles shift beneath my feet, and I turn to realize he has backed me up against the precipice. Inky darkness fills the air below me. I can't tell how far the drop is.

He moves so fast. All at once he has me by my shirt. My feet rise up off the ground, the collar of my shirt tight against my neck. I whimper and kick out, but my feet don't hit anything. Below me, the ravine opens hungrily. He lifts me up and pulls me close to his face so that I choke on the rancid fumes of whiskey.

"Why do you make me so crazy?" he asks, his voice breaking in agony.

And then he lets me go.

19

FACE OFF

The heavy tread of footsteps sounded outside the door. Emma quickly shoved the pages back into the folder just as Quinlan stepped inside.

Without hesitating, she shot to her feet. "Detective Quinlan, I think I know who killed my sister."

"Yes, tell him," I urged. I was still reeling from the sensation of Garrett holding me out over the precipice.

He stopped in his tracks. One eyebrow crept up his forehead in a skeptical arc. "That's interesting. I was just coming back in here to tell you the same thing . . . *Emma*."

For a moment what he said didn't register. Emma stood

rooted to the spot, unable to move a muscle as her mind raced to catch up with what was happening.

Quinlan gave her a cool smile. "When I swabbed your cheek, I couldn't help but notice you have two fillings in your molars. The thing is, Sutton Mercer has never had a cavity in her life. Must be all that nice organic food the Mercers buy. But according to the dental records we got from Las Vegas, Emma Paxton has two fillings. Right where yours are, as a matter of fact." He threw a set of dental X-rays down on the table.

Emma stared at them dumbly, adrenaline churning through her body. For one wild moment she thought about making a break for it. But then what? She might make it as far as the hallway, but she was surrounded by cops. The awful realization unfolded: There was no way out of this. She slowly lowered back to her seat.

Quinlan pulled out his chair and sat as well. He watched her for a moment, his face softening visibly. Emma had the impression that he felt almost sorry for her. "It's time to tell the truth, Miss Paxton. Come on, why not make this easy on yourself?"

Emma looked down at her fingers on the table in front of her, her mind racing. How much did he already know?

Quinlan sighed, pressing his fingertips together thoughtfully in front of him. "Come on, Emma. I can't help you if you're not honest with me." He opened Emma's file, pulling out the crime scene photos and dropping them on the table in front of her.

"Maybe it was just an accident," Quinlan said gently. "You girls were in the canyon, you got into some kind of argument. Things turned physical, and Sutton just . . . fell. You didn't mean for it to happen. But you have to help me out, Emma. You have to tell me the truth."

I watched warily. I knew what he was doing from long hours spent in the hot seat myself. He'd pulled this on me more than once—*it must be so hard for you, Sutton, being adopted, not knowing who your family is. Why don't you just tell me the truth?* He was trying to manipulate my sister into talking.

Quinlan's stone-gray eyes were implacable. Before Emma had time to process what he was saying, he threw his hands up as if he'd tried his hardest to reason with her. "All right. Let's see what's behind door number one, then." His knees popped as he slowly stood up, pushing his chair in behind him. He opened the door a crack and looked outside, holding a low conference with someone in the hall. Emma craned her neck, trying to see who was out there, but his body obstructed her view.

Then the door opened wider, and a female officer propelled Alex Stokes inside.

She was in handcuffs.

Emma's jaw dropped. Her best friend stood awkwardly

in front of her, staring down at the familiar checkerboard-patterned Vans she'd worn every day for the past two years. She was a short, elfin girl, tiny next to the Amazonian officer escorting her. She'd been crying, and her trademark turquoise Urban Decay liner had smeared across her cheeks. When Quinlan gave her a little nudge, she stumbled forward, lifting her tear-filled eyes to meet Emma's.

A lead weight seemed to drop on Emma's heart in that moment. Alex was in trouble, all because of her.

Quinlan's lips curled up in a cruel smile. "We can get your friend here on a half dozen charges. Aiding and abetting, obstructing justice, concealment of a crime. Hell, if the judge is feeling creative I might be able to get her as an accomplice to murder one." He made a *tsk*ing sound. "We got a search warrant for her phone, and it turns out she's been in contact with her dear friend Emma Paxton for the past *three* months. And Emma had all kinds of interesting stories about life in Tucson. How close she was with Sutton, how great life was with the Mercers. The most recent one was . . ."—he made a show of looking at a pile of papers in his hands—". . . one day ago! Look at that!"

Emma shot to her feet again, anger bubbling up from beneath her fear. "Alex had nothing to do with this. That should be obvious, if you read the texts."

Quinlan shrugged. "Maybe it's obvious. Or maybe you

two are talking in code. How can I know, if you haven't told me the truth?"

Emma stared at him, suddenly hot with anger. She clenched her fists, digging her fingernails into the soft skin of her palms. "I tried to tell you the truth, the day I got here." She didn't even have to channel Sutton for the attitude; cold fury squeezed her chest. "Maybe if you're going to charge Alex with anything, you should charge yourself too—with negligence, for not even bothering to look into my story way back in September."

The room went silent. Somewhere down the hall a phone rang over and over. The female officer glanced at Quinlan uncertainly. His smirk died away, but as he spoke he didn't break eye contact with Emma.

"Get her out of here," he muttered, jerking his head at Alex. The officer hesitated, but when Quinlan didn't move, she took Alex by the arm and guided her back to the door. Emma wanted more than anything to call after her friend, to ask her forgiveness, but she knew she couldn't show weakness in front of Quinlan now.

"So what's your story, then?" Quinlan asked finally, crossing his arms over his chest.

"Aren't you going to turn on your little tape recorder for this part of the interview?" she snapped. He scowled, reaching down to turn on the machine. She leaned back in her seat. "I came here to meet Sutton at the end of the summer. But she was the one who stood me up in Sabino Canyon, or so I thought. I waited forever, but she never showed up. Madeline Vega and the Fiorello twins found me on the bench and thought I was Sutton. The message had warned me not to say who I was, so I played along. I kept thinking Sutton would show up any minute and clear everything up." A lump formed in Emma's throat as she thought back to the hopes she'd had that first night, of meeting Sutton, of finding family. Of finally fitting in somewhere. Tears stung her eyes, but she kept her chin high, refusing to break Quinlan's gaze. "Then I got a note, one that said Sutton was dead and I had to play along. I still have the note—that, and the others the killer left. I stitched them inside a purple pillow on Sutton's bed. You can check."

Quinlan gave an impatient grunt. His eyes glittered darkly as he leaned across the table toward her. "Let me tell you what I think. I think you've been stalking your sister for a long time. I think you've been watching her on Facebook and on Twitter. Maybe you even took a little road trip here to Tucson to watch her. She had everything you wanted, everything you never had yourself—money, popularity, a nice house, a loving family. And you decided to take it. You came out here without luggage, without ID, because you knew you wouldn't need it, because you planned to take over her life." Emma shook her head violently, but he stabbed at the crime scene photos between them with his index finger. "You pushed your sister down that ravine. And then it was easy. All you had to do was step into her shoes. You waited one night, then headed to Nisha Banerjee's party, calling yourself Sutton. Luckily for you, your twin was a notorious practical joker, so if anyone suspected anything off, they could chalk it up to some kind of prank. You even came in here pretending to be yourself, so that you could have some semblance of an alibi if you got caught. A smart move, trying to make the truth look like a lie. But not smart enough."

"You're wrong," Emma said, slamming her hands on the table. She almost surprised herself with the force of her anger. As Emma Paxton she'd never talked back to an authority figure. She'd always been the get-along girl, the foster kid who didn't make trouble, a chameleon who could turn into whatever kind of person the adults in her life needed her to be. Now, though, she was possessed of a righteous fury all her own. "While you're busy harassing me, the real murderer is getting away with it. Don't you see? Someone's setting me up."

Quinlan gave her a long, measured look. Then he squared his jaw.

"I'm not going to lie. Sutton Mercer was a pain in my ass." His gravelly voice was almost deadly calm. Suddenly the room was so quiet she could hear the second hand on Quinlan's watch ticking. "But she was just a kid. She didn't deserve what happened to her. I can't prove you killed her. Not yet, anyway. But I'm going to make it my mission to dog your steps until you slip up. Because you will, Emma. Criminals always do."

"So can I go?" Emma asked, her voice shaking but clear.

Quinlan nodded. "Sure. We need both your BlackBerry and Sutton's iPhone, though. And we're impounding Sutton's car for clues. Someone at the front desk can give you a ride wherever you're heading tonight. I hope it goes without saying that you shouldn't think about skipping town."

Emma gave a jerky nod. "What about Alex? Are you going to charge her with anything?"

"We haven't decided yet." He shrugged. "That'll depend on how well you cooperate with us. Tonight she's probably going home to her mom. We're not planning to charge her yet. But we're keeping an eye on her."

Another surge of guilt swept through Emma at the thought of Alex's mom worrying, her face tight and anxious. She stood up and picked up her purse. From behind her, Quinlan's voice came again, this time with a taunting edge.

"I believe this is the part of your prank where everyone jumps out and says 'Gotcha,' Miss Paxton."

She turned to stare at him, and saw that he was smiling again. "The cat's out of the bag. Everyone in town is about to find out about the lies you've been telling—and that includes the Mercers. This game you've been playing, it's over." He opened the door to the interrogation room and bowed her out into the hall.

I would have been almost touched by Quinlan's determination to bring my killer to justice, if he hadn't been acting like such a total moron. It was bad enough that I was dead. Now the cops were going to go after the wrong person on top of that.

20

THERE'S NO PLACE LIKE HOME

Emma didn't know how she'd made it to the front desk a few minutes later. All the fury had leached out of her, and her limbs felt like they were made of stone, so heavy and stiff she couldn't believe she was able to move them at all. She stood in a fog while a receptionist with purple acrylic nails paged an officer to take her home. Finally, a tall cop with buzz-cut auburn hair seemed to appear out of nowhere. His name badge said CORCORAN. "Emma Paxton?"

She nodded silently. He gestured for her to follow him, and together they walked through the double glass doors. The sun had set. Beyond the parking lot, rush-hour traffic crawled past, brake lights glinting red in the gloom.

Corcoran didn't talk much as he drove Emma to the Mercers'. As they glided past shops and salons decorated in green and red for the holidays, she stared out the window, half listening to the crackle of chatter from the cop's radio. ". . . report of vandalism at the Snack 'n' Shack on Valencia," a muffled female voice was saying. "Unit fifty-three, please report."

"So did you do it?"

She turned to look at the officer, giving him an are-you-serious grimace. Did he think she was going to offhandedly confess to a beat cop—if she *had* done it—after Quinlan had already interrogated her? But he was staring straight ahead at the road with an earnest frown, like some part of the situation just didn't add up.

"I was a foster kid, too," he said matter-of-factly. "Here in Tucson."

She nodded mutely, unsure what he was getting at.

"I don't know why it is, but people don't trust you if you don't have family. Even if it isn't your fault." He shrugged. "You become a scapegoat for everything that happens, just because you don't fit into the natural order."

Emma swallowed hard. She looked back out the window, not trusting herself to speak. Were they trying to good-cop her now, trying to get her to confess just because some cute guy, close to her own age, was acting like he understood what she was going through? But Corcoran had fallen silent, like he'd said his piece and that was all he had to say.

When they turned the corner onto the Mercers' street, Emma's jaw dropped. The place was swarming with reporters. The whole street was lit up like a ball-park, a dozen vans lining either side of the road. Reporters checked their makeup in the side mirrors on cars and ran through their lines, beard-stubbled men with giant cameras hoisted on their shoulders trailing in their wake. It looked like the Mercers' neighbor, Mr. Paulson, was being interviewed in his driveway by a man with his hair plastered in a Ken-doll coif. Other reporters seemed to be mid-broadcast, using the Mercers' house as a backdrop.

I'd always dreamed of being famous, of having paparazzi follow me home and beg me for interviews. But this definitely wasn't what I had in mind.

"Stay where you are," Corcoran said to Emma, putting the car in park in the middle of the street. He opened his car door. The moment he did, the cacophony of dozens of voices filled the squad car.

"Are you Emma Paxton, or Sutton Mercer?"

"Emma, why'd you do it?"

"Did anyone help you kill your sister?"

Corcoran didn't even look at them. He walked around to the passenger side door and opened it, standing

protectively in front of Emma to keep the shouting reporters at a slight distance.

She met the officer's eyes. They were calm, clear blue,
and while she couldn't tell if he believed her story or
not, she could see a stubborn conviction there. This guy
wanted her to be treated fairly, she realized. Whether or
not she was innocent, whether or not she had lied, he
wanted her to have a fair shake.

"Ready?" he asked. She nodded, suddenly feeling
a little stronger. He might not be her ally—but for the
moment, he was close enough.

He helped her to her feet, then guided her quickly
through the crowd.

"Emma! Did you really think you'd get away with it?"

"Do you think your mom's mental illness is genetic?"

"Did Sutton put up a fight?"

Corcoran stood at the edge of the yard, his arms crossed
over his chest. "Go on, then," he said. "I'll stay here 'til
you get inside."

She nodded, staring longingly at the Mercers' front
door. All she wanted was to be inside, to sit down with
her family and tell them everything, as they'd already
done with her. As she walked up the driveway, she could
hear the manic clicking of the photographers' cameras all
around her. A man in a dark red blazer tried to launch
himself past Corcoran, microphone stretched out toward

her—but the officer grabbed him by the collar of his shirt and jerked him back.

Emma reached the porch and stood in front of the oak door with its lion-shaped knocker. She pulled out her keys, then fumbled and dropped them with a resounding clatter on the porch. Cheeks burning, she bent to pick them up.

But when she went to unlock the door, the key wouldn't fit.

Her heart tightened in the half second before she consciously understood. The locks had been changed. She wasn't welcome.

I stared down at the keys in my sister's hand. My house key had purple nail polish painted across the top, so I could always differentiate it from the others. How many times had I used it without ever realizing how lucky I was to have a home to go to? How many times had I let myself in, never realizing what a privilege it was?

Her hand trembling, Emma rang the doorbell. Inside she could hear Drake barking, deep and hoarse. The blinds were all drawn tight, but it looked like every light in the house was blazing—blades of yellow cut through the slats.

Something rustled behind the door. She waited. Behind her, the reporters were yelling questions, drowning each other out so they generated a loud, indeterminate roar. Corcoran stood at the curb with his arms crossed over his chest, staring stoically out at the crowd.

Suddenly a voice came from behind the door. "You can't stay here." Mrs. Mercer's voice was nasal and stuffy. It was obvious she'd been crying.

"Please, Mrs. Mercer, I just want to explain." She didn't want to plead her case here on the doorstep, with the press watching and taking pictures. She leaned toward the door, hoping to hide her face from their cameras. "Please just give me a chance to explain."

The door jerked open without warning.

My heart wrenched at the sight of my mother standing in the light-filled entryway, her face blotchy with tears. A frenzied, wild expression contorted her features, grief and rage twisting together. She still wore her work clothes, gray tweed slacks and a pink shell top, but she was barefoot and disheveled. She stared at Emma like she barely recognized her.

"I want you gone," she said shrilly, her eyes blazing.

"Mrs. Mercer, please . . ."

"You're just like your mother," hissed the older woman. Emma took an involuntary step back. "You're both liars. You're both insane. You don't care who you hurt, as long as you get your way."

"I'm not like Becky!" Emma gasped. A sense of desperation clawed at her chest. She had to make her grandmother understand. "I'm sorry I lied to you. I'm so sorry, but I had no choice!"

Mrs. Mercer gave a strangled sob, tears collecting at the corners of her eyes. "You had a choice, and you made it."

A dark shape moved at the back of the hallway, like someone was around the corner listening. Emma craned her neck to see who it was. "Where's Da— Where's Mr. Mercer? Can I talk to him?"

Her grandmother shook her head violently. "No, you can't. He doesn't want to speak with *you*. Not after what you've done to us."

"But if you'll listen for just . . ."

Mrs. Mercer's breath was fast and shuddering. She moved quickly, lunging toward Emma. Emma flinched, almost anticipating a blow. But instead of striking her, Mrs. Mercer wrestled the Kate Spade hobo bag off Emma's shoulder.

"This is my daughter's purse," she sobbed, tears flooding down her cheeks. Then she grabbed Emma's jacket in her fists, pulling it out of her arms. "And her coat. Not yours."

Emma stood motionless, her lip trembling. She didn't struggle. She didn't have the heart to. Mrs. Mercer was right. None of this belonged to her. Not the clothes, not the house—and not the family. She had nothing of her own.

"Now get the hell off my property," Mrs. Mercer spat.

I'd never heard my mother curse before, not even

when she was at her most frustrated. The sound of it now filled me with fear. She was acting like a different person. It was like the old Mom, the one I'd loved so much, who had taken me for ice cream the day I got my first period and who'd watched old romantic comedies with me on rainy, lazy Sundays, was gone. All that was left was this bitter, angry shell of a woman. Suddenly I realized that this was what my death would mean to my family—that this wasn't some adolescent fantasy where I'd get to hear everyone say nice things about me at my funeral and then ride a cloud to heaven. My mother had just realized that she'd lost me, and it was destroying her. This was my murderer's—Garrett's—legacy.

Mrs. Mercer started to close the door in Emma's face, but before she shut it all the way she paused. "Tell me one thing." Her voice was lower now, very soft.

"Anything," Emma whispered.

Her grandmother's eyes flitted over Emma's face, searching for something. Emma wasn't sure what.

"Did you do it? What they say you did?"

Emma took a deep, shuddering breath. "No."

Mrs. Mercer stared at her silently, her blue eyes, so much like Emma's own, suddenly soft. Emma wanted to say more, but she couldn't figure out where to start. She wanted to tell Mrs. Mercer how badly she had wanted to meet Sutton. How sorry she was, how scared she'd been, how desperately she'd wanted to tell the truth all this time. More than anything, she wanted to tell her how the last few months had felt like someone else's dream—that she had never had family like this, and that it'd meant more to her than anything. But before she could speak, Mrs. Mercer's expression hardened once more, and she gave a strangled cry.

"I just don't know how I can believe you." She gave Emma a long, searching look, her eyes wounded. Then she slammed the door. The lock clicked shut.

Slowly, Emma turned to face the street. Corcoran resolutely watched the reporters. They were in a frenzy, microphones bristling from the crowd, her name the only word she could make out in their screams. Step by step, she walked back down the slate path. She felt like she was moving through deep water, her body slow and heavy.

A microphone appeared under Emma's chin. She looked up to see the local reporter who had been covering both Nisha's and Sutton's deaths, now in a cobalt blue suit. Her hair was even bigger in person than it looked on TV. "Tricia Melendez from Channel Five. Can you tell me whether the rumors are true? Are you the girl who was presumed dead?"

Corcoran forced a way through the crowd, looking menacingly at the reporters on either side of him. They parted when they saw his uniform. He put a hand on

Emma's back and pushed her gently toward the car.

Once they were safely inside, he looked at her. "Where can I take you?"

She hesitated. Ethan's face bloomed in her mind, but involving him was the last thing she wanted. She'd already gotten Alex in trouble. She didn't want anyone else to suffer because of her.

But she didn't have anywhere else to go. She gave Corcoran Ethan's address.

I looked out the rear window. My home receded into the distance, smaller and smaller until finally we turned a corner . . . and it was gone. A sick, empty feeling opened inside of me. My mother didn't know that in banishing Emma, she was banishing me, too. It had been hard enough, not being able to touch my family or talk to them. Now I couldn't even watch them.

It was like I was losing them all over again.

21

SHELTER FROM THE STORM

Emma gripped the sides of the squad car's passenger seat as the officer sped around a corner. She craned her neck to look behind them at the reporters trailing in their wake, news vans and cheap rental cars harrying the cop's bumper like a pack of hungry wolves. She glanced at Corcoran. His lips were pursed in a tight, stoic line.

"Is there any way to keep them from following us?" she asked, her voice barely a whisper.

Corcoran didn't answer. His eyes flickered up to the rearview mirror. Then, without warning, he jerked the steering wheel into a hairpin turn, down an alley that ran behind a Starbucks and a Mediterranean deli. Emma watched three vans streak past. His hands steady on the wheel, he then floored the gas, and with an angry squeal of tires the squad car shot through the intersection just as the light turned red.

I thought suddenly of the times that Mads and Thayer and I had played *Grand Theft Auto* on our old PlayStation, back before I ever even thought Thayer was cute. This was even better. But Emma didn't seem so happy. Her pulse throbbed wildly in her ears, and she was clutching the door handle, her eyes wide. "That was some driving," she mumbled.

The hint of a smile flitted across Corcoran's lips, but he didn't say a word.

They drove the rest of the way to Ethan's in a circuitous route, making a wide loop to get back to the Catalina Foothills where he lived. Emma watched Corcoran out of the corner of her eye as he drove. She wasn't sure what to make of him, but he'd certainly gone out of his way to protect her from the reporters, which was more than Quinlan would have done.

Corcoran pulled up outside of Ethan's house and put the car in park. She sat for a moment, staring up at the faded bungalow, the porch light casting a feeble glow over the steps and the swing.

"I'll wait until you're inside," Corcoran said.

"Thanks," she said softly. She let herself out of the car and started up to the house.

Before she'd made it halfway up the walk, the door burst open. Ethan ran down the steps to meet her, a worried frown on his face. His hair looked ink-black in the darkness, but his face was pale. "What's going on?"

"The cops know." She stumbled, suddenly feeling faint. Ethan grabbed her in his arms and steadied her. "Quinlan figured out that I'm not Sutton, using my dental records. He has my friend Alex from Henderson—he knows I've been texting her as Emma all this time."

Ethan gave a sharp intake of breath. "And they think you did it?"

She nodded, rubbing her eyes with a fist. His arms were strong around her, her cheek pressed flat to his chest. His T-shirt had a Mexican sugar skull screen-printed across the front, and she found herself staring into its hollow eyes. It made her think of the crime scene pictures all over again, of her sister's body ravaged by time and elements. She squeezed her eyes shut against the thought, breathing in Ethan's warm vanilla smell.

"Who's that?"

She looked up to see that Corcoran's car was still there. She felt a little rush of gratitude. It was too dark to see the man's face behind the windshield, but she knew he was waiting to make sure she was all right.

"They kept Sutton's car to search for evidence, so he tried to take me home. But . . . the Mercers . . ." Her lip trembled. "They're furious, Ethan. They think I killed Sutton."

His chest rose and fell beneath her as he sighed. "Come on," he said, leading her up the stairs and through the front door.

Ethan's house gave off an aura of genteel neglect. The hardwood floors were scuffed but squeaky clean. The décor was dated—the floral wallpaper had a "grandma's house" kind of feel—and the air smelled stale, as if the windows had been closed for a long time. There was no clutter anywhere, no piled-up mail or half-folded stack of laundry. Emma felt dizzy, and her knees buckled. "Let's go into the kitchen," Ethan said quickly, catching her. "You look like you need a glass of water."

He led her down a short hallway into the Landrys' kitchen. Unlike the Mercers' pineapple-themed, cheerful kitchen, this one felt empty and soulless, with a few mismatched tea towels and a plain gray countertop. A two-year-old calendar featuring a picture of a Persian cat hung on the wall, flipped to March.

They didn't notice Ethan's mother until they turned on the light. She'd been sitting in the dark at a square table by the window, still and silent. She was bone-thin, her hair flat and dull, the corners of her eyes crumpled like parchment. When they came in she gave a small, startled jump.

"Hi, Mrs. Landry," Emma said nervously. She wasn't

sure how much Ethan's mother knew—did she follow the news? Would she welcome someone at the center of so much drama into her home?

The woman didn't say anything but stared silently at Emma for several beats. Emma didn't know if it was her imagination or not, but she thought she detected a glint of fear in the woman's eyes. *She knows*, Emma thought, her heart sinking. *Or at least she knows what I've been accused of.*

After a moment, Mrs. Landry got slowly to her feet and scuttled wordlessly toward the hall. Ethan didn't even look at his mother as she nudged past. He pulled out a chair for Emma and gently pushed her into it.

"Are you going to be in trouble for having me here?" she asked tremulously.

"Don't worry," he said. "My mom just . . . isn't used to having guests. She'll get over it."

Though they rarely talked about it, Emma knew Ethan had a strained relationship with his mom. His dad had basically bailed when Mrs. Landry got cancer, and Ethan had taken care of her throughout the whole ordeal. But when his dad started abusing Mrs. Landry, and Ethan hit his father to make him stop, she called the cops on Ethan, not on his dad. Emma knew all of this only because she'd found Ethan's psych file a few weeks ago while looking for Becky's, and he'd confessed the whole story. *So many unhappy families*, she thought sadly.

As Ethan started to pour her a cup of water, Emma turned away—and saw Sutton's ghost looking back at her. She nearly jumped out of her chair.

But then she looked again—and of course it wasn't Sutton's ghost. It was Emma's reflection, haunted and pale in the glass of the window that looked out into the dark night. Her hair was tangled, her face smeared with tears.

Ethan handed her the water. It was in a keepsake glass printed with a picture of Miss Piggy on a motorcycle. "There's more," Emma said. "Ethan, Garrett was in the canyon that night. I saw the file for the murder case while Quinlan was out of the room. His car was in the parking lot."

His eyes widened. "You're sure it was his?"

"Yes." She took a deep breath. "And this afternoon, before I went to the cops, I went to his house."

Ethan sputtered, spitting out the mouthful he'd just sipped. "You *what*?"

"I'm sorry I didn't tell you first," she said quickly, "but I'm done playing the game by Garrett's rules. It's time to go on the offensive. Anyway, I talked to Louisa. She said that he came home really upset the night Sutton died, that he was out of control. And Ethan . . . he has a prescription for Valium." She dropped her voice again. "That's what was in Nisha's bloodstream when she died."

My mind flashed back to the look of rage on Garrett's

face, that night in the canyon. I knew why he'd killed me—he was in a jealous rage after he caught me with Thayer. But Nisha's death seemed less of a heat-of-the-moment act; drugging her and pushing her in the pool would have required deliberation and planning. What made him decide she needed to die?

A worried frown creased Ethan's brow. "You shouldn't have gone to his house. He's been warning you to stop looking for answers. What's he going to do when his mom or his sister tell him you were there?"

Emma smacked her palm on the table in frustration. "Ethan, what else can he do to me? I'm already wanted for Sutton's murder. If I can't prove that he killed her soon, I'm going to jail . . . and he'll walk free. I can't let that happen."

"I know," he said, rubbing his face roughly with his hands. "I just hate that you took a risk like that." He stared down into his water glass. "Everything points to Garrett, doesn't it?"

Emma nodded. All of the pieces fit—and from what she'd seen of Garrett's temper, it was easy to believe that he was capable of murder. "But I still don't have anything to take to the cops."

"What about that key?" he asked, leaning back in his chair. Emma felt in her jeans pocket, where the tiny silver key hugged her hip. She held it in the palm of her hand, squinting to try to make out what was etched on the metal tag it was attached to.

"It's too small for a car or a house. What could this go to?" She sighed. "For all we know it could be for his bike chain or something."

"I don't know, Emma." Ethan tapped the back of the tag, where the unmistakable S.M. was scratched. "Those are her initials."

They sat in silence for a moment, the key on the table between them. The events of the evening swirled furiously around Emma's head. In just a few hours, she'd lost the place she'd learned to call home, and the family she had come to love.

"What am I going to do?" she asked softly, tracing a line of condensation on her glass. "I don't have any money, anywhere to go. The few things I brought to Tucson are now evidence, and everything else was Sutton's. I don't even have a change of clothes."

Ethan put a hand on her knee, squeezing it almost painfully. "You're going to stay here. At least until we can get this sorted out."

"Ethan, no. I can't put you in any danger. Alex is already in trouble for helping me. And what about your mom? She doesn't want me here."

Ethan set down his glass and gazed at her, an earnest, tender expression on his face. "Emma, I love you. I know no one has ever stood beside you when you were in trouble, but no matter what it takes, I'm going to make you believe that I'm the one who will do that. I'm not leaving you."

Her heart gave a violent thump. Ethan was right—she had never depended on anyone in her life. After being abandoned by Becky, and surviving the stream of disappointing foster parents who followed, Emma had learned early on to rely on no one but herself. Her friendships and relationships had mostly been short and shallow, easily made and easily broken. Until Ethan.

"I don't want you involved," she whispered. "They're going to charge Alex with aiding and abetting—maybe even conspiracy. They could get you on the same things."

He pulled her close. "Nothing will happen to me." He tilted her chin up gently, gazing into her eyes. "Stay with me. Let me help you through this, and protect you."

Emma sighed and curled up against his chest contentedly. "I don't know what I'd do without you."

"Are you kidding? I don't know what I'd do without *you*. God, Emma . . ." His dark-blue eyes were wide and earnest. "I don't think I ever understood love until I met you."

She laced her fingers through his, her heart singing in her chest.

"So you'll stay?" he asked, stroking her wrist with his

fingertips. She shivered, and for the first time in days it wasn't in fear.

"I'll stay," she murmured.

"It's settled then." His face broke into a crooked grin, and he took her hand. "Want to go watch some TV, to take your mind off things?"

As she followed Ethan down the hall, Emma suddenly wondered—where would she be sleeping tonight? Her cheeks grew warm as she pictured Ethan's full-sized bed with its smooth, carefully tucked covers. Would they be sharing it?

The living room's walls had been painted a dusty rose color, a fussy vine pattern stenciled along the top in dark green. A clock with pictures of different American birds in place of the numerals hung over the TV, and an ornate gilded mirror loomed above a drafty fireplace, doubling the room in its reflection. Like the rest of the house, the room was spotlessly clean, though bare patches showed on the arms of the blue chintz sofa, and the flowered rug was mottled with stains.

Emma sat down next to Ethan, curling her legs up under her and snuggling into his shoulder. The TV popped on with a loud hum—and almost immediately, Nisha Banerjee's pictures came into focus on the screen. Emma's breath caught in her chest at the sight.

"Police say the intruder knew the alarm code to

the Banerjees' house, so the alarm was not triggered. However, Mr. Banerjee was home at the time, and he saw the masked intruder before he or she managed to escape," said a familiar brisk voice. It was Tricia Melendez, reporting the evening news.

A scowl creased Ethan's forehead. "I wanted to take your mind *off* this," he muttered, fumbling for the remote. She grabbed his arm.

"Wait," she whispered.

Tricia Melendez continued. "Officers responded to the scene within minutes, but the perpetrator had already fled the premises. The only information Dr. Banerjee could provide was that the figure looked at least six feet tall and was wearing a dark hooded sweatshirt."

The camera cut to Quinlan, his face deeply lined beneath the camera's bright lights. "It's possible this was some kind of prank. Miss Banerjee's death was a high-profile case, and unfortunately that can occasionally attract some petty harassment. Luckily nothing was taken or disturbed."

Emma gaped openmouthed at the screen, then jumped suddenly to her feet, running to the window and fumbling at the avocado-colored curtains. The Banerjee house stood silent and dark next door. She could see Nisha's window, the drapes pale and ghostly in the moonlight.

"Do you know what this means?" Emma exclaimed.

Her reflection stared excitedly back at her. She felt Ethan move behind her and turned to meet his eyes. "This means Garrett still doesn't have whatever Nisha was hiding." She gripped the sleeve of Ethan's shirt. "The evidence is still there!"

Ethan blanched, the color leaching from his cheeks. "Jesus," he murmured. "Emma, I hope you're not thinking of breaking in, too. Dr. Banerjee will never let you in now that he knows who you are."

But a flash of energy flared through Emma. Finally, after being helpless for so long, she'd found the break she'd been looking for. Whatever Nisha had, Garrett had murdered her because of it. Surely it would prove he had killed Sutton, if not both girls.

"We have to go over there," she said. "We should go now, before Garrett figures out a way back into the house."

She was halfway to the door when Ethan's hand gripped her wrist, spinning her back around to face him. "Are you crazy?" he asked, his voice hoarse with emotion. "Emma, Garrett was here. One house away. He ran away once he realized Dr. Banerjee was home, but he's not going to make the same mistake again. And if he sees you trying to get into Nisha's house, who knows what he'll do?"

She stared at him incredulously. "There's something in Nisha's house that could end this. It's worth the risk!" She pressed his hand in both of hers. "If I can solve this case, I'll be free. You and I can be together without all this . . . this craziness hanging over our heads."

Ethan's lips turned downward as he grabbed her by her shoulders. "If Garrett sees you over there, he'll *kill* you. Emma, *please*." He took a deep, shaking breath, and then exhaled. "Besides, Garrett's not the only one watching you. If the cops catch you trying to break in, they'll find a way to put you in jail. You said yourself they're just looking for a reason."

Emma glanced back at the widow, frustration mounting inside of her. The answers were so near, and yet she still couldn't get them. But maybe Ethan was right. She was being watched too closely. Reluctantly, she sank into the sofa, her hands curled into fists.

But at least there was hope.

In the window, the ghost of Sutton blinked back at her, hopeful and terrified. *I promise we'll solve this*, she thought desperately, hoping her sister could hear her. And then, as she watched, tiny patches of Sutton's face began to fall away, as though she were decomposing.

Emma stood and took a step forward to the window. It was raining. The raindrops were hitting the window, breaking up her reflection in the glass and destroying the tentative moment of connection she'd felt with her dead twin. *You're being silly, Sutton wasn't here at all*, she tried to tell herself, though she couldn't shake the sudden and acute sense of loss.

"I'm with you," I whispered. As always, my voice disappeared into the wide breach between us. But it made me feel better to say it out loud. Now that she was barred from my home, Emma was all I had. We were in this together—whether she knew it or not.

22

EMMA NON GRATA

Emma and Ethan spent the weekend mostly in hiding. It seemed like Corcoran's defensive driving had worked; none of the media showed up on the Landrys' doorstep. Still, they didn't want to tempt fate, so they drew the blinds and avoided the windows, curling up on the couch to watch a *Star Trek* marathon on cable. Every now and then they'd stop to sift through the details of the case or get a snack. The kitchen wasn't very well stocked, but they had enough for stacks of sandwiches, and on Saturday Emma showed Ethan her secret recipe for making jarred pasta sauce taste homemade: olive oil, a sprinkle of sugar, and a tiny splash of vodka.

On Sunday, they disguised Emma in an old flowered shirtdress that belonged to Ethan's mother so they could go to Goodwill incognito. Ethan even produced a blonde Farrah Fawcett–style wig from the back of Mrs. Landry's closet. They both laughed at her reflection in the mirror—she looked like she'd been stuck in a bomb shelter since the late seventies. But when they went out she was glad for the disguise. For the first time in a long while, no one paid any attention to her at all, either as super-popular Sutton or as accused-murderer Emma.

But on Monday, Emma knew there would be no disguise that could get her through the day at Hollier. She stood at the mirror of the Landrys' hallway bathroom, braiding her hair into a long side plait, a style she would never have worn as Sutton. For the first time in months she was dressed like herself, in a faded blue-and-white raglan T-shirt and a pair of perfectly distressed Rag & Bone jeans she'd scored for five bucks. As she looked at her reflection, she felt somehow vulnerable and exposed. She'd been hiding behind Sutton's persona for months now, her real self a secret that she revealed only to Ethan. Now everyone would see the real her. The thought was strangely terrifying.

She hadn't had the guts to reach out to any of Sutton's friends. Her relationship with them was built on a lie—and now they knew it.

A soft knock came at the door. "Are you ready?" Ethan asked.

"Ready as I'll ever be," she replied, opening the door. He smiled at her, grabbing the end of her braid and tugging lightly.

"It's kind of weird, seeing you like this. Like seeing Sutton in Emma-drag."

"I know," she admitted. "I feel like I'm still playing a role."

Ethan shrugged. "We all play roles. You just have to find the one that you like best."

She poked him in the ribs. "What role are you playing?"

He put on a mock-hurt expression. "Prince Charming, obviously."

Laughing, Emma followed him down the hall to the entryway. Staying with Ethan was the silver lining to this whole nightmare. She'd never spent so much time with a boy before, but it just felt . . . right. A perfect fit.

On the way to school Ethan played an old Arcade Fire album, humming under his breath. Emma idly opened and closed the glove compartment. She tried to steel herself for whatever would come.

The area around the student parking lot was clotted with news vans. Emma had anticipated this. She put on her shades and pulled the hood of her sweatshirt up over her head.

"You look like the Unabomber," Ethan said.

"At least they won't be able to see my face," she replied.

Dozens of students milled about among the reporters, trying to get on TV. Emma saw Celeste Echols speaking into a microphone that Tricia Melendez held under her chin, and she groaned aloud. Celeste had been saying something was wrong with her "aura" since they first met. She would be insufferable now.

Ethan parked the car, and they stepped out into the pallid winter morning. A crescent moon still hung low on the horizon. She met Ethan's questioning glance with a determined, let's-get-this-over-with nod.

The students loitering in the parking lot stared at her baldly. A crowd of muscular guys hanging out around a Ford F-250 stopped body-slamming each other to gawk as she walked past. Two twiggy freshman girls scuttled out of her way as if she'd menaced them. She caught sight of a half dozen girls from the tennis team clustered near the flagpole. They fell silent as she approached, their faces pale and eyes wide. Ethan took her hand, and she squeezed back, trying not to look right or left. She focused on walking slowly and deliberately, though a part of her just wanted to bolt toward the glass double doors to the school.

Then she saw who was waiting in the entryway. Principal Ambrose stood with her arms crossed over her chest and her legs planted wide. She wore a zebra-striped suit coat and a pair of purple trousers. Her skin was usually dull and sagging, but today she'd put on turquoise eye shadow up to her eyebrows.

I had the distinct impression that Ambrose had dressed up for the media attention. I could just hear her saying *Sutton Mercer was such a special girl*, with tears in her eyes. *So effervescent! I'd like to think I was something of a mentor to her.* Never mind that the only times Ambrose talked to me were the handful of times I'd been busted for a Lying Game stunt.

Emma stopped uncertainly a few feet in front of the principal. She glanced at Ethan, who'd gone strangely pale, then back to Ms. Ambrose. The principal's lips were pressed into a single thin line.

"You will not be allowed on the premises," she said in a smug voice. "Emma Paxton is not registered at Hollier."

Emma blinked, stunned. "But . . . what about school?"

Ms. Ambrose shrugged. "I expect they'll let you get your GED in prison. Now please leave, before I report you for trespassing."

The crowd surrounding Emma went absolutely quiet, a hundred pairs of ears straining so that they could later report everything they'd seen and heard.

"Can I at least clean out my locker?" she asked quietly. Her palms were suddenly moist with sweat. She let go of Ethan and grabbed her backpack straps in each hand.

"Those aren't your things," Ms. Ambrose said simply. "The police have confiscated the contents of Miss Mercer's locker."

Emma took two steps back, tears stinging her eyes. How could she be so stupid? She should have expected this. She turned to run when Ethan caught her hand.

"Here," he said, pressing his car keys into her palm. "Go home. Call me if you need anything." With that, he planted a firm, ostentatious kiss on her lips. Then he pulled away, giving the principal a defiant smirk, and shouldered past her into the school.

Bolstered by Ethan's kiss, Emma turned and walked with as much dignity as she could back toward Ethan's Civic. She was so focused on getting out of there that when Madeline and Charlotte stepped in front of her, it took her a moment to process. She stopped in her tracks.

Madeline looked as unkempt as Emma had ever seen her. Her hair was loose and unstyled, and while her balletic frame normally seemed willowy and graceful, the shadows under her eyes gave her a skeletal look. Charlotte stood next to her, her face pale beneath her freckles. She hadn't put on makeup at all.

"Tell us it's a prank," Madeline said, her voice tremulous. "Please. Tell us it's the best one yet."

Emma stared at Sutton's best friends, wishing desperately that she could tell them what they wanted to hear.

Even though their friendship was built on a lie, she'd grown to genuinely care about the girls. Underneath the petty jealousies and pranks, the Lying Game girls were fiercely loyal to one another. Emma wasn't quite sure when she'd stopped thinking of them as Sutton's friends and started thinking of them as her own—but like everything else of Sutton's, they weren't hers at all.

Emma looked down at her shoes, avoiding Madeline's gaze. "It's not a prank," she said softly.

A sharp pain cut across her cheek as Madeline slapped her. "You bitch!" she shrieked, her voice a full octave above its normal range. "What did you do to my best friend?"

Emma reached a hand to her stinging cheek, blinking back tears. The two girls swam in her vision for a moment before a tear finally fell.

"You guys have to believe me," Emma pleaded. "I didn't do what they say I did. I didn't mean for this to happen—I never wanted to lie to you."

Charlotte had gone even paler under her freckles. Her eyebrows were bright reddish-gold without her makeup, and they made her look wild-eyed.

"We trusted you," she hissed. "We told you all kinds of secrets, let you ride in our cars, let you in our houses . . . after you *killed* our best friend!"

"I didn't kill anyone!" Emma's voice came out louder

than she'd intended, reverberating around the parking lot. A few feet away a little conference of pigeons took wing at the sudden noise. She took a deep breath and said more softly, "I've been trying to figure out what happened to Sutton since I got here. If you help me, we might be able to figure it out together."

Madeline gave a bitter bark of laughter. "Help you? You've got some nerve. What makes you think we'd help someone who's been lying to us for months?"

"Madeline, we created an entire game about lying," I shouted, annoyed. "And you *have* to help her! She's my only hope!" But obviously I didn't get a vote this time.

"I hope you rot in jail," Charlotte said, her lip curling upward. "And I hope you dream of Sutton every night for the rest of your life. I hope she haunts you until you die." Then she headed back toward the school entrance without glancing back.

Madeline gave Emma one last look of loathing, and then turned to follow Char.

Emma stood frozen, watching them go, until she realized that the entire parking lot full of students was staring at her. With a nervous glance around, she quickly let herself into Ethan's car and locked the doors.

In the rearview mirror she could see the entrance to the school. Principal Ambrose still stood there, staring daggers at her. Most of the students started streaming toward the door now that the show was over. The clock on the dash read 7:58. The bell was about to ring.

Suddenly, Emma picked one face out of the crowd as if a spotlight shone over him. Garrett stood alone in the shadow of a ten-foot saguaro cactus growing in the desert-scaped bed separating the school from the parking lot.

His eyes were honed onto my sister like a laser beam. He stared at her for a long moment, his face motionless.

I stared at him right back, wishing I could unleash the full force of my anger on him. I might have been taken in by those eyes when I was alive, but now that I was dead I knew the truth: They were the windows to a soul that was as dead and rotten as my body.

23

A WALK IN THE PARK

Emma started Ethan's car, fumbling with the clutch so it rabbit-hopped a few feet before snapping into gear. She swerved toward the exit, narrowly missing a pudgy girl with a backpack shaped like a panda. A few feet away, Tricia Melendez stood close to her cameraman. Emma gritted her teeth. Without looking into the oncoming lane she hit the gas pedal hard, peeling out into the road just as the reporter started rushing toward the car. As the car roared away from the crowd, she could hear Tricia yelling: "Emma! Emma! Emma, what do you plan to do next?"

She'd never hated the sound of her own name so much.

Her eyes blurred with tears as she entered a neighborhood lined with pastel bungalows. In one yard a terrier ran alongside the chain-link fence, barking as she passed. A tottering old man with a pair of shears in one hand glared at her suspiciously from another.

Her heart sank as she glanced in her rearview mirror. A navy blue BMW was tailing her closely. She recognized it immediately—it was Thayer's car. He honked lightly on the horn, signaling her to pull over. Her heart picked up speed. If Madeline and Charlotte were pissed, he'd be livid.

Still, Emma took a deep breath, then pulled over. The guilt of hiding Sutton's death from him had been eating her alive. He deserved the truth, and a part of her believed she deserved what she was about to get.

She rolled down the window. Thayer held Emma's gaze for a long moment before speaking.

"I knew there was something weird about you," he said finally. "I knew it."

Emma swallowed hard. Her pulse throbbed in her ear. "I tried to tell everyone at first. But no one would listen." She winced, bracing herself for the onslaught of accusations.

But Thayer just nodded, eerily calm. "I know. Laurel told me."

With a sigh of relief, Emma got out of the car and

followed Thayer to an empty playground around the corner. A rusted merry-go-round pivoted slowly in the breeze. The jungle gym was shaped like a giant red spider, its long metal legs covered in footholds for climbing. Emma sat down on one of the swings, empty of energy, drifting listlessly back and forth. Thayer slouched against one of the swing set's support poles, crossing his arms over his chest.

"You acted too nice," Thayer said.

Emma glanced up at him, frowning. "What?"

"That's what Laurel said: You were too nice to be Sutton. You didn't do a very good job playing her." Thayer shrugged. "Well, I guess you did a fine job. Everyone bought it. Then again, it would have been crazy not to. I mean, *I* thought I was going crazy."

"Thayer, I'm so, so sorry—" Emma started, but Thayer cut her off.

"Save it," he said curtly. His eyes narrowed on Emma. "Just tell me—did you kill Sutton?"

"No." Emma looked down, shaking her head. Even though the whole world thought she'd done it, it somehow hurt more that Thayer thought she could have hurt her own sister. "I've been trying all this time to figure out who did." She glanced at Thayer, who was staring off across the street. "Ask Laurel—my first morning here, there was a note for me on her car. She thought it was a love note. But it was a threat from the killer. It said that if I didn't keep pretending to be Sutton, I would be next. It's in Sutton's room, if the cops haven't taken it." A cloud drifted over the sun, and the colors of the world dimmed like someone was turning down a knob. "I've gotten three notes since I got here. I told Quinlan about them. There's a purple pillow with a ripped seam in Sutton's room—I hid them all inside it and stitched it back up. Ask Laurel if the police came for it yet." Emma looked down at her lap. "And it wasn't just me he threatened. He said he'd hurt the rest of you if I didn't do what he said. You. Laurel. Laurel's parents. Everyone."

Thayer gripped the pole. "So some maniac has been watching you for months, making sure you kept fooling everyone into thinking you were Sutton?" There was an unavoidable note of skepticism in his voice.

"Look, I know it sounds crazy. It *is* crazy. But yes. Sutton's murderer has been watching every move I make." Emma paused. "My first week here, someone strangled me with Sutton's locket during a sleepover at Charlotte's, warning me to keep up the act. Then that light almost fell on me at homecoming court rehearsal, with another warning note. And . . ." Her voice grew small, but she kept going. "And I think whoever killed Sutton killed Nisha, too. I'm almost certain that Nisha learned something about

Sutton's death that night, and she died because of it."

Thayer's face went pale, but he didn't flinch. He stared at Emma with steady green eyes. "I guess that explains why you asked me so many weird questions when I was in jail. You thought I did it for a while, didn't you?"

Emma hesitated, then nodded. "I know now you're not capable of anything like that. But when I first got here I didn't know anything about anyone. Everyone was a suspect. You, Mads, Charlotte, Gabby, and Lili." She paused. "Even Laurel."

Emma fell silent, shivering in the morning breeze. For a few minutes the only sounds were the birds twittering in the low canopy of trees. A college-aged nanny wearing a jumper and tights pushed a stroller down the street. She started to enter the playground but seemed to change her mind when she saw two teenagers hanging out there during school hours. Emma swayed gently on the swing, the chains creaking overhead.

"Well?" Thayer asked after a moment's silence. "Who are your suspects now? Do you have any clues?"

Emma picked at one of her cuticles, her mind racing. Thayer might have information she needed, something that could help her defeat Garrett before he managed to frame her. Then this nightmare could be over.

But she thought of the notes she'd gotten, the warnings. She'd been one step behind Garrett ever since she arrived in Tucson. Ethan was already in danger just for helping her. She didn't want to risk any more lives.

"No," she lied. "And anyway, I don't want you involved. It's too dangerous."

Thayer stepped forward quickly, to stand directly in front of Emma. "I'm not stupid. I know you have a suspect." He lowered his voice. "You think it's Garrett, don't you? That's why you were asking me all those questions about him the other day."

Emma hesitated.

Thayer seemed to read her fears in her expression. He shook his head impatiently. "I'm not giving up on this." Grief flashed through his eyes, so raw she had to look away. His voice cracked. "Someone took Sutton away from me," he said fiercely. "And I want that person to pay."

The pain in Thayer's voice tore at me, fear and love warring for control in my heart. I wanted nothing more than for Thayer to stay safe, out of Garrett's reach. But at the same time, the violence of his feelings sent a little thrill through me. Thayer loved me—and he wouldn't let Garrett get away with what he'd done.

Emma clasped the swing chains, hanging her head with a sigh. A moment later Thayer crouched down next to her.

"Emma?" he prompted.

"Okay," she finally said under her breath. "But don't go

doing anything stupid, Thayer. You can't go after Garrett. You'll end up in prison, or worse."

"I don't care," he shot back, his hands clenching against his thighs. She tugged hard at his sleeve, forcing him to turn and look at her.

"*Sutton* would care," she said softly.

She was right. The image of Thayer in prison, staring at cinder block for the rest of his life, knotted my insides. But even worse was the possibility that Thayer could end up like me—murdered, lost to his friends and family forever.

Emma held Thayer's gaze. "Promise me. For Sutton's sake."

His jaw tightened, and he turned away from her. After a moment, he gave a short nod. She looked out over the tawny mountains, where fluffy clouds drifted against the deep blue. "Garrett was definitely in the canyon the night Sutton died," she said softly, hugging her knees. "When the cops took me in for questioning I saw a security photo that showed his car in the parking lot. And Louisa mentioned that he came home in the middle of the night. She remembered it because he'd been so upset. Something really freaked him out. She thought that he and Sutton must have broken up."

Thayer remained perfectly motionless, but she could see the muscles in his shoulders tense.

"I don't have a way to prove it, though. Everything is circumstantial. You didn't see anything suspicious in the canyon that night, did you?" Emma glanced at him out of the corner of her eye. Storm clouds were gathering across his face, grim and foreboding. A sudden fear dawned on her: What if she'd overestimated Thayer's self-control? What if he *couldn't* keep his promise? Before he'd gone into recovery, his temper had been almost as legendary as Garrett's. The way he looked now, she wasn't sure he wouldn't run after Garrett and tear him apart right this moment.

"Besides the headlights heading straight for me? No." Thayer's eyes narrowed. "So you think Garrett ran me down, too?"

Emma nodded, picking at one of the small distressed holes in her jeans. "He's violent. At first I chalked it up to the breakup. But I think it goes deeper than that." She met his eyes. "Everyone keeps hinting about something that happened to Louisa, something really traumatic. Do you know what they're talking about?"

Thayer blinked in surprise. "Yeah, I do. It was pretty fucked up."

My ears pricked. Thayer took a deep breath. "Last year, Garrett took Louisa to this party. It was almost kind of a joke—she was just this awkward, naïve little freshman. I think he got it in his head that he was going to initiate her into high school life or something. You know, get her drunk for the first time, introduce her to all his friends. But the party got really out of control." Thayer shuddered. "I was there. Not that I remember much of it—I was pretty blasted. Anyway, at some point in the evening Garrett lost track of Louisa. I guess at first he didn't worry much. I mean, it was a party. He just assumed she was swimming or dancing or whatever. But after a while he started to panic. No one had seen her in hours, and people were starting to leave. He tore the place apart looking for her. Finally he ended up calling the cops."

Emma suddenly realized she'd been holding her breath, and took a deep gulp of air. A part of her knew what was coming and didn't want to hear it—but she needed the truth.

Thayer's eyes were distant and glazed when he spoke again. "They found her in the pool house, unconscious. Pretty badly beaten up." His lip curled in disgust. "She'd been raped."

"Oh my God," Emma whispered. A queasy feeling spread through her body.

"They caught the guy," Thayer continued. "His name was Daniel Preuss. He'd graduated by then, but he'd been on the soccer team. He was a really good friend of Garrett's."

The memory rose up in me as Thayer talked. I hadn't been at that party—it'd been the week of the state championship, and I'd been in Glendale with the rest of the tennis team. Garrett and Louisa had been out of school for a few weeks, but I remembered when he came back. He'd looked so vulnerable, so lost. That made it easy to ignore his mood swings, his temper tantrums—because after each violent flare-up, he looked so anguished. I'd made excuses for him every time.

But he'd been more broken than I'd realized. I pictured his face that night in the canyon, twisted into a mask of rage, the terrible things he yelled at me. How jealous he'd been that I was out there with Thayer. How he called me a slut for wearing shorts, his breath angry and hot with whiskey. He hated the fact that I'd wanted to sleep with him—and hated himself for wanting to sleep with me, too. What happened to Louisa shattered him, and he'd punished me for his own fear and self-loathing about not being able to protect her.

Emma's stomach curled into a tight little ball inside her, her head spinning. "That's . . . awful," she breathed.

Thayer nodded. "Yeah. Garrett never really recovered."

In spite of everything, a twinge of pity shot through Emma's chest. She couldn't even imagine the kind of pain Louisa and Garrett had been through. Then again, she thought, the same thing had happened to her   someone had hurt her sister beyond belief, and she had to live with it. Sutton hadn't deserved what happened to her any more than Louisa had.

She looked up to see Thayer watching her closely. "So you think what happened to Louisa made him snap?" he asked.

Emma sat up, straightening her legs out in front of her. "Maybe. But it doesn't matter, does it? He killed my sister, and I don't care what his excuses are. He's dangerous, and I have to find a way to prove it."

Thayer was silent for a long moment, studying her face.

"You know, you're so much like her." He gave a sad smile. "Not just the way you look, I mean. When you get that determined gleam in your eyes, you remind me so much of her."

Emma found that she was leaning slightly against his shoulder, their arms just touching. She knew she should shift her weight, put more distance between them, but she couldn't seem to move. For just a heartbeat, something magnetic pulled her toward Thayer.

"But I'm not her," she said softly, forcing herself to move away. "And you have to keep your promise. I don't know what I'd do if Garrett hurt you, too."

Thayer's jaw clenched, and his hands curled into tight fists. But he took a deep breath and stood up, his eyes suddenly clear. "I promise. You know where to find me if you need anything . . . *Emma.*" Then he turned and strode off toward his car.

I watched him go, hoping against hope that Emma had made the right choice in telling him—and hoping against hope that Garrett wouldn't kill him, too.

24

GO GOOGLE YOURSELF

Emma drove back to the Landrys' house slowly, reluctant to spend the day inside and alone. She cruised for a while past organic markets and upscale boutiques, decorated for Christmas with garlands and bows and twinkling lights. For a moment she contemplated going into the public library—she could go online, maybe do some research from there—but the memory of the reporters shouting her name made her shudder. Anywhere she went in public, she ran the risk of drawing down the press.

Soon the storefronts disappeared behind her, replaced by large, elegant homes and the Santa Catalina Mountains beyond. She turned into Ethan's development and parked beneath the Landrys' carport. Across the street the entrance to the canyon was still blocked off, police tape draped across the drive. She wondered if the investigators were over there even now, slowly sifting through the dirt. The skin on the back of her neck crawled like it always did when she glimpsed the bench where she'd waited for Sutton that first day. Sometimes it felt like the canyon had eyes.

Movement from across the lawn caught her eye. She paused as she climbed out of Ethan's car, the keys frozen in her hand. Next door, Dr. Banerjee was shoving a battered suitcase into the hatchback of his car. It looked like there were already a bunch of bags piled haphazardly in the backseat. Nisha's father still looked haggard, his eyes swollen in exhaustion, but he'd straightened himself up since she'd seen him last. His hair was combed, and he wore a button-down shirt that was wrinkled but clean.

As he climbed into the front seat of his car, Emma caught his eye. She lifted her hand to wave, taking a step toward him. For a moment she almost called out for him to stop—if Nisha had left evidence that Garrett had killed Sutton, Dr. Banerjee was the only person who could help her find it. Then she saw the look on his face. His eyes were hard slits, his mouth twisted in disgust. Her hand dropped limply back to her side. He thought she was a murderer—just like everyone else did. He backed out of his driveway, shaking his head slowly as he did. His lips moved like he was muttering to himself. Then he turned out onto the street and screeched away.

Her shoulders slumping, Emma turned away in defeat. It looked like Dr. Banerjee was skipping town, and with him, her last chance to find out the secret Nisha had died for.

She let herself into the Landrys' house with Ethan's key. As she pushed the door open, she wondered if she should have knocked instead. But inside, everything was dark and still. The sounds of a daytime talk show came from under Mrs. Landry's closed bedroom door, and Emma sighed in relief. She hated to admit it, but running into Ethan's mom—seeing the startled, nervous look in her mousy eyes—set her on edge.

Emma got a Coke Zero from the fridge and trudged to Ethan's room. His bed was perfectly made, with hospital corners and everything, his plain white pillows stacked neatly at the top—she'd watched him make it that morning, his lip between his teeth in concentration. His OCD side was kind of adorable. She blushed a little as she settled onto the bed, thinking that she and Ethan had been cuddling here just a few hours earlier.

Propping herself up against the headboard with some pillows, she pulled his laptop onto her legs. She chewed on the end of a lock of hair, then typed "Emma Paxton" into the search field—and regretted it almost immediately. The case was everywhere, and Emma herself was the star of the show. It was like a horrible, nightmare version of the headlines she used to write about herself—only now they were real. *Rags to Riches*, one news site proclaimed in enormous type, and underneath: *Emma Paxton lived in squalor and dreamed of escape. How far would she go to get what she wanted?* Every bad picture anyone had ever taken of her was now online, looking somehow sinister. She recognized Clarice's house in several of them—Travis had obviously been snapping photos of her without her knowledge. One even showed her sleeping, her mouth open and her tank top's spaghetti strap hanging off one shoulder.

A website called On the Q-T had interviewed Clarice herself. Emma scrolled down the page, full of pictures of her old room and stories about how disturbed Emma had seemed. *She told me she was working at a roller coaster, but I heard afterward that she was involved with some kind of exotic dance troupe. She used to flounce around here in short-shorts and halter tops, but I'm so naïve I didn't realize what was going on.*

Emma clicked through link after link, her heart sinking. Not one person seemed to even *consider* that she might be innocent. A task force called CIT—Coalition of Identical Twins—called her a monster and demanded her immediate arrest. Former classmates from Vegas, most of whom Emma didn't remember ever talking to, portrayed her as a shady, calculating thug. Another blog interviewed Hollier students who swore up and down that they'd suspected her all along.

Meanwhile, someone at Hollier had put up a Sutton Mercer remembrance page, filled with pictures of Sutton, Elton John's "Candle in the Wind" playing as background music. A guestbook was already filled with comments from Sutton's classmates.

I read the page over Emma's shoulder. Would everyone talk about what a bully I'd been? Would they say I'd deserved what I got? Would anyone even miss me? But most of the comments were superficial. *I will always remember how pretty she looked for Junior Prom*, someone named *wildcat_chick* had posted. *I had such a crush on her in eighth grade,* another comment read, and *Remember her sixteenth birthday party? That night made Hollier history!* It seemed like no one really knew me underneath my shiny, popular exterior. Then again, I hadn't exactly let many people see past that part of me.

Emma seemed to realize the same thing. She opened Twitter, certain that she would find something from Gabby and Lili. Sure enough, they'd been commenting on the whole situation.

@LILI_FIORELLO: *Calling it now: It's a prank. This is too crazy to be real.*

@GABBY_FIORELLO: *Sutton Mercer wouldn't let herself be taken out by some flimsy black market knock-off bitch.*

@LILI_FIORELLO: *Joke is getting stale. Cross your heart and hope to die?*

And then, a few hours later, simply:

@GABBY_FIORELLO: *Sutton, we love you and will miss you forever.*

Both of them had changed their user pictures to black squares. Emma's heart ached. She knew Sutton and her friends had never been touchy-feely, but she also knew that below the surface, they cared deeply about one another. Then she suddenly realized: Gabby and Lili were twins, too. She wondered if they believed the rumors that Emma had killed her own sister. Maybe they were joining CIT at that very moment.

For hours Emma sat bent over the computer, reading story after story and searching for clues. When a car door slammed outside, Emma was shocked to see it was already three. Tiptoeing to the window that looked over the front of the house, she pulled aside a slat in Ethan's Venetian blinds—and froze.

A cop car had pulled into the driveway, and Ethan was getting out of the passenger door. He paused to say something to the officer in the front—Corcoran again. She recognized the buzzed auburn hair. Then Ethan nodded and walked toward the house.

She met him in the entryway. He looked tired but calm, his backpack slung across one shoulder behind him.

"What happened?" she exclaimed.

"It's okay." He went to her, dropping his backpack on the floor next to him. As he straightened back up, she saw a scar on his temple she'd never noticed before, curving out from his hairline. She wanted suddenly to kiss it. "I went in willingly."

Emma's jaw fell open. "What?"

"I couldn't just sit here and do nothing. They need to know you're innocent." He raised his hand and cupped her cheek in his palm. "I told them I was blindsided by the news that you were really Emma but that I didn't care. I said that I love you, whoever you are—and that I believed you were innocent."

His touch on her face made her feel momentarily light-headed. The chill that had swept across her skin when she saw the cop car was replaced by a warm tingle.

Ethan's voice dropped low. "And I told them I'd seen Garrett running up to the canyon, the night Sutton died."

She blinked. "Wait, what? If you saw Garrett the night of the murder, why didn't you tell me earlier?"

He looked from side to side, though they seemed to be completely alone in the hall. "I didn't really. But it was the only way I could think of to get the cops to look at him more closely. You saw his car in the parking lot security stills, right? I may not have seen him, but he was out there."

"Ethan, do you realize how deep a hole you're digging for yourself?" she hissed. "Don't lie to the cops again—not for me. Isn't it bad enough that *I've* been lying to everyone?"

His hand dropped away from her cheek, and he looked down at his feet. "I'm sorry. I just—I thought it would help."

A door opened somewhere in the house, the quick patter of a local used-car commercial drifting through. Ethan glanced furtively into the hallway. After a moment there was the sound of a toilet flushing, and then the door closed again and the TV became muffled and distant once more. Mrs. Landry had retreated back to her cave.

Emma took a deep breath. Garrett *had* been in the canyon, after all. Maybe Ethan was right—now the cops had to look into Sutton's ex. "You're right," she said, touching his shoulder. "Thank you. I'm sorry for snapping. I'm just so afraid that the cops are going to pull you into this, too."

He shook his head. "Emma, I'd do anything for you. I want to keep you safe." He stooped to unzip his backpack, and when he stood back up he shoved something in her hands. She looked down to see a burner cell phone, still in the package. "I also swung by Radio Shack and got this for you."

She shifted her weight. The box felt strangely heavy in her hands. "You've already spent so much money on me, Ethan."

"Yeah, but you need a phone," he said. "Now I'm just a call away. If you need me, I'll come running." He wrapped his arms around her waist, pulling her close to him. The contact sent a warm glow through her body, and she hugged his neck.

"So, I really need to catch up on my calculus," he said, resting his forehead against hers. "But when I'm done, how about we grab some takeout and have a picnic? I know a great little spot just a few feet from here where the paparazzi will never find us. It's right behind my house, in fact."

She smiled. "You mean your yard?"

"You've heard of it!" he teased. "Come on. You, me, the mood lighting of the citronella candle. The best tom kha gai in town . . ."

"I'm there," she said, laughing.

As I watched them, it was almost like my heart came unclenched for a moment. Even with all the madness in her life, my sister had found someone who really cared for her. When I saw the way he looked at her, it made me hope that someday, when this was all over, they would be able to move on.

And I was glad they'd have each other when—*if*—that time came.

25

EMMA PAXTON: MASTER OF DISGUISE

"Have a nice afternoon, miss." A thin, white-bearded man wearing a flannel shirt and an apron handed Emma her bag of groceries and gave her a quizzical look.

Emma tugged self-consciously at her skirt. It was Wednesday, and she was incognito again, in Mrs. Landry's blonde wig, a denim jumper embroidered with butterflies, and a red turtleneck sweater she'd gotten at Goodwill. Plastic dime-store glasses completed the look—she was a dead ringer for the Sunday school teacher she'd had during her few weeks with the Morgans, a particularly pious foster family back in Nevada. She couldn't believe it had come to this to just buy milk; but the reporters—or Garrett—could be anywhere.

She exited the store and walked across the parking lot toward Ethan's car, her shadow flickering across the asphalt at her feet. Next to the home improvement store was a Burger King, a line of cars stretching around the drive-through. Just as she dropped the groceries in the car, someone laid on his horn, impatient to make an order.

What she saw next made her stop in her tracks.

Travis had just stepped out of the Burger King, a thirty-two ounce soft drink in his hand. He paused in the doorway, pulling a pair of cheap aviators down over his eyes, before slouching up the street in the opposite direction.

Emma didn't waste any time. Slamming the car door shut, she followed him on foot.

The area was a cheap commercial zone, lined with big-box stores and chain restaurants. A thin strip of weeds ran between the road and the sidewalk, dotted with over-flowing trash cans. She walked slowly, letting Travis stay several feet ahead but keeping him in her line of sight. He wore a backward-facing baseball cap and saggy jeans hanging down almost off his butt. A wallet chain went from his belt loop to his back pocket. When he glanced behind him, she ducked into a crowd of people at a bus stop, trying to keep her face as bored as all the other commuters' expressions. When she was sure he'd turned away, she followed again.

Travis passed an abandoned mechanics' garage tagged with graffiti, then cut across the parking lot to a Days Inn Hotel. The pool shone behind the cast-iron gate, three small children in inflatable water wings squealing in the shallow end. Emma hung back and watched as Travis climbed the steps and let himself into one of the rooms.

She stood in the shade of a mesquite tree, uncertainty coiling inside her. Why was he still here? He didn't know anything about the killer—did he?

But her head snapped up as Ethan's words came drifting back to her. *If we had access to Garrett's texts or e-mail, we'd be able to see if he sent the link.*

They didn't have Garrett's phone. But the message might still be somewhere on Travis's.

With another glance around, she climbed the stairs to his door and knocked. For a moment nothing happened. She knocked again, louder. From the parking lot, a middle-aged couple in matching Hawaiian shirts paused as they climbed out of their station wagon, staring up at her. Emma swallowed, sweat gathering on the back of her neck. She lifted her hand to knock one more time, but before she could, the door jerked open.

Travis stood in the doorway, his hat off. He wore a white tank top snug across his meaty chest, and a thick gold chain dangled from his neck. His chin jutted belligerently at her. Behind him, Arnold Schwarzenegger filled the TV screen, roaring up the freeway on a motorcycle. "What do you want, lady?"

For a moment, she didn't remember that she was in costume. She blinked, then pulled off her glasses. "It's me. Emma."

His jaw fell slack. He looked her slowly up and down, his piggy little eyes bulging. The smell of stale tobacco and sweat hung around him.

"I need your help," she said, putting on the sweetest expression she could muster. "Everyone thinks I killed my sister."

"Yeah, I know," he said, grinning. "That one cop, Quinlan or whatever? He's been trying to get me to tell him all about you."

She chewed on her thumbnail, knowing she had to play this just right. "What have you told him so far?"

Travis shrugged, bracing himself against the door frame so he loomed over her.

"So far just about your freaky little habit," he said.

"You mean that video someone *sent* you?" she said, choosing her words carefully.

"Yup," he said. "Man, I liked watching that. Such a bummer they took it down."

Bingo. Garrett *had* sent him that link. Her heart swelled with excitement. If she could get her hands on his phone, she could prove it. She took a deep breath.

"I didn't kill Sutton," she said, a soft, pleading note entering her voice. "You believe me, don't you?"

He smirked. "I don't know, Emma. You were pretty violent with me. Always had a nasty temper."

Emma tensed, fighting the angry retort that was rising in her chest. She'd kneed Travis in the groin once after he'd tried to cop a feel. That was what had led to his framing her for the theft of Clarice's money.

Travis's voice dropped conspiratorially. "Besides, Tucson's a pretty nice place. The cops have me set up here all week—free HBO, room service. All for telling them anything I can about you."

She looked up at him, blinking through her thick lashes, her eyes wide and vulnerable. I was impressed—back in the day, I'd been a master of the puppy-dog-in-the-rain look. If only she could make herself cry on command, Emma would give me a run for my money.

"Why are you doing this to me?" She gave her voice the slightest tremble, pretending to wipe at the corner of her eye.

Travis glanced left and right as if looking for

eavesdroppers. Then he leaned forward, putting his mouth right by her ear as if to share a secret. His breath was rancid with sugar and pot. "The thing is, Emma, you're a real bitch."

It took all her willpower not to slap him in the face. But she had to play nice. Her lips slightly parted, she rested a hand on his bare bicep. Travis's eyes flickered down to where she was touching him.

"I'm desperate," she whispered, ignoring the surge of bile at the back of her throat. "I'll do anything. You have to help me, Travis. You're the only one who can."

He stared at her blankly for a moment, his malice overcome by surprise. She ran her eyes appraisingly over his body, trying to look seductive, hunting for the telltale rectangular outline of his phone. *There.* It was in his front pocket, just against his hip.

A slow smile spread across his face. "Anything, huh?" He stepped back from the door, holding it open for her. As she stepped past him, he slapped her on the butt, and she jumped. Her stomach lurched. For a moment, she wondered if she was making a huge mistake. Travis was dangerous.

But Emma was tough, too. And she needed that phone.

She reached up to take the itchy wig off her head, but Travis grabbed her hand. "Leave it," he murmured, his breath hot on her face. "I like it."

Emma dropped her hands to Travis's hips, leaving the blonde wig where it was. Slowly, she slid her hands into his pockets. His eyes closed, his breath coming quicker. Her fingers searched past stray coins and a baggie of something she was sure was pot before closing around the hard plastic form of his phone. As she wrenched it from his pocket, his eyes shot open.

"What—" But he didn't get to finish his question. She brought her knee up as hard as she could between his legs. His eyes crossed, and he fell backward onto the bed, clutching at his groin.

She was out the door and slamming it behind her before he could even move, taking the stairs three at a time, adrenaline coursing through her veins. By the time he wrenched the door open, she was already at the bottom.

"You crazy bitch!" he screamed, limping after her. "I'll kill you!"

"You'll have to get in line!" Emma yelled over her shoulder as she took off running. She zigzagged around an acne-scarred man dressed in the polyester blazer of a hotel staffer, then sprinted across the parking lot, leaping over medians and dodging cars. The muscles blazed in her legs, but she barely noticed. For a moment, she felt like she could fly.

And I was flying right next to her, chanting her name

like a cheer. Finally, my sister had gotten her hands on something that might be able to clear her name. And finally, she'd been able to hit Travis *exactly* where it hurt.

26

SHOW US YOUR TEXTS

Emma burst into Ethan's room thirty minutes later, the phone pressing sharply into her palm. He jumped up from where he'd been sitting at his desk, his mouth open round in surprise. She whipped the wig off her scalp and threw it down in victory, unable to wipe the grin from her face.

Ethan stared at the BlackBerry in her hand, then looked up at her wonderingly. "What . . ."

"It's Travis's phone!" She quickly explained what had happened, leaving out the fact that she'd had to faux-seduce him.

"Emma, you're amazing!" Ethan took the phone, a smile spreading across his face. She sank to the edge of his bed, running her fingers through her mussed-up hair. There wasn't enough soap in the world to get the memory of Travis off her skin—but it was worth it. She'd gotten the phone.

Ethan's fingers danced over the BlackBerry's keys, and she held her breath, watching him carefully. After a minute, he shook his head. "It looks like his text history and his e-mails have been cleared pretty recently."

Emma's heart sank. "So it was all for nothing?"

"Not necessarily." Ethan popped the SD card out of its slot and held it pinched between his thumb and index finger. "That stuff stays forever, if you know how to look for it. And it just so happens that your boyfriend is sort of a techno-geek." He shot her a grin as he stepped toward his computer.

"What are you doing?" Emma said.

Ethan stopped. "Plugging it in. Don't you want to see what's on it?"

"But . . . shouldn't we take it to the library or something?" Anxiety streaked through her. "What if someone can trace it to your computer? I don't want it to look like you had anything to do with stealing it."

He shook his head impatiently. "The nearest branch is

closed for the night. We can't wait for tomorrow. Emma, this could answer all our questions. This could be the solution we've been looking for!"

She rubbed her palms into her eyes. Then she nodded. "Okay. You're right. Plug it in."

Ethan turned back to his laptop, inserted the card into a small device, and plugged it into the USB port. Instantly a window popped open on his screen, listing the contents of the phone. Ethan clicked to view all the files at once—and blushed a vibrant red as Travis's entire pornography collection opened on his desktop.

He lunged forward, covering the monitor with his torso to shield it from her view. "I'm so sorry," he mumbled, fumbling to close all the images. Emma's own face was burning, too, but she couldn't keep a nervous giggle from escaping.

"That was all on his *phone*?" she exclaimed. "Like, that's what he takes with him everywhere he goes?"

"Just let me . . ." Ethan kept hiding the monitor from her with his body, typing furiously. The back of his neck was scarlet. And suddenly, Emma couldn't help herself— she laughed. After all she'd been through, after everything that had happened, they were so close to finding out the truth. The only thing stopping them was a few hundred pictures of boobs.

By the time Ethan managed to close all the pictures,

Emma had reined in her laughter. She moved closer to his desk and put a hand on his shoulder. He was still bright red with discomfort and was looking carefully away from her. "That was like my worst nightmare come true," he muttered.

She looked at the monitor over his shoulder. "Was there room for anything else on his phone?"

"We'll find out." Ethan's fingers flew deftly over the keyboard. He typed in several commands she didn't understand, then paused for a moment before striking hard on the "enter" button with his index finger. Pages of texts and e-mails immediately shot open. Her jaw dropped.

"Now who's amazing?" she breathed, leaning down to kiss his cheek. His flush, which had started to drain away, brightened again.

The most recent texts included an exchange between Travis and a girl named "Sapphire" that started with the line HEY GIRL WHUT U WEARIN? Ethan made a disgusted face. "You lived with this guy?"

"Child Protective Services didn't exactly give me a lot of choice," Emma said, leaning over "What's in his e-mail from back in August?"

He hesitated. "We're not accidentally going to find naked pictures of him on here, are we?"

She grimaced. "I never said this would be easy."

Emma watched as Ethan scrolled down to the e-mails from August. All of Travis's friends had e-mail addresses like *markdogg69* or *bluntmeister*. She rolled her eyes. Then she saw it. On August twenty-ninth, someone named *hollier_hell* had sent a message with the subject line *Check this out.*

She lifted a trembling finger to point to it. Ethan's eyes widened. "'Hollier_hell'?"

She tucked her hair behind her ears, catching a lock in her hands and twirling it around her finger. "Open it."

Ethan double-clicked on the message.

Hey man, thought you might like this video of your sweet little foster sister. Do me a favor and show her, too.

Below that was a link. Emma was willing to bet it would be dead now, but she was certain that back in August, it had led straight to the *Sutton in AZ* video that started it all.

"This is two days before the murder," she said, a clammy feeling descending over her body. That meant that Sutton's murder had been *premeditated*—not a crime of passion or an accident. And it meant that Garrett had been watching Emma, too; had known where she lived and with whom. It meant she'd been a part of his plan all along.

Travis had replied: *That is some freaky shit, bro. Thanks*

for the link. But what's in it for me if I show her?

Hollier_hell answered: *$5K sound good to you? But don't tell anyone about this. Delete these messages. If Emma leaves town you've done your job. Then meet me at 5784 W. Speedway in Tucson on September 15. I'll be there with the money.*

The last e-mail in the thread was from Travis: *I'm game. Sept. 15. Be there.*

Emma clenched her fists, her fingernails digging into her flesh. Travis had sold her to her sister's murderer for $5,000. "Ethan. Do you know that address?"

"I'm on it." A map flew open on the browser when he searched for the address. It was on the outskirts of Tucson, on the west side of town. When Ethan selected the pin on the map, the name of the business sprang up.

"Holy shit," Ethan muttered.

The address the murderer had given Travis was for Rosa Linda Storage.

Slowly, Emma reached over him. She slid open his desk drawer and pulled out the tiny silver key they'd found in Garrett's locker, holding it up next to Ethan's monitor. She stared at the scratched-out second word again.

Emma's blood went still in her veins. The glittering key dangled motionless between her and Ethan, catching the bright overhead light. There it was: Under the scratches and the scars on the metal, the second word was suddenly clear. It couldn't be anything but LINDA.

Emma pulled the burner cell out of her tote. Wordlessly, she keyed in the number on the website. Ethan opened his lips to ask what she was doing, but she held her finger to her lips. The line rang five times before someone finally answered.

"Rosa Linda Storage," croaked a man's voice in the receiver. Emma took a deep breath.

"Hi, this is the tenant of unit three-fifty-six," she said, using a brisk, important voice. "I'm calling to find out when my next payment is due."

A crackling silence came from the other end of the line. After a moment, the creaky voice replied, heavy with skepticism. "This is Arthur Smith?"

Her heart sank. She'd hoped it would be in Garrett's name—if it had been, all she'd have had to do was turn the key and Travis's phone over to the cops. But of course Garrett had covered his tracks.

She cleared her throat. "This is *Mrs.* Arthur Smith, yes."

"Oh, I'm sorry, Mrs. Smith." There was a rustle of paperwork. "It looks like your account is clear through the end of the month. Will you be paying in cash again?"

Emma ended the call, lowering the phone back to her bag. Then she looked at Ethan, his eyes round and questioning.

"Get your coat," she said. "We're going to Rosa Linda."

If I still had fists, I would have punched them toward the sky in excitement.

Finally, we were going to find out what was behind door number two.

27

MEMENTO MORI

Rosa Linda Storage was located on a desolate stretch of road on the outskirts of Tucson, between a run-down motel called the Flamingo and a boarded-up liquor store. A neon sign stood out front, several of the letters burnt out so that it said only OS LIN STOR. A chain-link fence wound around the property, the barbed wire dotted with incongruous red bows for the holidays.

Emma traced her sister's initials on the key fob as Ethan pulled into the parking lot. She knew that they wouldn't find old furniture or soccer equipment in that storage unit. Whatever it was, it had something to do with Sutton.

I knew it, too. I could feel the truth just out of my

reach, like a dream that fades from memory upon waking.

Ethan parked, and they stepped out into the packed-earth courtyard. Rows of storage units, shuttered and silent, branched off into the darkness in four directions. No one else was there at that hour.

"Are you ready for this?" Ethan asked, his voice low.

"I don't know," Emma admitted. She took a deep breath, the dry desert air filling her lungs and calming her. "Come on," she said, giving Ethan's hand a squeeze. "Let's get this over with."

They started down the aisle of buildings hand in hand. The floodlights that lit each unit made their shadows flicker grotesquely across the ground, misshapen and eerie. Their footsteps echoed in the stillness. Farther into the desert, a coyote gave a shrill yip.

The unit numbers were painted on the doors in bright orange, starting with 100. Emma counted out loud as they walked through the aisles. "One hundred fifty," she whispered. "Two hundred . . . three hundred . . . three fifty—it should be down here, Ethan." She jerked her head around a corner.

Unit 356 looked like all the others, the numbers stenciled across the folding leaves in the garage-type door. Emma had leaned down to fumble at the padlock when Ethan grabbed her elbow.

"Wait," he said, handing her a pair of knit pink gloves,

which no doubt belonged to his mother, from one of the pockets in his cargo pants. From another he extracted a pair of black climbing gloves and pulled them over his own fingers.

"Good call," Emma said, tugging on her gloves and grasping the padlock once more. The key was a perfect fit. With an almost inaudible click, the latch sprang free. Emma gripped the door's handle—and pulled sharply up.

The inside was completely dark. She groped along the wall to find the switch, and a single fluorescent bulb hanging in the center of the unit flickered to life. The unit was large enough to hold an apartment's worth of furniture or a few hundred boxes—but it was almost completely empty.

Almost.

In the center of the cavernous space, a single manila envelope lay on the floor just under the light. Next to it was a stuffed octopus missing one of its black button eyes. Emma knew that octopus. She'd hugged those blue knit legs countless times as a little girl, whenever she needed comfort. It was her Socktopus, one of the only things she'd brought with her from Vegas.

She slowly walked forward, picking up the stuffed animal and staring down at it. Socktopus had been in the duffel that was stolen from the bench in Sabino Canyon, her first night in Tucson. Whoever took it had acted quickly—it had only been unattended for a few minutes before she'd returned looking for it.

Ethan hung back, glancing at the open door every now and then as if afraid someone would spring out at them. "What is that?" he asked, frowning.

"My mom got it for me," she said. Her voice sounded far away, even to her. "When I was little."

For a moment the dingy storage unit faded, and she could feel Becky tying two of the octopus's arms around Emma's neck in the store so it hung down on her back like a cape. *So he can protect you,* Becky had explained, a rare smile lighting up her pretty face.

Emma blinked away her tears, and the dusty unit came back into focus. She tucked Socktopus under her arm, leaning down to pick up the envelope. For a moment she fumbled at the brad that held it closed, her fingers wooden and clumsy through the gloves. Then a pile of papers and photos slid out in one large stack. On top was a disc in a clear jewel case, labeled SUTTON IN AZ in red Sharpie.

"The video," Ethan whispered.

She nodded, but she was already rifling through the pages behind the disc. There was a printout of the very first message Emma had sent Sutton. *This will sound crazy, but I think we're related. We look exactly the same, and we have the same birthday.* Behind that was a page with Sutton's e-mail and Facebook passwords. And behind that were photos—a thick stack of glossy black-and-white photos.

Emma had gotten so used to seeing Sutton's face everywhere that for a moment, she thought the pictures were of her twin. But that wasn't right—in the very top picture, the girl stood behind a ticket window. Emma's heart skipped a beat. It was the New York–New York roller coaster in Vegas, where she'd worked the summer before coming to Tucson. In the picture she was busy counting change for a customer, completely unaware that someone had a lens trained on her.

The next picture caught her and Alex, running side by side on a trail through Red Rock Canyon. Another showed her reaching up to pull something off the top shelf at the public library. In a third she was walking into Clarice's house, an expression of utter despondence on her face. The photos were grainy, taken surreptitiously and at awkward angles—but she was clear in all of them.

The old Emma had been an expert at staying anonymous and invisible, at keeping low to the ground so she couldn't get hurt. The old Emma would have been embarrassed to realize that someone had been watching her all that time.

But the new Emma? The new Emma was pissed.

And so was I.

Emma shuffled the pictures to the back of the stack of paperwork, and leafed through the rest of the pages. She frowned at one that was simply a list of numbers. For a moment she didn't know what she was looking at. Then she recognized one of the numbers.

It was the Mercers' alarm code.

Her jaw dropped. Beneath that code was the Chamberlains'. And below that was another set of digits she recognized: 0907.

September seven. Mrs. Banerjee's birthday.

Nisha had given Emma that same code nearly a month earlier so she could access the mental health files at the hospital. Emma was willing to bet that was the alarm code for their house, too. Garrett had used it to break into Nisha's house, to find what she'd been hiding there, but Dr. Banerjee had scared him away.

Except Dr. Banerjee was out of town now.

"Ethan," she breathed, holding up the sheet of paper. "We can get into Nisha's house. We can find the evidence!"

Ethan stared at her. "Emma, we need to go straight to the cops. The stuff in here is enough to put Garrett away."

"But it's not," she argued. "There's nothing here that points to Garrett. It's rented under a fake name, paid in cash—and I'm willing to bet there aren't any fingerprints on any of this stuff," she added bitterly. "The only thing that links Garrett to this unit is the key we found, and that's our word against his. But whatever Nisha had was damning enough that Garrett killed her for it."

Ethan let out a breath. He glanced around the storage unit, then back at her. "Okay. You're right. We'll swing by Nisha's and look around one more time. Then we'll go to the cops and give them what we have."

She nodded, excitement bubbling in her chest like fresh water from a spring. She felt lighter than she had in weeks. They were so close now—just a little more evidence, and they'd be able to prove what Garrett had done to her sister.

"We should leave the stuff here, how we found it. It's a crime scene now." She slid the paperwork and the photos back into the manila envelope and carefully put it back on the ground. Then she picked up Socktopus, hugging him to her chest once more before setting him next to the envelope.

They locked up the unit and went back to the car. Ethan hit the highway, driving carefully but fast. The desert spread out on either side of them, disappearing into darkness just a few feet from the road. Emma clutched the key to the storage unit in her hand.

Hell yeah! I shouted silently, wishing I could slap my sister five. Garrett was finally, *finally* going down.

28

A MESSAGE FROM BEYOND THE GRAVE

Emma pushed through the wrought-iron gate leading to the Banerjees' backyard, Ethan right behind her. The house was completely dark, the windows gaping like empty eye sockets. The only light was the moon catching on the surface of the pool, vague and shimmering. The sight made her queasy. It was easy to imagine Nisha, face-down, her long hair billowing around her head.

"I hate it back here," she whispered. Ethan nodded. He slid his fingers through hers and squeezed.

Two enormous French doors connected the patio to the kitchen. To the left, an alarm panel glowed softly red. Emma approached it cautiously, her nerves humming. She couldn't risk making a mistake. If the alarm went off, Dr. Banerjee would change the code again, and who knew what he'd change it to. For a moment her fingers hovered over the numbers, about to punch in 0907. Then she thought of Garrett, and how he'd already broken in.

"Dr. Banerjee changed the code," she whispered. "Of course. He would have, after finding Garrett in his house. There's no way it's Mrs. Banerjee's birthday anymore."

Ethan's face fell. "You're right. We can't . . ." But he trailed off as she spun back to the panel. Before she could second-guess herself, Emma typed in a new number: 0420. Nisha's birthday. For a moment, nothing happened. She held her breath, bracing herself for the blare of alarms cutting through the silent night, ready to run as fast as she could back to Ethan's house.

But then, after what felt like forever, the light turned green. She heard a soft click inside the door. They were in.

She turned to face Ethan, a triumphant grin spreading over her face. His jaw hung slack, his head whipping from the panel to her and back again. "How did you know the right code?"

She shrugged. "A hunch."

Ethan swallowed hard. "Jesus, Emma, you could have set the alarm off."

"A girl's got to get lucky sometimes. Even me." She opened the door silently and stepped inside, her eyes adjusting to the deeper gloom of the kitchen.

The room had been scrubbed top to bottom since she'd last seen it. A strong smell of Pine-Sol lingered on the air, and the bronze fixtures winked in the scanty light. Next to the door, a bowl sat on the floor, overflowing with cat kibble.

I followed Emma's gaze around the room, remembering the parties and tennis dinners I'd attended at Nisha's house, standing around the kitchen island with my friends, eating carrot sticks and gossiping. Now the house was silent and empty, like the very walls were in mourning.

A small sphere of light appeared out of the blue. Emma spun around to see Ethan, holding a pocket Maglite out in front of him. It was attached to his key ring. He handed it to her. "We should keep the lights off," he whispered. "We don't want anyone to see us from the street. I'll check the living room and Dr. Banerjee's office. You take her bedroom. Meet back here in five minutes?"

"Okay," Emma said, leaning up to kiss his cheek. Then she turned and slipped into the hall, sending the flashlight's beam ahead of her.

Motes of dust swirled in the pale light. The pictures along the hall seemed to leer at her, grotesque in the dark. She flinched as she stepped on a squeaky floorboard, the low squeal sounding as loud as an alarm in the thick silence. What if Garrett chose this moment to rebreak into the house? What if he arrived only to find that she and Ethan had beat him to the punch? She shuddered at the thought of what he might do.

At Nisha's bedroom door she paused. Even though she'd already searched this room once, she couldn't shake the feeling that the evidence was here. She knew from her years as a foster kid that the only safe hiding place was somewhere personal, close to you.

Her heart thudding against her ribs, Emma paused in the doorway, sending the orb of light slowly over Nisha's things but carefully avoiding the window. Everything was just as it had been the last time she visited. Crystalline vials of perfume sat on top of Nisha's dresser, next to a small collection of tennis trophies. The creased spines of books faced out from the shelf, neat and alphabetized, and the bedspread was smooth and unruffled. Next to the Compaq laptop on the desk lay a DVD case for the BBC *Pride and Prejudice* miniseries—Nisha must have been watching it before she died.

Nothing seemed out of place. Emma hit her fists against her thighs in frustration, her nails digging into her palms. Nisha had found something important—and it was still *here*. Emma could feel it in her gut. But where would she have hidden something that important?

The thought came to her slowly, like a lens coming gradually into focus. Emma had hidden plenty of things herself—she'd spent her childhood protecting her scant treasures from nosy foster parents and kleptomaniacal roommates. She inhaled sharply. It seemed too much of a long shot, too simple an answer. But it was worth a try. Creeping on the balls of her feet, she pushed the door to Nisha's bathroom open. A small night-light flashed on from the outlet by the mirror. She knelt down by the cabinet and started opening drawers.

There, in the gloom beneath the sink, was an enormous, Costco-sized carton of Tampax.

She froze, almost afraid to move. Afraid her last decent hope would be quashed. Boxes of tampons had been her go-to hiding place for years. But Nisha couldn't possibly have had the same secret spot . . . could she?

Slowly, she pulled out the box. Her heart felt still in her chest. She groped inside the carton, past the rows of individual boxes, and at the bottom her fingers closed on something that felt like a tube.

It was a plain manila folder, rolled into a tight spiral and rubber-banded several times. Emma's head spun as she peeled away the rubber bands and smoothed the folder flat on the ground. Paper-clipped to the outside of the folder was a piece of pink Hello Kitty notepaper. She recognized Nisha's neat handwriting right away.

Sutton, I'm so sorry. I had a bad feeling about this after we talked, and I had to check. You need to know the truth.

Holding her breath, she flipped the folder open.

On the top page, the words UNIVERSITY OF ARIZONA MEDICAL CENTER RECORDS were typed in a large bold font. Under "department" someone had scrawled the word *psychiatric* in black pen.

When I saw the name written on the form next to PATIENT, it didn't register at first. The letters were like hieroglyphics, strange and illegible. But then the world snapped into a painful, horrifying clarity.

The name sparked something in my memory, and with a deafening roar began pulling me back to that night in the canyon. And I knew with sickening certainty that finally, *finally*, I was going to relive the last moments of my life.

29

THE LAST MEMORY

I can't breathe. The shirt collar digs into my throat, crushing my windpipe. I kick my legs furiously, but already I'm seeing spots, and Garrett is much too strong for me. Far below my feet the wind rushes through the ravine with a lost, lonely howl. Garrett's face is inches from mine, twisted into a mask of fury that's almost unrecognizable in the moonlight. I dimly register that my shirt is tearing as he shakes me back and forth. I'm going to die here, in this canyon where I used to go camping with my dad, where Thayer and I stole some of our first kisses, where Laurel and I used to tell ghost stories.

Finally Garrett lets go, and a scream erupts from the depths of my ragged lungs, echoing off the walls of the canyon.

But I don't fall far.

I land in a heap on the ground, crumpled at Garrett's feet. Inches behind me I can feel the ravine yawning wide. My heart roars in my ears, adrenaline singing in my blood. I'm alive. My fingers curl through the dirt, raw and stinging. My face feels wet, and I realize that I'm crying.

Garrett looms over me, shuddering violently as if the force of his rage might literally tear him apart. Then he turns his face to me, and it's as red and tear-streaked as my own. He's crying, too.

I stare up at him, suddenly unable to move, my heart aching. We stay like this for a few minutes: me sitting motionless on the brink of the cliff, Garrett standing there, bruised and broken by his own anger. And in spite of everything that's happened, I feel sorry for him.

At last he sits in the dirt next to me, his cheeks slick with tears. "I'm sorry." He reaches out to touch me, but I flinch. He pulls his hand away, looking as wounded as if I'd slapped him.

I wipe at my eyes. The wind makes my tear-streaked cheeks feel raw.

"Were you going to throw me over the edge?" I ask, my voice small in my ears. Garrett gapes at me.

"Sutton, I would never . . ." He trails off. Slowly he holds his hands up in front of his face. Horror dawns in his eyes, and it's like he's looking at someone else's hands, like he's just now realizing how strong they are, how beyond his control. How close he had been to hurting me. He looks up at me again, and this

time it's fear that pinches his face. "I don't want to hurt anyone," he whispers.

I don't say anything. It doesn't matter what he wants anymore. Garrett has been too volatile for a long time. The attack on his sister cut something inside of him loose, and he has been out of control ever since.

The stars gleam bluish-white overhead. Garrett is slow to catch his breath, and even after he does, the occasional sob seizes his lungs. Somewhere nearby I hear twigs breaking—probably a possum or raccoon, some night creature waddling clumsily through the bushes.

"Garrett, I need to know. Did you . . . steal my car and chase . . . me?" I ask, not wanting to say Thayer's name for fear of setting him off once more.

Garrett's jaw drops, and I can already see the answer in his shocked face. "Someone stole your car and chased you?"

My head swims with the mysteries of this never-ending night. "Yeah . . . kind of."

Garrett looks sickened. "Do you really think I'd do something like that?"

Our eyes meet. I force myself not to look away. "I don't know anymore, Garrett."

He bites his lip so hard a drop of blood wells up. Then, slowly, he crawls close to the edge of the ravine, until his feet are dangling over the side. His body sways slightly with the alcohol still clouding his brain.

"Be careful, Garrett," I say, an edge creeping into my voice. "This is a really sharp drop."

He looks up at me, and in the dark his eyes look like fathomless pits. His face writhes in torment, a frantic, miserable expression shifting over him. My heart is suddenly in my throat, and I'm not sure why.

"Wouldn't it be easier if the only person I hurt was myself?" he whispers. Another shiver passes through him. His hair sticks up like a blond halo around his head, bright against the wide darkness beyond him.

"Garrett." I'm kneeling now, my bare legs aching beneath me. The scrapes on my knees burn against the stony outcropping. "Things will be better. I promise. But you have to back up for me."

He shakes his head. "Things won't be better," he says softly. "Not for me." He leans forward, his eyes wide and staring into the abyss. "Maybe I could make them better for everyone else, though."

The fear from a moment ago is back, but now it's different—now I'm not afraid for myself. I inch closer to him.

"Do you really think Louisa would feel that way? Or your mom?" The wind swirls up from the ravine, cutting right through my hoodie, so sharp I can feel it in my bones. "How do you think they'd feel if they lost you?" I swallow hard. "How do you think I'd feel?"

I can hear the faint echo of my own voice dancing through the chasm below. How would I feel? I know I don't love Garrett.

But I do care about him. When we first got together, I thought I could help him get over the things that had hurt him. I thought if I were pretty enough, charming enough, fun enough, if I could distract him enough, he'd just get better.

Now that seems insanely narcissistic, even for me.

"Please, Garrett," I say, my voice shaking. I hold out my hand to him. "Come off the ledge, okay? Please."

He stares at my hand, his face strange and distant. His eyes seem to have a hard time focusing, his head wobbling on his neck. For a moment we're frozen in place, and I can't breathe.

Then his hand clasps mine, and my shoulders sag with relief.

His palm is moist, and the salt of his sweat burns the stings and cuts I've accumulated all night long. I pull him toward me, away from that nightmare abyss. He stumbles against me. I put my arms around him to steady him, and we stand like that for a moment. I can feel the tremble that's seized his body, fluttering against my heart.

"We should get out of here," he whispers. The scare seems to have sobered him up a little. His pupils are enormous in the darkness, his eyes focusing more clearly now.

I let go of him. I'm suddenly tired to the bone, my body limp as a rag doll. For a moment I think about climbing down with Garrett. His car will be in the parking lot, and he will be able to take me home. He seems clear-headed enough to drive now, and I can tell how bad he feels, both for accosting me and for almost dropping me.

But I don't feel safe with him. I know how hurt he's been, and I know he doesn't mean to lash out—but I've been making excuses for him for months now.

"You go ahead," I say. My voice is soft but firm. "I want some time alone, okay?"

He frowns at me. "It's dangerous out here at night. I don't think I should leave you."

I shake my head. "Look, it's been a crazy night. I need some time to process it all, okay? I'll be all right. I'll head down to Nisha's when I'm ready to get out of here. But right now I just need a little space."

He doesn't let go of my hand. For just a moment he looks into my eyes, and I can see everything he wants to say there—how sorry he is, how sad he is, how much he loves me. I look away, toward the bright city lights.

"Will you call me tomorrow?" he asks, a slight tremor in his voice.

I hesitate. I want so badly to break it off with him, once and for all. I want a brand-new start when I walk off this mountain. But if I set him off again, who knows what he'll do?

"Yeah," I say. "I'll call you tomorrow."

Tomorrow, when he's sober, when we're not in the middle of nowhere, I'll rip the bandage off. I'll end it and tell him my decision is final. But for now this is the best I can do.

He reaches out to take my hand in his. We stand that way for a minute, him cradling my fingers in his palm. Something about it—how tender he's gotten, and how ashamed—twists my heart. Then he pulls away, still a little shaky on his feet, and turns wordlessly, walking slowly down the trail to the parking lot. I can hear him even after he disappears from my sight, breaking branches and stumbling.

A profound silence settles over the canyon when he's gone. All of the city sounds—barking dogs and sirens and cruising motors— have died away.

It's a strange feeling. All day long, I'm surrounded by voices that tell me where I belong, what I should be doing, who I am. But tonight, in this deep, dark silence, I can decide that for myself. I climb onto a low boulder and stare out over the city. It's beautiful and calm from here. People are asleep in their beds, never suspecting that one lonely girl is looking at the twinkling lights outside their homes.

I've only been out here a few hours, but it feels like years have passed. I've learned so much tonight, about who I am and where I came from. About who I want to be. It's hard to know what tomorrow will hold—I'll have to face my dad again, after discovering his secrets. I'll have to face Laurel, who's spent the night in the ER with Thayer. Then I think about the e-mail draft on my phone. I quickly pull it up, but just as I suspected, the top corner is flashing with NO SERVICE. *I reread it, and a little thrill goes through me. I mean every word. The moment that I have a signal again, I'm sending this to Thayer. And my secret twin sister—I will find her, if it's the last thing I do.*

And deep inside my sore, stiff body, I feel a sense of peace. Everything is going to be different, starting tomorrow.

I stand up, brushing the dirt off my thighs. I've had enough soul-searching for one night. It's time for my pajamas and a cup of my mom's peppermint tea. Time to get down the mountain and find a ride home.

But then someone clears his throat behind me.

I turn slowly to see a guy standing there. He's tall, with high cheekbones and dark hair. His frayed hiking shorts show off his muscular calves. On his hands he wears black climbing gloves, and a bashful smile plays around his lips.

It's Ethan Landry.

"Oh. Hey," I say, jerking my neck backward in surprise. "What are you doing out here?"

Even in the pale moonlight I can see him blush. He kicks at a stone with the tip of his sneaker. "Sorry to startle you. I saw you on the trail from my house," he says, gesturing to the darkness below us. "I was watching the stars. There's a meteor shower tonight."

"Oh."

Ethan watches me intently, and I suddenly feel self-conscious. There's blood caked on one leg where I scraped myself, and I've fallen in the dirt a half dozen times. I run my fingers through my hair and come away with a leaf in my hand.

Ethan steps closer, and I can see him more clearly now. A concerned frown crumples his brow. It seems odd that he's out so late, but Ethan's always been a little bit odd—I remember him carrying around a tarantula in a jar in junior high, and getting in trouble during gym class for looking at the flowers in the outfield when he was supposed to be playing baseball. He's not exactly in my circle—he's cute enough, but he's always been so shy. Then recently, he walked in on a *Lying Game* prank gone out of control. It was Laurel's stupid snuff film, and Ethan had pulled her off me and then stayed with me while my head cleared.

Now he shifts his weight, shoving his hands in his pockets. "Are you okay? You look . . . well, you look like you've had a long night."

"Oh, yeah . . . I'm okay." My smile trembles a little and then collapses. "It's been a really weird night, is all."

He touches my shoulder, his hand warm through my shirt. "Do you want to talk about it?"

And suddenly, I do. My voice shaking and weak, I tell him everything. About Thayer coming to town, and how we fought, and how someone ran him down. About my dad being my grandfather, and Becky appearing after I'd wondered about my birth mother so long. About how Garrett had been getting out of control, so angry and so hurt he lashed out at everything around him. It all comes flooding out of me. Ethan doesn't try to interrupt or offer advice. He just nods every now and then, watching me steadily through his long lashes.

"I feel like a different person than when I climbed up here," I finish. "I know that sounds lame. But so much has happened."

"It doesn't sound lame," he says. "You've been through a lot tonight." His eyes are focused on my face. I'm suddenly aware that I've just told him things I'm not even ready to tell my best friends—and I barely know him. The thought makes me a little nervous. But Ethan's such a good listener, and he never told anyone about the snuff film. I feel implicitly that I can trust him. When he puts his arm around my shoulder, I feel safe for the first time all night.

"Please don't tell anyone," I whisper. "I'm not really ready for people to know all this."

"Of course," he says. "I'll keep all your secrets, Sutton."

My face breaks into a smile. I feel so much lighter after unloading everything that's happened. Confiding in Ethan feels so natural, so comfortable—I wonder how we've been in school together since we were kids and yet barely ever talked. He's always been so quiet, almost standoffish. Then again, I probably haven't seemed like the friendliest person to him, either.

The more I think about it, the more I realize that it's not just school where I've seen Ethan. We've crossed paths countless times, at the coffee shop, at the movie theater. Sometimes he's hanging out alone at the park when I go to the tennis courts, sitting on a bench reading a paperback. We've orbited each other for years, and we've never connected. Not until tonight.

I smile up at him. "I never had a chance to tell you thanks. For, you know, helping me that night. When my friends were pranking me."

He shrugs. "You guys sure play rough with each other."

"Yeah." I give an embarrassed laugh. "That one got really out of control."

"Friends aren't supposed to hurt each other that way." His voice sounds strangely choked. I put my arm around his waist and hug him.

"You're right," I say softly. "You should be able to count on your friends."

The stars are vibrant overhead now. I tilt my head up to look at their bright light. One in particular catches my eye, pure white and so steady it doesn't flicker like the others do. It's so beautiful I don't notice Ethan's hand on my chin for a moment. Then he's leaning over me, his lips soft against mine.

A surprised jolt runs through me. Ethan Landry isn't a boy I've ever even imagined kissing. For a moment I'm so stunned I don't move. Then I put my hands on his chest and push him gently away.

"Oh, Ethan, no. I'm so sorry if I've done anything to mislead you, but I just—I like you as a friend." My voice is as soft as I can make it. "I'm in love with Thayer."

"Don't say that, Sutton," he murmurs. I stare up at him, and his eyes are filled with earnest tenderness. "I've been in love with you for years."

"In love with me?" I can't help it. I laugh. It sounds shrill and cruel even to me, and I instantly feel bad. "You don't even know me," I say, lowering my voice.

"Yes, I do. I know everything about you," he says. His voice is strangely calm and commanding, as if there's no room for argument. As if he could convince me to love him by reasoning with me. "I know you've been trying to sleep with Garrett Austin all summer. I know you've been sneaking around with Thayer Vega. Neither one of them deserves you, but you don't seem to get that. I know you're adopted and that you've always felt like your family couldn't possibly love you as much as they love Laurel. I know you're afraid Nisha's going to beat you out for the state title this fall, because you've barely practiced all summer. I know you need your friends to be afraid of you so they don't get too close to you— and so you won't have to feel hurt if they ever abandon you."

My mouth falls open. Somewhere at the back of my mind, an alarm goes off. This has to be some kind of joke. Some kind of prank. But he's not done.

"And I know something you don't know." A smile sneaks up the corners of his mouth, like he's been waiting a long time to tell me this. "I know where your twin sister is. Emma. I've been watching her for weeks. I found her for you, Sutton."

For a heartbeat, I feel like I'm paralyzed. Then the anger comes, a quick, savage spike. I didn't even know about Emma until a few hours ago. How the hell did he?

"Have you been out here spying on me?" My voice rings with a hard edge. I push away from him, taking a step back. "That's not cool, Ethan."

A shadow flits across his face. "Aren't you listening? I found

Emma. For you. Do you know how hard that was? I even went to Las Vegas to make sure I had the right girl. It was uncanny—you're totally identical."

"That's not the point!" My muscles tense. Something about this is all wrong. "Ethan, I don't know how you knew about Emma, but . . ."

"I told you." His voice is calm but insistent, like he's reasoning with a child. "I found her for you. Because I love you."

I feel sicker every time he says it. How long has he been following me? Listening to my conversations? He knows things about me I haven't even told my best friends. Things I haven't even told Thayer. And he's been planning to give me my sister, as a present—like she was some kind of thing. But maybe that's how he thinks about me, too. As a thing, to be fought over and won.

"Jesus, Ethan." I shake my head, disgust curling my lip. "I don't think you know what love is."

Then I'm turning away from him, determined to start back down the mountain, but his hand darts out to clamp around my wrist. He pulls me back toward him, leaning in to kiss me again. His mouth is almost sickeningly sweet. Panic shoots through me, and before I can think about it, I bite down on his lip—hard. He throws me to the ground, his hand flying to his mouth in pain.

"Are you insane?" I shriek. Then I see his eyes, with their long, dark lashes. Empty and implacable. And I realize: He is.

I scramble away from him, stumbling to my feet just as he lunges, and break into a sprint down the trail, trying to put distance between us. Cacti and brambles claw at my ankles. Behind me, I can sense Ethan more than hear him—his feet make almost no sound on the hard-packed earth, but I can feel him in my wake, his hands just inches from me. I think back to the headlights in the darkness, bearing down on me and Thayer—my car. I'm suddenly certain that it was Ethan behind the wheel.

But I'm faster than he is. I make a mental note to thank Coach Maggie for every sprinting drill she's ever made me do as I leap lightly over a small boulder. I'm going to get away from him—I'm going to head back to the visitor center, and the instant I have service I'm going to call 911 and have his creeper ass dragged off to jail. I'm going to go home to my family, to Thayer, and I'm going to put this whole god-awful night behind me forever.

My sneaker catches on something and curls under my foot, and my feet dance dangerously under me as I try to keep my balance. To my left the ravine opens hungrily. Before I can move he grabs me around the waist, pulling me off my feet. His breath is hot against my ear. "I don't understand why you're fighting this," he growls, his arms so tight I can't breathe. "You're supposed to love me! We're supposed to be together."

He spins me around to face him, his teeth bared in frustration. Below us, I can hear the wind howling through the chasm. Pebbles slide away from my feet, sounding like raindrops as they fall. I scream, my voice tearing through the night. A burst of anger shoots through me, burning hotter than my fear. He's a liar, a manipulator—and he's been stalking me.

"I'll never love you," I hiss, spitting in his face.

He gives a howl of anger, and twists my wrists so hard spasms of pain shoot up my arm. I writhe in his grip, and for a moment we're motionless, grappling silently for control.

Then my feet are sliding out from under me, my body slipping out of his grasp, and I am falling. The last thing I see is his pale, shocked face, his hand still outstretched toward me. Then the darkness swallows me, and the world is nothing but wind and stone.

I fall. Or rather, I tumble. My body careens off every outcropping of stone and every protruding branch. I flail around, grasping for any kind of handhold. For a minute my fingers close around a clump of exposed roots. Then the roots tear free from the earth, and gravity has me again.

When I land, my lungs claw inside my chest for what seems like ages before I can take a breath. The world is brilliant with agony, shimmering and surreal. When my eyes focus again, I can see a shard of bone protruding from my left leg.

From somewhere nearby I can hear something scrambling around. I try to pull myself up on my elbows, but everything goes white with the effort. Sweat and blood drip down into my face. And he's here now, standing over me. Ethan.

"Please help me," I croak. "My leg's broken. I can't walk."

Ethan kneels down next to me. For a minute his face is cloaked in shadows. He fumbles around next to me—I can't see what he's doing. Every time I try to move my head the world spins. But *then a cool white light illuminates the angles of his face. He's pulled my iPhone out from my purse—I can make out the polka dots on its Kate Spade cover.*

"There's no service down here," I say. Pain ripples out from my leg in sickening waves. "Please. You have to walk back to the parking lot and call 911."

He looks down at me, his face strangely blank in the electronic glow of the phone. It's almost like he doesn't recognize me. For some reason this scares me more than anything that happened at the top of the cliff. I start to cry, my body heaving in choked, painful sobs.

"I can't believe you made me do this," he says, his voice hollow with disappointment. "After everything I did for you. I didn't want this. I thought you were different, Sutton."

Then he's kneeling down over me, fumbling at my shirt collar. His fingers close around the locket at my throat, and he pulls so sharply the chain breaks.

"Give it back!" I scream, my breath ragged. "Give it back, you asshole!" But he's already moved away from me, into the shadows. The gentle twinkle of the stars has become pulsing and rhythmic. They throb in time with my heartbeat, flaring and then fading, flaring and fading.

Then he's back, looming over me. He's nothing but a dark shape blocking out the stars behind him. There's a jagged, pointed rock in his hands. He holds it high overhead.

"If I can't have you, no one can," he says.

I close my eyes, but I can still hear it whistling through the air as he brings it down over my head.

Before I can even scream out, the world explodes in light—the grand finale of a summer fireworks display—and then, just as quickly, my world goes suddenly, finally dark.

30

THE ENVELOPE, PLEASE

Emma stared down at the records in her hand. Written in black ink across the top form was the patient's name.

Ethan Landry.

For a moment she thought about stuffing the paperwork back in the envelope, back into the Tampax box under the sink. She'd had the chance to look at this once before, when she'd broken into the hospital about a month earlier. But she had chosen not to invade Ethan's privacy—and she still didn't want to.

Ethan had been honest with her about the whole thing. When she'd asked him about the files, he told her the story: how his dad had been beating his mom, and Ethan had intervened, hitting his father over the head with a beer bottle—only to have his mother call the police on him. She'd reported him as "violent" and had him admitted to the psychiatric ward. Emma's heart ached when she thought about it. In a way, Ethan had been abandoned by his family, just like she had.

But her eyes moved across Nisha's note again. *Sutton, I'm so sorry.* She'd been so certain that the evidence Nisha found was some kind of proof that Garrett killed Sutton. But it seemed obvious from her note that Nisha had no idea Sutton had died. What had she called and texted so frantically about, then? Why had Garrett come to kill her if she didn't have evidence against him? Emma's fingers clutched the folder sharply. She didn't understand any of this.

But I did.

"Get out of there!" I screamed, terror churning inside me. The whole world was upside down. My sister was alone in a house with my murderer—and she trusted him. She *loved* him. She didn't suspect a thing.

Emma bit her lip. Whatever Nisha had seen in Ethan's file had clearly freaked her out, even if it had nothing to do with Sutton's murder. She glanced back into the bedroom. On the other end of the house she could hear movement, drawers opening and closing as Ethan searched Dr. Banerjee's study. As quietly as she could, she shut and locked the bathroom door, and started to read.

REASON FOR TREATMENT: *Patient was referred to our facility for court-ordered psychiatric services upon his family's relocation to Tucson. This was a condition of Ethan's acquittal in the San Diego Family Court System.*

Emma's blood ran cold. She glanced at the date at the top of the records. They were almost eight years old—Ethan would have been ten. A child. What could he have possibly done at ten that required an acquittal?

In April, Ethan (age ten at the time) was seen playing with a neighborhood girl (age eight) in a culvert near their home in San Diego. A city worker who'd been assigned to clear a nearby drainage ditch testified that he witnessed Ethan strangling the girl, but by the time he was able to intervene, the girl had died.

When interviewed by police, Ethan claimed he had only been playing and that he had not intended to kill the girl. Due to his young age he was tried in family court, where he was acquitted of manslaughter. It was felt that Ethan displayed remorse for what he claimed was an accident, and that he hadn't properly understood his own strength when roughhousing with the victim.

Emma felt like something was clamped down around her lungs, cold and metallic and painful. This wasn't what Ethan had told her. For a moment she thought it had to be a mistake, or a joke. Maybe Nisha had been trying to get into the Lying Game and had mocked these up to mess with her. But somewhere at the back of her mind

Emma knew the records were real. The papers shook in her fingers. She turned the page quickly, her breath short and hard.

Over the course of our sessions, Ethan confided in me that he had considered the deceased to be his "best friend," but that she'd been playing with another child from the neighborhood just before her death. Again and again, he told me that "you weren't supposed to have more than one best friend." Ultimately, Ethan confessed to me that he'd killed Elizabeth Pascal on purpose, then lied to the authorities. Due to the double-jeopardy clause I am unable to make this observation to the court, as Ethan has already been acquitted.

Her mind reeling, Emma shook her head as if someone were reading the notes out loud to her. The shrink had to be wrong. She must have misunderstood what Ethan told him. The little girl's death had been an accident, a mistake, and Ethan had been carrying this guilt for his entire life. No wonder he hadn't wanted to tell Emma the truth. He must have been tormented by the memory. She kept reading, faster this time, looking for the words that would reflect *her* Ethan, the caring, thoughtful boy she had fallen in love with.

Ethan is incredibly gifted at playing to an audience. I have caught him in dozens of lies in the past six months, all engineered to manipulate my opinion of him. In our first sessions he seemed confused and saddened by what he had done; once he'd made sure

I could not do anything to indict him, however, he couldn't seem to resist telling me the details of what must now be called a murder. He has a need to show off and reveal the depths of his own cleverness, which in this case has led to his confession for a crime he can no longer be charged with. I am of the opinion that Ethan has antisocial personality disorder with obsessive tendencies, possibly bordering on psychopathy. It is likely that he will display violent behavior again.

She whipped through the pages of the report, looking for a note that said obviously this had been a huge mistake, that Ethan Landry couldn't have hurt a fly. She tried to find the word CURED rubber-stamped across a page in green ink. But the transcripts attached to the report didn't seem to challenge the doctor's opinion. *"If she wasn't going to be my friend, she didn't matter anymore. She deserved what she got,"* Ethan said in one session. In another, he boasted: *"The police officers in San Diego are stupid. They were really easy to trick. You're actually pretty stupid too, Dr. White, but that's okay. I like talking to you anyway."*

The taste of bile filled Emma's mouth. Even as her brain spun, making frantic excuses and explanations—this wasn't *her* Ethan, the shrink was wrong, the reports were fake—in some dark corner of her mind, thoughts were cascading into one another like falling dominoes.

Only Ethan had known she wasn't Sutton. None of Sutton's friends or family had figured it out. But Ethan, a boy Sutton barely knew, had confronted Emma that very first week in Tucson. *You're not who you say you are,* he'd told her. *You're not Sutton. You're someone else.* She remembered, with a cold, sick dread, that she'd immediately accused him of killing her sister—how else could he have known that Sutton was gone? He'd recoiled as though she'd slapped him, his face gray. *Sutton's dead?* he'd repeated, clearly shocked. And Emma—trusting, naive Emma—hadn't questioned him again. She'd simply broken down and told him the whole story, desperate for an ally.

Another domino fell. Ethan lived across the street from the canyon. Ethan had a telescope that was always angled in that direction. Ethan had been positioned perfectly to watch Sutton on her last night alive—and to watch Emma arrive and leave her duffel bag on a park bench.

Time froze as Emma quickly rewound through the last four months, replaying every moment, every conversation with Ethan. How he'd fed her information and encouraged her to pursue different suspects. How he'd tried to keep her away from Thayer, and then Garrett. How desperate he'd been to keep her from Nisha's house when she'd wanted to look for the evidence. How Ethan had arrived late to dinner at the Mercers' the night Nisha had died—how he hadn't been in school that day. And she knew he was an expert hacker.

Her heart froze over in her chest, hard and metallic, heavy with certainty. Ethan had killed Nisha. Ethan had killed her sister.

And now she was alone with him in a dark house.

Footsteps echoed in the kitchen, and she froze.

"Here, kitty, kitty," came Ethan's voice. It sounded strangely distorted, like it belonged to a stranger. Emma listened furtively, and then fumbled in her purse for the burner cell.

Her hands were shaking so hard she had to try a few times before she managed to dial the right number. When the line began to ring, she crammed her fist in her mouth to keep from letting out a sob.

"Hello?" Laurel's voice cut through the dense silence. Emma flinched, covering the speaker with one hand. Down the hall she heard something clatter onto the tile. "Hello? Who is this?"

"It's me," she hissed. She cupped her hand around her mouth, her knuckles white around the phone. "Emma."

"Emma?" Laurel's voice shot up an octave. "What's going on? Are you okay?"

"Laurel," Emma gasped, swallowing a frantic sob. "It's Ethan. He did it, there are these files at Nisha's house, and it sounds like he's killed before."

"Emma, wait, slow down," Laurel instructed.

But Emma couldn't stop, the words tumbling from her

mouth. "I don't know what to do. I'm alone in Nisha's house with him . . ."

Emma trailed off as footsteps echoed down the hall. Her jaw started to shake. She fumbled the phone, then jammed her finger against the power button and shoved it into the depths of her bag. The file was still in her hands. She glanced wildly around the room, looking for somewhere to put it. Just outside the door, a floorboard creaked.

Quickly, she shoved the file back under the sink, back behind the Tampax box. As she stood up again and opened the bathroom door, she came face-to-face with Ethan.

"Were you talking to someone in here?" he asked.

"Just . . . just myself. It helps me think," she said, clasping her fingers together behind her back so he couldn't see them shaking. All she could think about was the file, inches from them both. She forced herself not to look toward the sink. "Did you find anything?"

He shook his head. "Nothing. What about you?"

"No, nothing." She knew as soon as she'd said it that she'd answered too quickly. Her voice was shrill in her ears. He blinked, staring at her strangely. Then he exhaled loudly.

"Whatever Nisha had on Garrett, I guess she hid it really well." He glanced around the room. For a moment she could have sworn his gaze lingered on the cabinet. Then he looked back at her. "We just have to hope that the stuff in the storage unit is enough to put Garrett away."

She nodded silently. Her insides felt stripped raw. Ethan stood before her, the same Ethan he'd been ten minutes earlier. The same Ethan who told her he loved her, who covered her face in tender kisses. The same Ethan she'd given her virginity to. But he'd never been that Ethan, not really.

He slid his fingers through hers, as he'd done a thousand times before. But now the touch sent a howl of panic sweeping through her. That hand had killed her sister. She fought to control the tremor of fear running up and down her body. She couldn't let him sense it.

"Let's go," Ethan whispered. "There's nothing for us here."

"You're right," she said, and let him lead her down the hall.

Agassi crouched over his bowl, eating his kibble with a crunch that seemed loud in the silent kitchen. Ethan pushed the patio door open, then turned back to face her. For a moment her legs refused to budge. She stood frozen in the middle of the room, her eyes wide and staring, her heart hammering in her chest. For a split second she thought she saw Ethan's expression shift, an uncertain frown flickering over his face. She swallowed hard, then followed him out the door.

Her only hope was to play along like nothing had

changed and get to the police station. Once she was there, once she was safe, then she could start to think of a better plan. She forced a smile as they pushed back through the wrought-iron gate to where Ethan had parked his car. "I can't believe this is almost over," she whispered.

"Me neither." He ran his fingertips lightly up her arm. She shivered at the touch, her throat constricting in a wave of revulsion.

Ethan opened the passenger-side door of his Honda. Panic ripped through me as I realized my sister was going to get in with him. I wished I could grab her shirt and pull her back.

Emma seemed to have the same thought—she paused with one sneaker on the footboard. Fear clawed at her stomach, but there was something else churning there too, a softer, sadder emotion. Ethan stood next to her, waiting to close the door for her the way he always did. He gave her a curious look. She reached up to put her hand on his cheek.

"Thank you, Ethan," she said. And slowly, she stood up on her tiptoes and placed a single, soft kiss on his lips.

She didn't know whether she had kissed him to lull him into a false sense of security—or to say good-bye.

Ethan gave her a long, tender look, his hand touching her lips. Then he shut the door carefully behind her, walking around the car to get in on the driver's side. Emma clutched the sides of the seat as they pulled away from the house, her knuckles white and aching.

The scant houses they passed were draped in red and green lights, plastic reindeer perched on roofs or in Xeriscaped yards. One family had hung a giant neon candy cane over their four-car garage. The roads were winding out here, and she felt disoriented in the darkness. Emma's stomach pitched with every turn, her breath shallow and fast. She watched Ethan from the corner of her eye. He drove with both hands on the wheel, his face washed out by the pale blue dashboard light. It gave him a spooky, alien look. Not quite human.

It only slowly dawned on her that something was not quite right—they should have hit a main road by now. She stared out the window, trying to figure out where they were. When she saw the neon candy cane for a second time, she turned to look at him.

"I think you missed the turn," she said, her voice tight with anxiety.

Alarm bells started to go off at the back of my mind. I stared silently at Ethan. He didn't take his eyes off the road.

"I know you found the records, Emma." His voice was so low she almost thought she was imagining it for a minute. "You know as well as I do that we're not going to the cops." The car hummed into gear as he slowly pushed down on the gas pedal.

For a moment Emma's eyes went out of focus, the world blurring around her. She could feel the car accelerating. Ahead of the car she caught sight of Nisha's house, and Ethan's next to it—but they weren't slowing down. He was heading straight for the desert.

She didn't think. She groped along the car door, her fingers finally landing on the lock, and wrenched the door open before he could react. Bracing herself, tucking her head against her chin and rolling up into a ball, she jumped out of the moving car.

The impact knocked her teeth against one another, the vibrations resonating through her skull. Gravel and asphalt tore at her skin as she rolled toward the ditch. For a moment she couldn't breathe, her lungs flat in her chest. She heard the car's wheels screech to a halt, yards away. There was no time. She scrambled to her feet, gulping for air. Then she started to run, blindly, desperately.

Ethan had circled the block—she would have sensed it if she hadn't been so terrified. Now his house loomed in front of her. Next door the Banerjee house was dark and silent—but farther down the block there were lights in the windows. Strangers—but her only hope. She put on a burst of speed, screaming at the top of her lungs. "Help! Help!"

With a snarl of the engine, Ethan's car cut across her

path, between her and the houses she'd been running for. She stumbled, bouncing against the passenger-side door before catching her balance. The car idled in front of her, and she could just make out his face, tense and focused. He was inches away—if he wanted, he could jump out and grab her in a heartbeat.

She had no choice.

She bolted away from him—straight toward Sabino Canyon, with Ethan on her heels.

Just as I had the night he killed me.

31

ENDGAME

Emma ran blindly, hurtling into the depths of the canyon. Branches clawed at her ankles and whipped across her face. Ethan's car door slammed somewhere behind her, but she didn't turn to look. Adrenaline soared through her blood, and she flew into the trees beyond the parking lot. A crow screamed from the top of a boulder, warning the forest of her coming.

The trail was steep, and her sneakers knocked dirt loose as she climbed. Behind her she could hear Ethan scrambling for purchase, gaining on her. She whimpered, desperation coursing through her. It was like a nightmare—except in a nightmare, you could wake up.

The deeper she got into the canyon, the stronger I could feel its hold on me—the awful, magnetic pull that drew me there. Out here the world seemed sharper and more terrifying. But out here I also felt stronger, the senses that I shared with Emma somehow clearer. This was where my body had been broken. And now my sister was running toward the same fate. "Emma, you have to go back!" I screamed. "You have to get out of here!"

Tucson opened out below as she reached the overlook. Far away she could hear the rush of traffic, the thud of someone's car stereo. She risked a glance behind her and saw Ethan's form steadily following her. A strangled sob twisted her lungs, and she bolted again, trying to pick up speed.

Her foot caught on a half-buried root on the trail. For a moment she kept her balance, her legs dancing beneath her. But then Ethan was on top of her, tackling her to the ground. Her head bounced against a rock, and her eyes filled with stars.

When her vision cleared, she was gazing up at Ethan. He knelt over her, his eyes burning, his lips drawn back in a tight grimace. Then she felt metal against her neck, and looked down to see the edge of a knife in his hand.

The world tilted around me, and for a moment I

couldn't tell where my memory ended and Emma's present began. They were one and the same. And now she was going to die . . . just the way I had.

"Why are you doing this?" she whispered. His hand dug into her shoulder where he pressed her down in the dirt. She wondered if this was how it happened with Sutton, if he'd chased her, pinned her, and thrown her off the cliff. A sob shuddered through her throat.

Ethan frowned and gritted his teeth. "I did everything, *everything*, for you. God, Emma!" The muscles in his neck tightened as he spat the words out. "I warned you so many times to stop digging. And you wouldn't. It's like some kind of sick compulsion with you, isn't it? Why couldn't you just be happy with the life I gave you? Why did you have to ruin everything?"

Emma stared pleadingly up at him. At the back of her mind she wondered fleetingly if Laurel was looking for her even now—but Laurel thought she was at the Banerjees'. No one was coming to help her.

"Why did you kill my sister?" she asked, desperate to keep him talking, to buy any time she could. "Was it because of the science fair prank?" The Lying Game girls had done something to Ethan in eighth grade that had cost him a scholarship. Was killing Sutton some kind of long-delayed revenge?

Ethan's derisive snort echoed around the canyon.

Nearby some small animal scrabbled away through the brush.

"That? That was years ago. That doesn't matter to me anymore."

"What, then?"

For a second his expression shifted. His eyes softened, and he looked sad, regretful even. He shook his head. "I didn't mean for it to happen," he said softly.

"Liar!" I shrieked, an electric rage spiking through me. Emma's body tensed beneath his, and she closed her eyes, as if trying to hear something far away. I'd been able to communicate with her once before, the night that she met Becky out here. Could I do it again?

Slowly, Ethan pulled the blade away from her throat and sat back, though he kept the knife at his side. Emma could see it clearly now—a leather-handled hunting knife with a long, tapered blade, the moon catching on the polished steel. She tried not to stare at it.

"I loved her," he said shortly, his lips curling with bitterness. "I came out here to tell her that. I thought I could make her see that we were meant to be together."

A fresh wave of anguish crashed over Emma. Confusion and betrayal whirled through her head. He'd loved *Sutton*? Was that all he'd ever seen in Emma? Had he only wanted her as a substitute for the sister he couldn't have?

Ethan stared down at Emma, but something in his

eyes was far away and vague. For a moment she thought about taking her chance, trying to wrench free of him and run, but the sight of the knife kept her still. "I'd been in love with her for years, even though she treated me like garbage. I knew she wasn't ready yet, that I had to be patient. Then I came out here that night, after everyone else had left her. After everyone had hurt her and lied to her and abandoned her." His fingers curled into her shoulder as he spoke, digging painfully into her skin. "I thought for sure she'd see that I was the only one who'd been there for her all along. But all she wanted was Thayer Vega."

I thought about the shapeless form behind the wheel of my car, bearing down on Thayer. I heard the sound of bone cracking once again.

"So you ran him over?" Emma whispered.

Ethan's eyes flashed. "I wish I'd killed him. I've always hated that guy. I hated him when Sutton liked him, and I hated him when you did. He didn't deserve to be in her life. I had to show her that."

Tears ran down Emma's face, leaving hot salty trails on her skin. "So you and me—it was always about Sutton. It's just because I look like her."

"Emma, no!" he breathed, his eyes suddenly soft. "You have to believe me." He seemed lost for words for a moment, his shoulders knotted in agitation. Then he took a deep breath. The pressure of his hand on her shoulder disappeared. Slowly he helped her sit up, crouching by her side, but the knife still gleamed dangerously in his hand.

Emma's eyes darted frantically around. The light filtered down through the trees, making filigree patterns over the clearing. Beyond the brush the lights of the city glittered. A boulder jutted into the middle of the trail, and beyond it the path looked steeper than ever. There was no escape. Her only hope was to keep him talking.

A jolt of recognition ran through me. I knew that boulder. This was where Garrett and I had argued. The clearing showed signs of recent disturbance—the cops who had canvassed the area for clues to my death had left footprints and broken branches in their wake—but there was no sign that anyone was nearby at this hour. A few more yards up the path, the tree line broke to reveal the ravine, opening up beyond.

Ethan took her hand in his free one, a shattered look on his face. "I never meant to fall in love with you," he whispered. "I didn't know there was someone out there who could make me feel this way."

He looked so earnest, so hurt, that despite everything, a reluctant pang shot through her heart. Part of her wanted so badly to believe him—wanted to forget everything she'd just learned and go back to ignorantly, stupidly loving Ethan. If there was a way to undo what she'd learned, Emma might have done it. Because she had loved him, more than she'd ever loved anyone. And that was the most painful part.

But then she thought of everything he had done to her over the past three months. The light crashing next to her, the threatening notes, the locket tight around her neck as he strangled her. He'd made sure she felt scared and alone, that she had no one to turn to except him. He'd forced her to stay quiet, to lose her own identity, and to alienate the only family she had in this world. That wasn't what you did to someone you loved.

She looked down at his hand in hers, her skin crawling with aversion. But she didn't dare pull away. A vague glimmer of hope sparked at the back of her mind. Maybe if she seemed understanding—even loving—then he wouldn't kill her. At least not yet.

"So, all those pictures of me we found in the storage unit—you took those?" she asked.

He nodded. "At first I was trying to find your mom. I knew Sutton was adopted. I still remember when she had to read her family tree report in ninth grade, how upset she got." His gaze went distant again as he stared off into his memories. "She was so beautiful that day—she was one of those girls who looked even prettier when she cried."

Emma suppressed a shudder. "So you started looking for her birth mom."

"Yeah. I started investigating the Mercers and almost right away realized Becky must have been their daughter. I hacked the hospital records—and that was when I realized there were two of you."

"Hospital records are really hard to get," Emma said. She tried to sound impressed, maybe even a little admiring, but inside was nothing but cold, metallic terror.

He warmed to her tone easily, though—as if he fed on her approval. His eyes brightened as he spoke.

"It was pretty easy from there. I found all your information online. I made a few trips to Vegas to check you out, make sure I had the right girl. I even rode the roller coaster one day. I walked right up to you and bought a ticket."

Emma stared at him, trying to conjure up an image of him at her kiosk. It seemed impossible that she wouldn't have noticed him—for months now she'd been staring at him every day, preoccupied by how cute he was, obsessed with the curve of his lips, the curls in his hair. But then, all that time, she hadn't seen him for what he really was—a murderer.

"As soon as I realized how crazy Becky was, I knew she wasn't going to be the romantic present I'd hoped her to be." He chuckled, then glanced at her and sobered.

"But you? You were *perfect*. I couldn't wait to tell Sutton all about you. You were the proof of how much I loved her—more than Thayer or Garrett or anyone else. None of them could give her a *sister*." He sighed. "She would've been so excited to know I could lead her to you, if she'd just listened to me. But things didn't go right, and I had to use you a different way."

Emma swallowed. "What about those e-mails on Travis's phone?"

He gave a crooked grin, unable to hide his satisfaction. "Fake. I had that file doctored up for weeks and was just waiting for a chance to use it. I did send him the link, but I didn't have to promise him anything. Guys like that are so predictable. I knew he'd show it to you."

She nodded. A heavy feeling of resignation settled on her—one by one, all the pieces of the puzzle were coming together with implacable finality. Even as her heart thrashed in her chest like a frightened bird, a sickly, dull weight pressed down on her. Ethan had thought of everything. All along, he'd had the reins. "And you knew about the video because you'd walked in on the prank happening. You knew it had to be on Laurel's computer, and you hacked it. Just like you hacked Charlotte's alarm codes to break in and give me back the locket." She licked her dry lips. Her hand felt like wood in his, but she squeezed it softly, her eyes still on the knife shining in the moon. "That's pretty brilliant, Ethan."

She knew right away she'd said the right thing. He blinked in surprise, a flush of pleasure tinting his cheeks, and she remembered what the psychiatrist had written, about how Ethan couldn't keep from bragging about his crimes. "And what about Nisha?"

Again his expression fluttered, like he was fighting some feeling that lingered at the back of his mind. "I didn't have a choice. I knew she'd found those records. After you told me you'd seen them in the hospital, I had a feeling she'd go looking for them. That Monday she was acting weird when she got in from her volunteer shift— usually she at least said hi when she saw me out on the porch, but this time she wouldn't even look at me. Just scurried into the house with her manila folder clutched in her hands. I called the hospital to ask if they could fax my records to a new shrink, and they told me then the records had gone missing." He shrugged sadly. "She was going to ruin everything. So I spiked her water bottle with my mom's Valium. Then it was just a matter of giving her a little push."

A little push. I shuddered, imagining Nisha rolling slowly into the pool. Imagined her lungs filling with water. Imagined her opening her eyes and staring through the rippling blue at the figure standing overhead, watching her die.

"You two were going to ruin everything," he said. His eyes narrowed, and he stared at Emma like she'd just said something wrong. She flinched at the sudden mood swing. "I had everything taken care of, but you had to keep digging." He raised the knife high overhead, his teeth bared like a lion's. Emma cringed, waiting to feel the blade on her flesh. But instead he drove it into the ground, giving a frustrated grunt. "You had *nothing* when you came here. I saw what was in your bag. One stuffed animal and some threadbare clothes? Oh, and the journal. Page after page after page of how sad you were, how much you wanted a family, how poor Emma Paxton was so *alone*. How you wanted a boyfriend." Emma stared at him. Her heart shriveled in her chest, as if some disease were ravaging it to ash. Ethan's eyes blazed. "I gave you everything you ever wanted. You should be *thanking* me!"

Emma kept her face very carefully still, holding back the tears and the pain that threatened to burst through at any moment. "You can't kill me," she whispered. "If you do they'll know I didn't kill Sutton. They'll figure it out, and they'll come find you. You need me. I'm your cover."

He shook his head. "Don't you get it? I don't *want* to kill you. I *never* wanted to kill you. I just wanted to take care of you, Emma, and now you're going to make me hurt you. Just like she did." His fingers slid out of hers, tightening instead around her wrist. "It'll be a really sad story. They'll all think you committed suicide out of remorse for what you did to Sutton."

A chill shot through her, and she shook her head furiously. "No, Ethan. It doesn't have to be like this." She looked deeply into his eyes, sickened by what she was saying, hoping he'd buy it. "You're right. I should be grateful to you. I *am* grateful to you. It's all just been confusing. But I don't care what you've done. I want to be with you."

His jaw went slack, all the fury rushing out of him at once. An uncertain frown creased his brow. But she could see that he was listening.

"It's too late, Emma." Her wrist ached dully in his grip, but she didn't break his gaze. "Now that you know, it's too late."

"Why?" Emma said softly. "If you really love me as me, not as Sutton, then nothing else matters. We can run away together. Somewhere no one knows us. We can go anywhere." She twisted her hand in his grip so she could stroke his fingers lightly.

She could see in his face, in the way he leaned just a little bit closer, that he wanted to believe her. But doubt clouded his features. It almost broke her heart, how hopeful he looked, how badly he wanted what she proposed.

Almost.

"You'd do that?" he asked. He let go of the hilt of the

knife, bringing his free hand up to hold her face. His hand was cool and dry, but the touch of it made her skin crawl. Somehow she managed to smile and nod.

"Ethan, I love you. I'd go anywhere with you."

He let go of her wrist then, pulling her into his arms. She rested her head against him, just the way she'd done dozens of times before—right into the crook between his neck and shoulder, in the place that felt like it'd been made for her. She choked back a sob. She *had* loved Ethan, so very much.

Then she brought her elbow into his ribs with every ounce of strength she had.

His arms flew to his side, a grunt of pain escaping his lungs. She grabbed for the knife as she scrambled away, but her fingers closed on air. No time. Her only chance was to put distance between them. Her fingers clawed at the dirt, her feet sliding across the trail, desperate for purchase. His hand closed on her ankle, and he snarled in fury. She kicked out as hard as she could, but his grip was too strong. Then she opened her mouth and let out a guttural, blood-curdling scream.

I screamed with her, wishing the whole city could hear my cries. I had already died at Ethan's hands, and now the same thing was going to happen to my twin while I watched, helpless.

Ethan clapped his hand over Emma's mouth, his

pupils wide and dark. "I thought you were different," he hissed. "But you're just like your sister. Another lying bitch."

Emma bit down on his hand, hard. The metallic taste of blood flooded her mouth. Ethan swore and pulled his hand away, and she screamed again.

"You're a monster!" she shrieked, her voice ricocheting off the canyon walls. "You think I'd go anywhere with you after what you did to Sutton?"

He gave a wordless roar, his muscles tightening as he shoved her hard to the ground. This time he pulled a bandana out of his pocket, wadding it up and shoving it so far in her mouth she gagged. And then the knife was suddenly at her throat.

Emma stared up at him, tears coursing down her cheeks as he opened a thin, shallow cut on her neck. A white-hot fury coursed through me at the sight, so pure and strong I felt like I could rip straight through the veil between life and death.

And then, somehow, I *was* Emma. Or I was a part of her—not possessing her, exactly, but somehow joining my soul to hers for a moment, lending her the strength of my anger. With a sudden motion, her right leg broke free from below his, and we brought her knee to his groin with all of our combined might.

He groaned, his grip on her wrists slackening for just as

long as it took her to roll out from under him. Then she was on her feet. She gasped for breath, and for one split second she thought she saw something impossible.

Her sister—shimmering and translucent in the moonlight—was next to her, standing fiercely over Ethan with her fists balled up. And then, just as quickly, she was gone.

Ethan was already on his feet again. His face was twisted beyond all recognition, a mask of hatred so utterly different from the boy she'd fallen in love with. She staggered away from him, pivoting on her heel to run—but lost her balance and sprawled forward.

Ethan towered over her, the knife in his hand. A single drop of her own blood clung to the blade. "You Mercer girls are all the same," he said and lunged toward her, the knife flashing before him.

For a split second, time froze. Emma saw her own reflection, pale and frozen, in the blade.

But then a low snarl sounded from somewhere behind Ethan, and suddenly he was flying headfirst into the dirt. Thayer fell on top of him, clinching his arms behind his back.

From far below, the sound of sirens echoed up through the mountain pass. Thayer twisted Ethan's wrist until the knife fell out and clattered into the dust. Ethan struggled, spitting blood and dirt out of his mouth.

Laurel stepped out from behind them, her arms crossed over her chest. "You're right. We Mercer girls are all alike," she said, her voice cold. "We're bitches you don't want to mess with."

32

BACK IN THE STATION

"Please, tell me again what happened after you hung up with Miss Paxton." Detective Quinlan handed Laurel, Emma, and Thayer each a cup of hot chocolate, his eyes bright over the deep lines of exhaustion carved underneath. It was after midnight, but the arresting officer had called Quinlan at home. He'd arrived at the station still buttoning his shirt, his hair disheveled but his expression alert and edgy.

"I called Thayer," Laurel said. Her cheeks were flushed from the cold. She darted a furtive glance at Emma, then turned back to Quinlan. "He picked me up, and we went to Dr. Banerjee's house, though I didn't see Ethan's car anywhere. We looked in all the windows and couldn't see anyone inside."

The three of them were sitting on a vinyl couch in a room that was clearly meant for children. Cartoon tigers and monkeys grinned from the jungle-themed wallpaper. A dairy crate of broken toys sat on the floor next to a rug decorated with a hopscotch pattern. Emma stared blankly at a wooden labyrinth game atop of a stack of *Highlights* magazines. Her eyes traced the lines of the puzzle, her thoughts as lost and wandering as if she were in a real maze.

So far, Quinlan had let Laurel and Thayer do most of the talking, and she was grateful. She tried to take a sip of the hot chocolate, but her hand was shaking, so she carefully set it down. Her body ached to the bone. Images shot randomly through her mind, unbidden and startling. The glint of the knife in Ethan's hand. Sutton's decomposed body, her empty eye sockets staring out at the sky. Ethan's face leaning toward her for a kiss, his eyes heavy-lidded. Ethan's fingers laced through her own. She shuddered at each one. Everything she'd known, everything she'd believed had been a lie—and now there was nothing left for her to hold on to.

"How did you know they'd gone to the canyon?" Quinlan asked, rubbing the stubble on his jaw.

Laurel stared down into her hot chocolate. "It was a

hunch. We thought he might take her back to the same place he'd killed Sutton. We knew we were right when we saw his car near the entrance. So we called the cops and followed them."

Quinlan's mustache twitched. "After the 911 operator told you not to give chase."

"We weren't just going to sit there and do nothing," Thayer broke in angrily. "We didn't know how long it would take the cops to get there."

"And it's a good thing we did follow," Laurel added sharply. "He was about to kill her."

Emma looked up at the detective then. His normally hard gray eyes had softened, and they came to rest on her. She swallowed. "They're right. Ethan would have killed me if they weren't there to stop him." The EMTs had bandaged the cut he'd made at her throat—it had scarcely scratched the surface, but now it seemed to throb with her heartbeat.

She reached for her cup again and took another sip of the hot chocolate. It was the cheap, just-add-water kind, but it was soothing and sweet. The knots in her stomach loosened a little from its warmth. Thayer and Laurel sat protectively on either side of her. Laurel's leg was touching Emma's, and Thayer's hand rested between her shoulders, warm and gentle. She didn't feel safe, exactly—she wasn't sure she'd ever feel safe again. But they had rescued her and hadn't left her side since. Through the swirling, heart-breaking confusion of shock and grief, a sense of gratitude filled her. She'd lost so much. But she hadn't lost them.

I focused on Thayer. He was pale and tired, the vulnerable expression in his eyes contrasting with the fierce set of his jaw. That was what I had always loved about him—how strong he was, and how deeply he felt.

Quinlan clasped his hands around one knee, jogging his loafer up and down. "I owe you an apology, Miss Paxton. You and Sutton both." He sighed, opening a bristling file folder. "We've actually been interested in Ethan for a little while now. I've been going over the parking-lot surveillance photos from the last few months, and he shows up in dozens of them. He's out there all the time. It seemed like . . ."

"Too much of a coincidence," Emma said miserably. He nodded.

"Detectives don't believe in coincidences," he said. "So we started to look into him. At first I thought he was your accomplice. That you guys had hatched this plan together, maybe, or that he'd fallen for you and you'd roped him into it. But this morning we found out he had a sealed record. We put in a subpoena to open it, but it didn't get finalized until tonight, after we'd already taken him into custody."

Laurel stuck her chin up haughtily. "Then it's a good

thing Thayer and I were there, since you were taking your sweet time."

Quinlan rolled his eyes. "Please don't turn your little gang into a pack of vigilantes, Miss Mercer. That's the last thing I need." He turned back to Emma. "Of course, the investigation is ongoing. But between what happened tonight, and what I've seen of his medical records, we have probable cause to hold him. I've got a CSI team on their way to his house now, and another one at the storage facility. Ethan's a smart kid—I'm guessing he'll have done a good job hiding the evidence. But if it's there, we'll find it. We always do."

Emma nodded, feeling as if she were miles away from the interrogation chamber, miles away from Quinlan and Laurel and Thayer. She felt hollow to the core. Ethan had been lying to her all along. She'd loved him, and the whole time, he'd just lied and lied.

But it was over. Ethan had been caught, and it was only a matter of time before the cops found all the evidence they needed to charge him. So I couldn't help wondering— why was I still here? I hadn't been sure what to expect, but I'd always pictured *something* happening right about now. Pearly gates, or a long tunnel with a bright light at the end, or a cosmic escalator leading to some heavenly mall where my halo would double as a platinum card. But I was still here, still my sister's silent shadow. Would I be here forever, haunting her until she died and joined me in the afterlife?

The door flew open, and Mrs. Mercer rushed in, followed by her husband. They'd obviously dressed in a hurry—Mr. Mercer still had on the ratty UC Davis T-shirt he often wore to bed, and Mrs. Mercer had pulled on sweatpants and a wine-stained blouse that looked like it'd been at the top of a laundry hamper. Thayer and Laurel both stood to meet them. Emma's grandmother embraced Laurel tightly, her lips an anxious line in her face. Mr. Mercer, meanwhile, grabbed Thayer in a bear hug. Thayer looked embarrassed, but he patted Mr. Mercer on the back and smiled weakly.

Emma watched them from the sofa, her heart aching. For the first time, she thought she fully understood how they'd felt after finding out who she really was. She had done to them exactly what Ethan had done to her—she'd pretended to be someone she wasn't. She couldn't blame them for wanting her out of their lives.

But then Mr. Mercer let go of Thayer, his eyes shining as he sat beside Emma, and pulled her into an embrace.

For just a moment she went stiff in his arms. Then her body started to tremble, and she put her arms around his neck. Tears prickled her eyes. "I'm so sorry for everything," she murmured, her voice muffled against his shoulder.

"I know," he whispered, rocking her back and forth. "It's going to be okay."

Emma didn't know if anything would ever be okay again. Having Mr. Mercer's shoulder to cry on was a comfort she didn't deserve, yet she couldn't bring herself to pull away.

That was the thing about family. They were a comfort *none* of us deserved. I thought about the last angry words I'd said to my father, and the constant bickering with my mom while I was still alive. But they loved me anyway, no matter what I'd done.

Finally Mrs. Mercer settled on the couch next to Emma, her hands twisting around each other nervously. She gave Emma a lingering, uncertain look, then took her hand. Her blue eyes were serious and piercing.

"It's not fair that you've been facing all of this alone," she said softly. "I'm still struggling to understand it all . . . but I know you must have been terrified this whole time."

Emma nodded, tears prickling her eyes again. "I wanted to tell you so badly."

Mrs. Mercer squeezed her hand. "There's a lot we'll have to get used to. Do you think you can give us time to work through all these feelings?"

Emma frowned up at her. "Time?"

"We lost two daughters," Mr. Mercer said, his voice breaking. "We don't want to lose another."

"We'd like it if you'd come stay with us. At least for the time being," Mrs. Mercer said. "I know you're eighteen, and maybe after all this you're ready to move on. But we'd like a chance to get to know you, Emma. As yourself."

Emma opened her mouth to reply, but words refused to form. She glanced at Mr. Mercer, and he nodded encouragingly. Quinlan sat quietly in an armchair, as poker-faced as ever, but she thought she could see a twinge of sympathy in the corner of his mouth.

"Of course she's coming to stay with us," Laurel said briskly. "I didn't just save her ass in the middle of the woods so she could run off again." She looked steadily at Emma.

Emma stared around the room at her family, all of them waiting for her answer. They may not have forgiven her yet—but they wanted to try. And if they could do it, maybe she could forgive herself.

"I'd like that," she said, smiling through her tears.

I sat in their midst, surrounded by my family again. And I could feel their love for me, even across the divide between the living and the dead.

33

HOME

"There's been yet another twist in the sensational case of the Tucson Twin Murderer," Tricia Melendez's voice reported from Sutton's laptop. "On Wednesday night, eighteen-year-old Ethan Landry was arrested for kidnapping, assault, and attempted murder. The victim? Emma Paxton, Sutton Mercer's twin sister, and, until Wednesday, the chief suspect in Sutton's murder."

Emma lay curled on Sutton's bed Saturday morning, staring dully at the screen. She'd propped the computer on Sutton's nightstand, where she could see it from the nest of pillows. She'd been watching since she'd woken up, clicking through different blogs and news agencies to hear twenty different versions of the same event—the fact that Emma Paxton had been cleared of all charges, and that Ethan Landry had allegedly killed Nisha Banerjee and Sutton Mercer.

In just a few minutes she'd have to move. She'd have to get up, even though her body felt like it was made of lead, and go downstairs to join the Mercers. That afternoon, Sutton would finally be buried—and finally be at peace.

Would I? I'd been imagining my funeral for months, but now that it was here, I wasn't so sure. Would this last good-bye from my friends and family finally lay me to rest? Or would I linger in Emma's shadow for the rest of her life, voiceless and powerless and utterly alone?

"Police are now saying that Landry lured Paxton to Tucson under the pretense that she'd meet her long-lost twin." Tricia Melendez couldn't keep a note of glee out of her voice. She stood in front of the police station, wearing a tweed Armani jacket that was a step up from her usual polyester—it looked like she'd gotten a pay raise. "When she arrived, he sent her notes and threatening messages to force her to impersonate her sister so he could cover up his crime. The investigation is still ongoing, but one source told Channel Five that a storage unit on the outskirts of Tucson was raided on Wednesday night, and while it'd been registered under a false name, the attendant was able to ID Landry as the person who opened the account. No word yet on what the unit contained, but at this time it seems safe to assume police found some damning evidence inside."

Emma smiled slightly, wondering what Tricia Melendez would say if she had opened the unit to find a threadbare stuffed animal waiting patiently inside. Socktopus was still being held as "evidence," but she wished she had him here. She knew it was childish, but she wanted to tie him around her neck for protection, the way Becky had so long ago. A part of her still felt like she needed all the protection she could get. Maybe a part of her always would.

Ethan. A dark, fathomless chasm opened in her chest every time she thought of him—his earnest, lake-blue eyes; his laughter; his lips on hers. Every time a fragment of their conversation came floating through her mind, their flirtations and their promises, a cold, empty space opened inside her where something had been torn away— something pure and trusting and fragile. She didn't know if she would ever trust anyone again.

"Yesterday, I spoke with Beverly Landry, the mother of the accused, as she left the courthouse," Tricia Melendez continued. Emma bolted up on the bed, staring at the screen. Mrs. Landry stood uncertainly on the steps of the courthouse, her mousy hair tied in a lopsided bun.

In the bright light of day, she seemed more scared than hostile, her eyes wide and vulnerable in a thin, sunken face. "I saw him cross the yard to the Banerjee girl's house at around three in the afternoon the day she died," Mrs. Landry said, leaning nervously toward the microphone. "And a few weeks ago I found a green duffel bag shoved in a back corner in the attic. It had a journal and some girls' clothes in it. I tried to tell myself he'd just stolen it. But . . . but it scared me. I was afraid to ask what else he'd done."

Emma felt an unwilling lurch of sympathy for the woman. No wonder Mrs. Landry had been so uncomfortable with Emma. She'd known all along who Emma was, what her son was capable of—and she either didn't want to believe it or was too scared to intervene.

The camera cut back to the reporter. "The Tucson District Attorney's office plans to charge Landry with two counts of murder and one count of attempted murder, along with fraud, conspiracy, blackmail, kidnapping, and assault," she said. "The request for bail has been denied. This is Tricia Melendez, signing off."

Emma walked to Sutton's desk and snapped the laptop shut. The day before, she'd met with the Tucson District Attorney, a stout, brisk woman in a red power suit. She'd agreed to testify in court and to provide any evidence she could in the case. They'd offered her immunity from prosecution—the D.A. told her they could have charged her with fraud and identity theft if they wanted to—but that wasn't why she'd agreed to testify. She'd sworn to bring her sister's killer to justice, and she planned to follow through to the end. The idea of being in a room with Ethan again, even separated by the witness box and a dozen burly bailiffs, made the hollow place inside her feel even more raw. But the trial was months away. She had time to steel herself, to try to heal, before then.

According to the D.A., Ethan's laptop showed hacks into Sutton's and Emma's personal information—their phones, their computers, their medical files. There were also copies of all the photos he'd taken of Emma on his Las Vegas trip, and dozens upon dozens of Sutton. He'd encrypted everything, but the forensics lab had some guy who was more or less a savant, and he'd managed to retrieve it all.

She lay back in the nest of pillows, suddenly exhausted again. It had been so easy for Ethan to fool her, to make her love him. He'd been her perfect boyfriend, funny and sensitive and thoughtful. Had the entire thing been an act to keep her in Tucson? Was there any small part of it that had been real? And did she even want it to be? She wasn't sure what was worse: getting played by a monster—or being in love with a killer.

A soft tap came at her door. Emma gave a little start

and glanced at the bean-shaped clock over Sutton's window. It was just after one—soon they would have to leave. "Come in."

Mrs. Mercer opened the door a crack and peeked in. Her smile was almost shy, but her blue eyes were warm. "How are you doing?"

"I'm almost ready," Emma said. They stood in awkward silence for a moment, Mrs. Mercer's face framed by the barely opened door.

"Can I come in?" she finally asked. Emma blinked. She hadn't realized her grandmother was waiting for an invitation.

"Of course! Sorry, I . . . of course. Come in."

Mrs. Mercer opened the door and entered the room, sitting carefully on the bed. She was wearing a neat black suit, and her bobbed hair had been combed sleekly back. If not for the creases at the corners of her eyes, she could have been Becky's older sister. She crossed her ankles and looked around the room, the ghost of a smile playing around her lips.

"It feels so strange in here. It's like she's just around the corner—in the bathroom, or in her closet. And then you're here, looking just like her."

Emma wasn't sure what to say. In the past few days, she and the Mercers had been tentative and polite with one another, like they were approaching each other slowly from a great distance. Emma knew that they needed space to grieve for Sutton, and she'd tried not to intrude. But at the same time they seemed to want to get to know her. Yesterday Mrs. Mercer had asked what her favorite meal was, and that evening at dinner a chicken pot pie had sat steaming in the middle of the table, along with a leafy side salad and a carafe of sweet tea. Mr. Mercer had invited her to go on a walk with him and Drake, and as they'd walked he'd asked questions about her life before Tucson. They all seemed to be gently avoiding the topic of Sutton or Ethan—Emma assumed their grief and anger were still too fresh—but their overtures were sincere, and it was a start.

The one holdout was Grandma Mercer, who'd flown in the night before for the funeral. When she'd come in, she'd stared at Emma for a long time, her eyes red and glassy, before heading up the stairs to the guest room with cold dignity. "She was fond of Sutton," Mr. Mercer whis pered to Emma. "This is all a shock to her. But she'll come around." So far, though, Grandma Mercer hadn't shown any signs of "coming around." She referred to Emma only as "that girl" and had made a point of sitting as far from her as possible at dinner. Emma tried not to take it to heart, but it was hard.

"I know this is difficult for you, too," Mrs. Mercer said now, meeting Emma's eyes. "You have no idea how much

I wish we'd known about you before all this happened. We would have come for you a long time ago." She smiled sadly. "But there's no sense in wishing for what can't be changed."

"I wish I could have met her," Emma blurted out. She hugged herself, clutching at the gray wool cardigan she'd put on for the funeral. When she looked up, Mrs. Mercer was wiping away a single tear.

"I know." She patted the bed next to her, and Emma sat down. Her grandmother took her hand and squeezed it. "And I hope you know this was no one's fault but Ethan's."

Emma didn't answer. Her own lies had almost allowed him to get away with murder. If only she'd tried harder that first day, insisted to the police that they check her records. If only she hadn't been so afraid.

Mrs. Mercer shook her head, seeming to read her thoughts. "We don't blame you, Emma. How many of us have made mistakes in our lives? If Ted and I had been able to support Becky better, maybe she wouldn't have kept you a secret. If Becky hadn't made such a mess of her own life, maybe she could have cared for you both, or she could have had the sense to give you both to us. If you hadn't been a secret from everyone, Ethan never could have used you the way that he did. Of course it hurts that you felt like you had to lie to us. But you were carrying a terrible, painful burden, all by yourself. I don't know that any of us would have done differently than you did." Mrs. Mercer's lip trembled for a moment. "We've all made mistakes. But it was Ethan who chose to take my daughter's life. No one else."

Emma swallowed hard. She wanted to believe Mrs. Mercer. She wanted to forgive herself. Maybe, with time, she'd be able to.

I laid my hand over Emma's. "I forgive you," I whispered, wishing I could absolve her of her guilt.

Mrs. Mercer cleared her throat again. "Ted and I have been discussing things, and we'd like you to stay here— if that's what you want, of course." Her lashes fluttered. "You can finish up high school at Hollier. We'll meet with Principal Ambrose so you can adjust your schedule to be your own. And we'll help you look at colleges. Your grades from Las Vegas are very impressive."

Emma turned pink. She suddenly realized that this was the first compliment Mrs. Mercer had given her as herself, as Emma. Somewhere in the hollow ache of her chest, a tiny ember glowed to life.

Mrs. Mercer went on. "Sutton had a college fund. I think she'd understand if we used it for you."

Of course I understood. After all that had happened, after everything Emma had done for me, she deserved this.

Emma glanced up to meet her grandmother's eyes,

so like her own. "Thank you," she whispered, her voice breaking. "I just—I never knew, before coming here, what it was like. To have a family."

Mrs. Mercer hugged her tightly. Emma could smell her Elizabeth Arden perfume and a faint whiff of Earl Grey tea.

After they pulled apart, they sat for a moment in silence. Emma glanced around the familiar bedroom. Half-melted candles sat in glass jars on the white wood desk, wine bottles full of dried flowers lining the windowsill. Sutton's pillows crowded every surface, thick and plush. On the dresser, trinkets and mementos were arranged carefully around the large-screen LCD TV—luminous shells, a tiny box inlaid with mother-of-pearl, a white ceramic owl. The room smelled of mint and lily of the valley, just as it had on the first night Emma had arrived. She hadn't changed much of it since she'd returned to the Mercers' home as herself. A small pile of books stood on the nightstand, and a vintage Hermès scarf she'd bought at Goodwill lay where she'd draped it over the back of a chair. She'd left all of Sutton's old photographs pinned to the corkboard behind the desk—but she'd added a few of her own, too. One of Alex standing in front of the Bellagio fountain, the colored lights playing across her face. And one of Emma and Laurel, arms around each other's shoulders.

So much had happened to her here—in this house, in this room. So much of it had been painful, but that didn't erase the good. She'd finally found her family. She'd finally found where she belonged.

Mrs. Mercer followed her gaze. "This is your room now," she said softly, running her hands over Sutton's pink comforter. "We could redecorate it, however you want it."

Emma shook her head. "I want to keep it this way, just a little longer. It makes me feel close to her."

Mrs. Mercer smiled. "Me, too." She went to the door and put a hand on the frame. "We'll leave in about a half hour. Come on down when you're ready." With that, she was gone.

Emma sat in the silent room for a moment. Next door she could hear Laurel's music through the wall, the bass line thumping. Downstairs, Grandma Mercer and Mr. Mercer bickered about the tie he'd chosen to wear.

These were the sounds of a normal family—one that she actually belonged to. And that would hopefully grow by one more, eventually. She thought of the secret she'd told the Mercers as soon as they'd gotten home from the police station: that Becky had another child, somewhere in California. She'd be twelve now. Emma didn't even know what her name was, but the Mercers had vowed to track her down, too. Hopefully she was happy, wherever she was, but if she wasn't—well, the Mercers had a big house.

But that could wait. Today, finally, Emma could say good-bye to one sister. She'd worry about her other one tomorrow.

34

THE QUEEN IS DEAD
(LONG LIVE THE QUEEN)

Sutton's funeral was held in a beautiful Spanish Revival church in the Catalina Foothills. Cream colored adobe walls arched up from thick red carpets, and bunches of flowers had been arranged on every surface. Every pew was packed—the entire school was there, along with what seemed like half of Tucson. Emma's eyes scanned the crowd. Sutton's teachers sat mingled with the students. Principal Ambrose perched awkwardly at the front, a black pillbox hat on her stiff hair. A half dozen police officers were there, too, shining in their dress blues. Quinlan sat next to a pretty Asian woman Emma was shocked to realize must be his wife. Corcoran sat behind them, his face as stoic as always.

In front of the altar was a blown-up picture of Sutton. Unlike most photos of her, where she mugged for the camera or smirked or gave a movie-star pout, this one showed a quiet, inscrutable girl. Her eyes were wide and clear, her lips parted in an enigmatic smile. The expression wasn't malicious or sly, but it hinted at the presence of a secret self, deeper and more beautiful than anyone could have guessed.

I followed my sister's gaze as she looked out over the crowd. There were so many faces I barely recognized, people who'd flitted through my life without any real connection. Kids I'd passed in the hallway, people I'd rolled my eyes at, neighbors I'd only spoken to once or twice. The sheer size of the crowd made me feel strangely sad. Who here had I missed out on knowing?

Emma sat in the front row with the rest of Sutton's family, her hands balled up in her lap. Next to her, Laurel was sobbing into Mr. Mercer's handkerchief, her shoulders shaking. Mr. and Mrs. Mercer clung to each other as if to a lifeline. On the other side of them sat Grandma Mercer in a sleek black suit, her lips pressed into a savage red line of grief.

Emma stared ahead at the gleaming wooden coffin, dry-eyed, the ache in her chest too enormous to comprehend. She had been living with the loss of her sister for four long months—four months when she couldn't grieve, when she lived under constant terror. Now that she had the chance to say good-bye, she wasn't sure what to feel. She'd lost someone she'd never even met. But in a way, she felt closer to Sutton than anyone. She thought again about the shimmering form in the canyon. Translucent, blindingly beautiful. She and Sutton had been connected by something deeper and stronger than she could understand—and she didn't know how to let go of that.

And neither did I.

Across the aisle from the Mercers sat the Lying Game girls. Charlotte twisted a handkerchief in her fists. Madeline and Thayer sat side by side, Thayer's arm tucked protectively around his sister as she wept. He looked shell-shocked, his gaze glued intently to Sutton's photo. Even the Twitter Twins, who were usually buoyant, leaned against each other for support. Gabby stared at the ground, tears plopping straight down from her button nose. Lili turned her face away into her sister's arms, her shoulders trembling.

The Mercers had asked the hospital chaplain to perform the funeral—they'd never been a religious family, but Father Maxwell had known Sutton since she was a little girl. He wept openly as he delivered the eulogy, reminiscing about the rambunctious, joyful child he'd seen grow into a promising young woman. Emma barely listened. The priest's words were compassionate and well chosen, but there was no way he could speak to the Sutton she knew. Because even though they'd never met, by now she knew Sutton better than anyone. She knew the parts of her that had been haughty or selfish—but more than that, she knew the parts that had been loyal, and fierce, and passionate. She knew her sister had been a fighter. Sutton had lent her some of her strength, that night in the canyon.

She almost didn't notice when the priest gave the final benediction. Then all the guests were on their feet, a low murmur rising up in the packed church. People crowded around the Mercers to pay their respects. Laurel was already wrapped in a hysterical hug by their pottery teacher, Mrs. Gilliam, and Mr. Mercer was deep in a low conversation with Dr. Banerjee, two men bonded in the loss of their daughters. Suddenly Emma felt claustrophobic. She edged away from her family toward an alcove behind a column. After so long living as Sutton, and then as a wanted woman, it felt strange to slip away and become invisible, just like the old Emma had been.

She backed up into someone and stumbled. "Oh! I'm so . . . sorry." She trailed off as she turned to see Garrett Austin, dressed in a black suit and a pale blue tie. Her cheeks burned as their eyes met.

"Um, hey," he said, flushing as red as she was.

"Hey," she echoed. Beyond the little alcove, the church's sound system had started to play a delicate acoustic guitar track. Garrett took a deep breath.

"You have no idea how sorry I am," he said, not quite meeting her eyes. "I can't believe how I treated you."

Emma shook her head. "You didn't know."

"It doesn't matter." He shifted his weight, shoving his hands in his pockets. "Even if you *had* been Sutton, I shouldn't have acted the way I did."

"It was a . . . confusing situation, I'm sure." Emma tugged at her skirt to even the hem. "I'm sorry I couldn't tell you before. The whole birthday thing—I know it looked like I just threw that in your face. I didn't mean to humiliate you. I just couldn't . . ."

"I know," he said quickly, blushing a shade deeper. "I get it." He leaned against the column, avoiding her eyes. "The truth is, Sutton was about to break up with me. I knew it that night I saw her in the canyon. When I saw you the next day and you didn't say anything about it, I couldn't believe my luck. I thought Sutton had changed her mind." He looked down at his shoes. "Did you ever hear about what happened to my sister?"

"Yes," Emma murmured, biting her lip.

"I know it's no excuse. But I've just been so . . . so

angry since it happened. I don't know why I can't move on." A single tear cut down his cheek. "Sutton was more patient with me than she should have been."

Emma listened, her heart twisting with sympathy. "That's a lot to work through by yourself." Impulsively she grabbed his hand, squeezing it in hers.

He shook his head. "Well, I'm done making excuses. I'm starting therapy on Monday. If I'm so unstable that someone can suspect me of murder, I need help."

"So you heard Ethan was trying to frame you?"

"Yeah." He shook his head wonderingly. "That guy . . . I mean, he had us all fooled. We all thought he was crazy about you."

A knot formed in Emma's throat. She glanced away, turning toward a small marble crucifix nestled into an alcove. "Yeah," she said, her voice barely more than a whisper. "So did I."

Garrett opened his mouth, as though he was about to say more, when suddenly some kind of commotion started in the nave. He and Emma turned around to face the crowd, who all seemed to be looking up at the wall behind the altar. The guitar music jerked to a halt, and the lights flickered out.

A disembodied voice spoke over the intercom, echoing through the church.

"Sutton Mercer . . . we salute you!"

Emma barely had time to realize that it was Charlotte's voice before the staccato drumbeat of Fun.'s "We Are Young" started blaring out of the speakers. At that exact moment, a projector hidden at the back of the church kicked into gear. Images flashed above the altar, videos of Sutton and her friends, edited to the music. One showed Sutton, Madeline, Charlotte, and Laurel toasting one another with flasks in the hot springs they used to sneak into. In another, someone held a shaky camera to Sutton's face on a roller coaster. She screamed with laughter, her hair billowing around her face. There was footage of Sutton cannonballing into Charlotte's pool, footage of her singing karaoke with Laurel and dancing with Thayer. In one she, Gabby, and Lili got into a food fight, the Twitter Twins overpowering her and squirting a crown of whipped cream into her hair, all of them giggling.

And finally, there was a cut of Sutton doing a pin-up pose in a slinky silver dress. She was on Charlotte's patio, and behind her one of the Lying Game's exclusive parties raged.

"You can't keep a good diva down," she said coyly, her voice amplified through the church. Then she blew a kiss at the camera, and the video went dark.

Emma realized that her cheeks were streaming with tears. As the lights came back up, a long and echoing silence descended. Mr. Mercer had broken down, his face hidden in his wife's shoulder. Half the tennis team was sobbing—Clara wailed out loud, her cries cutting through the stillness.

As I watched the video, my friends' final tribute, my heart felt like a flower opening its bloom to the sun. Pops of color and light filled my mind, and suddenly everything—every memory, every moment of my life—came flooding through me. Everything I thought had been lost was returned. I remembered pouring pretend tea for my mother from her antique tea set. I remembered my father handing me a set of binoculars, pointing to where a red-tailed hawk nested in a tree above. There I was, playing with Laurel in a pillow fort on a rainy night. Meeting Charlotte on the school bus in third grade, and Madeline at recess the next year. Getting my first tennis racket for Christmas. Swimming in the Pacific Ocean on a vacation, staring out at the miles and miles of lonely blue. Printing the official Lying Game cards at Charlotte's house, giggling over the titles we'd invented for ourselves.

Kissing Thayer for the first time, and the second, and the third. All our kisses, every sun-drenched moment we spent together, came back in perfect focus.

Every prank, every secret, every adventure came back to me. And it was all so beautiful, so vibrant, so real. It was my life. Ethan couldn't take that away.

At the back of the church Emma heard scuffling. The lights came back up, and she turned to see an old woman with curly gray hair escorting Lili and Gabby out of the audiovisual booth by their ears. The Twitter Twins raised their fists in "heavy metal" devil horns as they followed. Father Maxwell was hurrying to take the microphone from Charlotte at the altar, and a man wearing a bow tie was shooing Madeline from the light control box.

But before the Lying Game girls could be removed from the building, someone started to clap.

Emma couldn't pinpoint where it started, but once it did, the applause built up, louder and louder. Someone wolf-whistled on his fingers. A girl Emma had never seen yelled, "I love you, Sutton!"

"Sutton, we'll miss you!" someone else cried behind her. And soon everyone was clapping and stomping, calling out for Sutton.

"Hollier will never be the same!"

"You're the only prom queen we'll vote for!"

Grandma Mercer was clapping harder than anyone else, Laurel weeping next to her. The pursed-lipped old lady let go of Gabby and Lili in shock, and they ran to join Charlotte and Madeline under a statue of the Virgin Mary. Then the four of them joined in the applause, and turned toward the portrait of Sutton, with tears glistening in their eyes.

I hovered over them, the applause vibrating through my being. For a moment, I could almost mistake it for a heartbeat.

35

MAKE NEW FRIENDS, BUT KEEP THE OLD

A few minutes later, Emma stepped out into the gentle afternoon sun. The reception had been arranged on the patio in front of the church, beneath clusters of fragrant eucalyptus trees. Already some of the funeral attendees had filled paper plates with vols-au-vent, cucumber sandwiches, and shortbread-and-jam cookies. Emma spied Dr. Banerjee, looking frail but talking animatedly to Coach Maggie. Quinlan was there too, sipping a glass of lemonade and chatting with Father Maxwell. Louisa stood with Celeste, sharing crudités off a single plate. Knowing what Louisa had gone through, Emma couldn't help but stare at her. Somehow she'd managed to put all the darkness behind her and move on. If she could come out the other side, then maybe Emma could too.

"Emma?" An uncertain voice spoke softly to her left. She turned to see Alex Stokes, a full head shorter than Emma and pixie-shaped, wearing a black slip-dress and Doc Martens laced halfway up.

Emma's face lit up. "Alex!"

Alex hurried forward and threw her arms around her. "I knew you didn't do it," she said, her voice muffled against Emma's shoulder. "I'm so sorry I showed the police those texts. I didn't know what else to do."

"It doesn't matter," Emma said. "They would have gotten them eventually. I'm just sorry you got pulled into the whole thing. And I'm so, so sorry for lying to you."

Alex pulled away from the hug to stare up at her with round, sympathetic eyes. "It sounds like it was . . . complicated."

"Yeah," Emma murmured. She bit her lip. "I'm not ready to talk about the whole thing yet. But I promise, I'll tell you everything as soon as I am."

"I'll be here," Alex said, squeezing her elbow.

The doors to the church opened again, and the entire Lying Game clique stepped out together. Their eyes were red, but they emerged with an It Girl dignity that would have made Sutton proud. Charlotte's lips were painted Bitch Queen Red, and Madeline lifted her chin with prima ballerina hauteur. Lili and Gabby were arm in arm, Lili in lace tights and black eyeliner, Gabby in a pearl necklace and matching earrings. Laurel was with them, too, her honey-blonde hair swept back from her face, an embroidered handkerchief clutched in one hand.

Alex glanced at the clique, then back at Emma. "They seem, uh, nice."

A grin broke across Emma's face. "They're not. But it's okay. They're actually pretty amazing."

Charlotte was the first to meet Emma's eyes. She came slowly down the steps to where Emma stood, the other girls trailing behind her. Laurel gave her an uncertain smile, but the others' faces were stony. Next to her Alex shifted her weight.

After a long moment, Charlotte held out her hand to Emma.

"We haven't officially met," she said softly. "I'm Charlotte Chamberlain. I'm very sorry for your loss."

Emma swallowed. Then she took Charlotte's hand in hers. The other girl's palm was warm and soft. She held it for a moment, and then she pulled Charlotte toward her into a hug.

"I'm so sorry, Char," she whispered. Charlotte trembled in her grip, then hugged her fiercely back.

"We're sorry we didn't give you a chance to explain," Madeline said, throwing her arms around Emma and

Charlotte. Emma could feel both girls crying again.

"I don't blame you," she said. "Sutton was your best friend. And I lied to you for months."

"Yeah, but you didn't have a choice," Charlotte sniffled. "I can't believe you were trying to solve her murder all on your own."

"*I* can't believe Ethan—" Lili started, but Laurel shot her a dirty look.

"Too soon," she hissed.

After a long moment, the girls broke apart awkwardly. Emma knew it was strange for them. She'd gotten to know them, but they didn't know her at all. Would they even like someone like Emma? She was so different from Sutton. But in spite of everything, she'd had fun with the Lying Game girls. They'd made her take risks she'd never have taken in her old life, and given her courage in a time when she'd needed it most. She liked to think that she'd rubbed off on them, too, a little. Since she'd stepped into Sutton's life, the clique had become a little warmer and more accepting of one another.

"This is my friend Alex. From Henderson," she said, and Alex nodded slowly. Emma tensed a little—this worlds-colliding moment felt weird. Alex was the kind of girl the Lying Game had loved to punk. And Sutton's friends were the kind of girls Alex used to call "fashion victims" and "trend whores."

Lili looked Alex up and down. "I love your boots," she said. "I had a pair of knee-highs, but the dog ate them."

"That sucks," Alex said. Lili nodded seriously.

"Henderson is near Las Vegas, right?" Charlotte asked. "We went there once, last summer, on a Lying Game trip. Sutton talked her way into getting us the Presidential Suite at the Bellagio." She smiled sadly. "It must be fun living there. There's so much to do."

"It's okay," Alex said. "Not as much fun without Emma."

"So . . . will you stay in Tucson, now that this is all over?" Madeline asked Emma tentatively, and she nodded.

"I hope so. The Mercers asked me to live with them." She glanced at Alex. "I'll miss you so much, but I've never had family before. I need to do this."

"I know," Alex said. "I get it. Besides, it's not like you're *that* far from me. Maybe you'll take another Lying Game trip soon, and come visit." She struggled a little over the name of their clique, but no one else seemed to notice. Emma smiled.

Charlotte exchanged a glance with Madeline, who gave a tiny nod. "Speaking of Lying Game, we were thinking sleepover, this weekend. Would you want to come?"

Emma flushed with pleasure. "I'd love to." She paused, then went on. "There's one thing I won't do, though."

Madeline cocked her head curiously, but Laurel looked like she knew what Emma was about to say.

"No more pranks. I can't do it anymore."

The girls were silent for a long moment. Charlotte looked down at her black Jimmy Choos, and Madeline hugged herself. Behind them, the Twitter Twins' jaws had dropped in shock. Alex just raised an eyebrow questioningly. But Laurel nodded.

"I'm with Emma on this," she said. "It's hurt too many people. And my snuff film prank was the one that Ethan used to . . . you know . . ." She trailed off.

Madeline took a deep breath. "You're right. Maybe it's time to be just boring old popular girls for once. We *are* fabulous enough not to need a gimmick, you know."

Charlotte swept her hair behind her shoulder. "I've been thinking it's time for a while now. We're not kids anymore."

Emma glanced at Lili and Gabby, who looked mutinous. Lili leaned in to whisper something in Gabby's ear, and Gabby nodded. They had only gotten into the club a few months ago and clearly weren't happy to be done with it so soon.

Oh, well. The Twitter Twins could go rogue, as long as they didn't prank Emma.

"Anyway, we don't have time for pranks right now," Charlotte said. "I need to find a new swimsuit for Barbados.

I can't just sit in a cover-up the whole time if I'm going to get any color." She smiled shyly. "Emma, you're still invited if you want to come. A little beach, booze, and boys might be just what the doctor ordered to recover from . . . from all this." She gestured helplessly around. Emma patted her shoulder gratefully, truly touched.

"Thanks, Char. But I need to spend this Christmas with my family." She met Laurel's eye, and they both smiled.

"More for us," Madeline said brightly. "We'll bring you back some rum."

Emma laughed. Suddenly, the sun on her face and the December breeze playing against her bare legs felt almost heavenly.

I watched my friends comforting each other, their eyes shining with tears, their smiles tentative in the winter sun. I knew how much they'd miss me—that they'd all carry that sorrow for a long time, deep in their hearts. But they would be all right. They would live, and thrive, and remember me with love, and eventually, they would let go of me, the way the living always had to let go of the dead.

Then I saw something that wrenched my heart in my chest.

Thayer, hands in his pockets, lingered off to the side. Alone. And watching Emma.

YOURS FOREVER

Thayer stood slightly apart from the crowd, leaning against the low white wall that surrounded the church's property. He'd come in a perfectly tailored Burberry sport coat and slacks, no tie. His dark hair fell down over one eye, and his hands were shoved deep in his pockets. When he saw Emma approach, he raised his hand a little.

"Hey," he said.

"Hey," she replied. Silence drifted down between them. She watched Garrett join Celeste and Louisa, wiping tears from his eyes. Grandma Mercer had stepped down from the church, Mr. Mercer at her arm. Laurel walked swiftly to her side and took her other arm, murmuring in her ear.

A few feet from Emma and Thayer, a pair of mourning doves perched together in a cactus. They cooed softly at each other, back and forth, like they were deep in conversation.

"How is it the thorns don't hurt them?" Thayer asked abruptly.

Emma cocked her head questioningly. He nodded at the birds.

"I guess because they're so light," Emma said. She swallowed, trying to push down the lump in her throat. "Thayer, I am so, so sorry."

Slowly he drew his gaze toward her. His hazel eyes were pained but clear. "I'm not mad at you, Emma." He gazed down into her face for a long moment, then looked quickly away. "It's just . . . You look just like her. Even knowing everything, there's a part of me that wants to kiss you."

"But it'd be all wrong," Emma said. She smiled sadly. "I'm not Sutton. I wasn't even a very good stand-in."

He laughed softly, one cheek's perfect dimple revealing itself. "Don't sell yourself short. You're not her. But you're pretty amazing."

He drew his wallet out of his back pocket and pulled out a folded piece of computer paper. As soon as I saw it, I knew what it was. A tendril of electricity connected me to that letter.

"The cops gave me this," he said, staring down at the note. "They found it on her phone. I guess Ethan must have tried to delete it, but their forensics guy retrieved it from the SD card. She wrote it, that night in the canyon, and saved it as a draft in our secret e-mail account. I think—I think she wouldn't mind if you read it."

Emma's throat felt constricted as she took the note in her hands. Carefully, she unfolded it.

Dear Thayer,

I am still processing everything that's happened to me tonight. I feel like my entire world has been turned upside down. But all this uncertainty has made one thing clear: I love you. I love you so crazy much, Thayer, and I want to be with you.

I know I've done a lot to hurt you. I don't want it to be that way anymore. Wherever you've been, I don't care. I'm not mad. You can tell me when you're ready to—but it won't make any difference to me. You're the only one for me. I know this kind of love comes along once in a lifetime. I'm not going to let it go.

Yours forever,

Sutton

Tears welled up in Emma's eyes. She wiped one away

quickly before it could fall and stain the note. She looked up to see Thayer, a haunted, aching look in his hazel eyes.

"All those weeks when she suddenly wasn't e-mailing me anymore, I was so confused," he said, his voice breaking. "I thought we were over. I thought that the things I said to her that night in the canyon had made her hate me. And all that time, she was . . . gone."

"Not gone," I murmured. "I'm still here. Still missing you so much."

"You couldn't have known," Emma said. "Ethan covered his tracks too well."

"Ethan." Thayer's face darkened. "I owe that guy a few times over."

"Well, he's getting what he deserves." Emma's voice was steady, but even as she spoke she felt the cold that crept up around her heart every time she thought of him. Thayer blinked away his scowl, looking at her with concern.

"Are you okay?" he asked, leaning slightly toward her. She suddenly remembered that night at Char's party, when Thayer had asked her the same question.

Don't I look okay? she had teased.

And Thayer had said, *You look perfect, as always. I asked how you felt.*

Thayer, always so perceptive. She sighed. He seemed to see right through her, just the way he'd always seen through Sutton.

"I keep telling everyone I'm okay. But the truth is, I'm not. I don't know if I'll ever be okay." Her voice broke for a moment, and she paused. "I'm just glad it's all over. Until now I was so scared I couldn't really grieve for her."

Thayer reached out and hugged her close.

"Thank you, for what you did for her," he whispered.

"Thayer," I whispered, close to his ear. For a moment I imagined I could feel the heat from his body, the softness of his skin. "I will always love you. But we both have to move on. I want you to be happy. I want you to live."

Tears glistened in his eyes. He rested his head on Emma's scalp. "Good-bye," he whispered. Emma didn't have to ask who he was talking to.

37

GOOD-BYE

The next afternoon, Emma stood at the mirror of Sutton and Laurel's shared bathroom with a tube of lip gloss in one hand, staring into her own marine-blue eyes. It was still surreal, to look in the mirror and see herself. She'd been someone else for so long. And after everything she'd been through, she wasn't quite sure who her real self was anymore.

Earlier that morning they'd all gone to the farmers' market to pick out a Christmas tree together. Now she could hear Mrs. Mercer and Grandma Mercer in the living room downstairs, rearranging the furniture to make room for the decorations. Overhead, Mr. Mercer and

Laurel's footsteps creaked in the attic as they retrieved boxes of ornaments. All day a gentle quiet had permeated the house—not an awkward silence but a peaceful one. It was the quiet of wounds starting to heal, of deep sadness that needed room to breathe.

Emma's eyes darted to the picture postcard she'd slid into the corner of the mirror, alongside all the photos of Sutton's friends and the concert tickets and the fashion magazine clippings her twin had hung there. The postcard had a photo of the Alamo at sunset, and said GREETINGS FROM SAN ANTONIO in a blocky font. On the back, a scratchy, untidy hand had scrawled only *I'm doing okay. —B.* It had arrived the day before, addressed to Mr. Mercer. He'd left it by Emma's plate at the breakfast table.

Becky still didn't know the truth—that Sutton was dead, that Emma was now here in Tucson with the Mercers. But it was a relief to know that Becky was safe. Emma liked imagining different versions of a new life for her mother: She pictured Becky strong and healthy, putting weight back on her skeletal frame so the severe, haunted look vanished from her face. She pictured her painting houses in bright colors, or selling fruit from a roadside stand, or learning to guide a skiff down the river from some patient, kind mentor. More than anything, she wanted to believe Becky could change. She wanted to believe they all could, if they wanted to.

Her eyes moved back to her own reflection as she raised the lip gloss to her mouth. But what she saw in the mirror made her drop the tube in shock, and it clattered into the sink, forgotten. For less than a heartbeat, she saw her there, a shimmer, a flicker. Sutton.

Her twin stood right next to her. She wore the same pink hoodie and terry-cloth shorts she'd died in, her hair in long loose waves around her shoulders. Their eyes met in the mirror. The ghost of a smile played around her lips . . . and then she was gone.

"Sutton?" Emma whirled around to look behind her. But even as she turned, she knew she wouldn't see anyone there. She turned back to the mirror, to her own high cheekbones, her own turned-up nose. The line between Emma and Sutton had been so blurred for so long. Where did her twin's life end and hers begin?

My sister would have the rest of her life to figure out who she was. But I had a feeling I would always be a part of her—that somehow, we'd changed each other.

A light knock sounded. "Come in," Emma called softly. Laurel opened the door. She fixed a stare on Emma for a long moment.

"What's up?" Emma asked.

Laurel shook her head. "It's still just spooky. Sorry. I know you're probably tired of hearing that. It's like you're Sutton, but . . . not." She came and stood next to Emma, running a brush through her honey-blonde hair.

"No, you're right. It's spooky to me, too," Emma said, staring into the mirror again. She was wearing her vintage 1970s Tootsie Pop T-shirt and a DIY denim skirt she'd made from an old pair of jeans. She'd braided her hair loosely back and trimmed her own bangs—they'd been in her eyes since she came to Tucson. "This stuff doesn't even feel like me anymore. But Sutton's clothes don't feel like me, either."

Laurel pinned her hair up in a sloppy bun. "Well, that just means we have to have an identity-crisis shopping trip soon. Maybe this week we'll hit La Encantada."

"That sounds awesome," Emma said. Their eyes met in the mirror, and they both smiled.

"Anyway," Laurel said, flushing with pleasure, "I think they're waiting on us to start the tree. Are you ready to go down?"

Emma took a deep breath. This was what she'd dreamed of for so long. A family Christmas. Now that it was here, she was oddly nervous. What if it wasn't what she'd expected? Maybe the Mercers would resent her being there. Maybe they didn't want her to come down and help.

"You think it'll be okay?" she asked, biting her lip.

Laurel raised an eyebrow. "You lived through black-mail, kidnapping, and assault, and you're worried about trimming the tree? Come *on*." She threaded her arm through Emma's and gave her a reassuring squeeze. Together, they went downstairs.

Mrs. Mercer had hung a garland along the banister already, and the smell of vanilla and cinnamon wafted through the house. In the living room, they'd moved an armchair to make room for the silvery green fir. Someone had already strung tiny winking lights around its branches. Bing Crosby crooned from the surround-sound stereo, and a platter of sugar cookies sat on top of the baby grand's lid. Drake —wearing plush reindeer antlers—lifted his nose to sniff hopefully at the plate.

The Mercers were already there, a fire crackling in the fireplace. Mrs. Mercer sat sorting through a box of decorations on the floor, while Mr. Mercer stood looking thoughtfully up at the tree, wearing a bright red Santa hat. Grandma Mercer was there too, her hair perfectly waved, pearls at her neck and throat. Emma swallowed. Grandma still hadn't spoken to her more than was absolutely necessary.

"Oh, God, they've already got 'White Christmas' going," Laurel groaned, rolling her eyes, but Emma could tell she secretly liked it. Mrs. Mercer gave a satisfied little smirk.

"That's right," she said. "And after this we have John Denver and Judy Garland to get through, too. "

Laurel pretended to gag, and Emma giggled. She'd always liked Christmas music—it was one of the few things you could enjoy for free during the holidays. She'd spent plenty of holidays walking the Vegas strip, listening to the Bellagio fountain show play "It's the Most Wonderful Time of the Year" and looking at the lushly decorated Christmas trees the casinos put up. She hummed along now, picking up a cookie from the tray and biting into it.

Grandma Mercer glanced at Mr. and Mrs. Mercer, anxious creases at the corners of her eyes. Mr. Mercer put a hand on her shoulder, some unspoken communication passing between them. He nodded earnestly at her, as if in encouragement. Emma's heart skipped a beat.

Grandma Mercer swallowed and turned toward Emma. Her eyes scanned Emma's face, taking in the features so like Sutton's. She cleared her throat. "There's something I'd like for you to have, Emma."

Emma's ears perked up at the sound of her name. It was the first time Grandma Mercer had said it out loud. She shot a look at Laurel, who smiled, the firelight dancing in her bright green eyes. Then the older woman pressed a small box into Emma's hand.

She held it in her palm for a long moment, unable to bring herself to disturb the pretty little package. It was jewelry-sized, tied with a satin bow. She could count on one hand the number of gifts she'd received in her life, as herself. Now she hardly knew what to do.

"Go on," Grandma said, her voice tinged with exasperated amusement. "Open it, already."

Emma took the ribbon in her fingers and pulled. Inside was an ornament, a simple five-pointed star in sterling silver. Engraved across the front in cursive was her name. Beneath that was her birth date.

"That was what I gave each of the girls for their first Christmases," said Grandma, a sad smile unfolding across her face. "Sutton and Laurel. And poor Becky, too, ages ago. I thought . . . I thought you'd like one, too."

Emma couldn't speak. She stared down at the ornament in her hand, her lips parted. The star became blurred as her eyes filled with tears. But for the first time in a long time, they weren't tears of fear, or grief, or frustration. She was crying with happiness.

She suddenly realized that everyone in the room was watching her. Mr. and Mrs. Mercer were both smiling softly, and Laurel hugged her knees to her chest on the sofa, looking pensive. Grandma Mercer gave her a worried, shaky smile. Emma wiped quickly at her eyes, looking around at all of them. "Thank you," she whispered. "It's beautiful."

"We thought this year . . . you could help us hang Sutton's, too," said Mr. Mercer, his voice breaking slightly.

Emma nodded, her throat tight with emotion as Mr. Mercer handed her the other star. For a moment it was cold and hard, and then slowly it warmed to her skin. She held them, one in each hand, engraved with the same date. Then she turned to the tree and carefully hung them side by side, so close that their edges touched.

The sister stars, she thought. *Finally together.*

I watched them all a few minutes more. My mom trying to sing "O Holy Night," laughing when she got the words wrong. My dad putting his arm around Grandma Mercer, tears glittering in her eyes as she found an ornament I'd made in first grade with my school picture. Laurel holding up her stocking, loudly asking if they all thought it was big enough. Drake, under the piano, slyly opening the crumpled napkin containing Emma's forgotten cookie. And Emma. Emma, unpacking the ornaments one by one, running her hands lovingly over them. Wondering about the history behind each one—where it had come from, what it meant, who picked it out. But there would be time to learn all that, time to hear her family's stories and become a part of them.

And then I felt myself drifting, slowly detaching from the world I'd always known. For a split second, panic shot through me. I wasn't ready. I didn't want to leave them. But then my eyes fell on the tree, on our little silver stars. Laurel had hung hers just below Emma's. I understood then. We were a constellation. We would always be together.

I turned toward Emma, the twin sister I never got to meet in person, who'd lived my life and brought me peace, even though it had nearly cost her everything. "Thank you," I whispered.

In the reflection of the stars, I saw my form glowing brilliant silver-gold, getting brighter and brighter until I couldn't even look at myself. I was turning into energy, pure and vibrant. I took a last look at my family, my constellation, beautiful and bright.

"Remember me," I said, knowing they would. And then, as fast as a shooting star, I was gone.

∽ ACKNOWLEDGMENTS ∾

Thank you to everyone who made this series possible, including Lanie Davis, Sara Shandler, Katie McGee, Josh Bank, and Les Morgenstein at Alloy, as well as Kristin Marang and her digital team. Also thanks to Kari Sutherland and the Harper team for all their good thoughts and proper direction. And to Jen Graham: You are truly amazing and beyond helpful. I don't know what I'd do without you!

Also a shout-out to the people at Alloy Entertainment LA and ABC Family—I love what you have done with the TV show, and I hope the fun continues! And thanks, too, to all the readers of this series—I hope you've followed the mystery to the very end. I love hearing from you—please don't stop the tweets, letters, and comments. Hooray!

PRETTY GIRLS DON'T PLAY BY THE RULES...
THEY MAKE THEM.

DON'T MISS SARA SHEPARD'S
KILLER SERIES THE LYING GAME—AND CHECK
OUT THE ORIGINAL DIGITAL NOVELLAS
THE FIRST LIE AND *TRUE LIES* ONLINE.

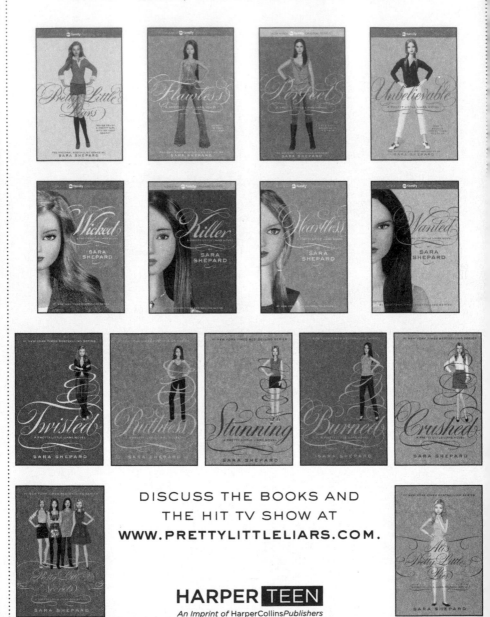